BROKEN BONES

A DCI LIAM BRODIE NOVEL

JOHN CARSON

Boldwood

First published in Great Britain in 2025 by Boldwood Books Ltd.

Copyright © John Carson, 2025

Cover Design by Dan Mogford

Cover Images: Getty Images

A CIP catalogue record for this book is available from the British Library.

Paperback ISBN 978-1-80557-364-7

Large Print ISBN 978-1-80557-363-0

Hardback ISBN 978-1-80557-362-3

Trade Paperback ISBN 978-1-80656-056-1

Ebook ISBN 978-1-80557-365-4

Kindle ISBN 978-1-80557-366-1

Audio CD ISBN 978-1-80557-357-9

MP3 CD ISBN 978-1-80557-358-6

Digital audio download ISBN 978-1-80557-359-3

This book is printed on certified sustainable paper. Boldwood Books is dedicated to putting sustainability at the heart of our business. For more information please visit https://www. boldwoodbooks.com/about-us/sustainability/

Boldwood Books Ltd, 23 Bowerdean Street, London, SW6 3TN

www.boldwoodbooks.com

To my wife, Debbie, who was by my side when this adventure started, and her faith has never wavered.

1

EDINBURGH

He knew the place would have a smell, just not like this. Old and musty, the dust from the shelves flew off with the slightest encouragement. It was cloying, invading his nostrils no matter what he did.

Edinburgh had died centuries ago, and with it, its citizens. Then they had started again, building right over the top of the old place, leaving behind in its wake a series of tunnels and chambers.

This was where Detective Chief Inspector Liam Brodie found himself now, in the underground book depository of the Central Library in the middle of the city. A cavernous space filled with row after row of ancient books and papers which reeked of another era, of history clawing at his throat.

The fluorescent lights above his head lay dormant, switched off to save money. To save the killer from being put in the spotlight.

Years ago, Brodie had told somebody: if you think there's a housebreaker in your home, don't switch the lights on. You know your way around your house in the dark; an intruder doesn't.

It was clear that this killer thought the same way, except he knew his way around thousands of square feet of what was essentially an ancient warehouse. This space had been built a long time ago, and the walls were made of thick stone, yet they didn't quite keep out the hum of the traffic moving overhead. Buses hissed as the drivers applied the air brakes, car horns blasted as impatient drivers tried to get out of the city at the tail end of rush hour, desperate to get home and out of the cold winter chill.

This place was where knowledge came to die. Books written and bound by human beings a long time ago, people who had once thrived in the dirty city that had risen from the ashes of the plague and had killed many less fortunate than themselves. They were left waiting on a shelf, hoping some-body would come along and give them a new life. Liam Brodie wasn't here for that. Somewhere among the long rows of shelves, a killer was waiting for him.

Brodie was down here alone, but his team was upstairs, covering every exit with the help of uniformed officers. Alone. The thought unnerved him for a moment, as every tiny sound was like a ghost from the past walking through him, making him shiver.

The space was in darkness, save for a light in a far corner, a lamp sitting on a desk. He had been told what to expect and had been given a brief description of the area, but he hadn't been prepared for the sheer number of shelves and books.

His shoes had scuffed on the old stone floor, so he had taken them off and left them at the entrance, something he regretted now as the cold seeped into his feet. It made him silent, though, as he slowly walked towards the light in the far corner, careful not to bump into any of the shelving, disturbing the sleeping tomes.

He heard another noise and stopped to listen, pressed between two rows of shelves in the narrow passageway they created. Adrenaline rushed through him, but he had to stay calm. The killer they had been chasing for months had made one fatal error, and rushing now could make him disap-pear forever. Or until the next kill.

Brodie was a little over six foot two and had worked out in the gym in his younger days, bulking up his body. Which had come in useful in a few bars when a fight had suddenly broken out, but not so much in here, where the metal shelves seemed to conspire to squeeze the life out of him.

Older sections were near the back, where the desk and the lamp were, marking the halfway point between what they had called the modern section and the ancient section. The brick walls gave way to rough-hewn stone as he moved silently towards the light.

Then he heard it, the movement of paper, then the sound of a page being ripped out of a book. He turned in that direction, holding his breath for a moment, waiting for the sound to come again. This was where the killer got the pages he'd left on the dead bodies. Most of them, Brodie thought, but not the book he'd bought in the second-hand bookshop. The book that had been his downfall.

He started to shiver, wishing that he'd kept his overcoat on, but he'd known the bulky coat might hinder him in a struggle. Down here, it was climate-controlled but still felt chilly. Or it could just be his adrenaline level dropping. Whatever it was, he stayed focused on the light in the corner as he got closer to it.

He heard more movement now, a slight shuffle, a rustle of paper again. He brushed up against the metal rack, once again smelling the mustiness of the old books. These passageways were narrower than the main ones, like the one he was heading to now. He didn't realise he was holding his breath at first, but let it slowly out as he tried to look through the shelving, past the books, towards the source of the light, but he couldn't quite make it out. He moved his head sideways, peeking round the corner, putting his weight on his left leg, not wanting to hold on to the shelves. He slowly entered the passageway, watching where he put his feet. There were rows of shelves opposite, filled with musty old books and darkness.

The killer stood at the end of the passageway, his back to Brodie. He wasn't a tall man, nor particularly big, but he must have presented an imposing aura to the women he'd killed.

He was dressed in black trousers and a white shirt. No jacket. He had dark hair, and his head was tilted down, looking at something. Brodie looked up and saw a convex mirror up high on the wall that marked the end of the depository. There was a cart for pushing books around near the desk with the lamp, and the mirror would be used on the off chance that somebody else was down there.

The desk was in this passageway, wider than the ones surrounding it. It was a sturdy old desk, its surface cluttered with papers and books. A single lamp cast eerie shadows on the walls. The killer was engrossed in his task, unaware of Brodie's approach.

Brodie approached slowly, taking it easy, watching where he put his feet. And still the killer sensed he was there.

He looked up into the convex mirror.

He was holding a book in his hands. He kept staring into the mirror as Brodie got closer. Maybe seventy-five feet separated them, and yet he didn't move. Brodie wished he had kept his shoes on as he kept on walking forward.

'It's over,' he said.

Yet it wasn't.

The killer dropped the book onto the desk and, without looking back, turned left round the corner and ran out of sight. Brodie ran, his shoeless feet silent on the old stone, and was about to shout when he realised that doing so would give his position away.

He took his extendable baton out as he turned the corner. A narrower passageway of metal shelves was opposite the wall, the light from the lamp throwing shadows around. There was no sign of the killer in here.

The bastard had the advantage; he knew his way around here. Had spent many hours down here, by all accounts. All in plain sight. Why not? Nobody on the upper levels knew he was a sadistic killer.

'You can't get out,' Brodie shouted. 'The place is surrounded and the dog handlers will be down here in a few minutes. If you think you can walk out of here, I'll make sure there's a hundred-pound German shepherd hanging off your bollocks.'

His voice echoed around the huge cavern, into the deepest corners of the subterranean room.

No answer.

He listened. The silence was absolute. He edged forward, ducking at one point to see if he could look through the shelving to see a pair of legs standing still, or dark hair poking about a rack, but there was nothing.

More shelves created passageways, leading to the left, opposite the foundation wall. He kept his shoulder close to the wall in case the killer jumped out. The paint was starting to peel here, as it hadn't been touched up in many years. It was a dull cream colour, and Brodie wasn't sure if this was intentional or if the years were taking their toll.

The light from the lamp was fainter around here, getting dimmer as the shelves got further away. Was the killer running for the doorway as he stood here like a lemon? If so, he wouldn't get far.

Brodie couldn't hear running feet, but maybe the killer had done what he had, and taken his shoes off. He moved forward as quietly as he could, looking down each passageway, but still nothing.

It seemed even more ancient and musty down at this end, if that was possible. Brodie had been in some dumps in his time, but this place – where books went to die – took the biscuit. He could understand why the killer would want to spend time down here; nobody else would voluntarily venture into this place.

He stopped and stood still, thinking he had heard a noise to his left. Then nothing.

Brodie was about to step forward, his eyes starting to adjust to the darkness again, when he sensed the killer right behind him. Had this aisle been wider, he might have been able to turn faster, but he didn't quite make it before the knife was rammed into his back. Had he not turned at all, the knife could have sliced his spinal cord, but the blade slid in and caught one of his ribs.

As the pain screamed through his body, he felt himself being dragged backwards, and a hand grabbing the knife handle and pulling.

He knew the darkness was coming for him, could feel his grasp on life letting go. He had underestimated the killer and now he was paying the price.

Brodie thought this was going to be his last day on earth as he reached up in one last, futile attempt to try and make the assailant let go, but he was too weak. His mind was exploding with the pain. It was game over.

Then he felt the hand let go without touching it. Then he heard shouting as his mind slipped from reality. He reached out and caught himself on a shelf, holding on for dear life, knowing that if he fell to the floor he was dead.

Another figure was there. A woman. He knew her but couldn't remember her name for a moment. Was she real? He thought so, but couldn't be sure. The light was hazy, like seen through morning-fuzzy eyes. He wanted to rub his eyes but couldn't remember how. He was closing down. Maybe this woman was an angel.

'You bastard!' she shouted, and then clarity came back to him for a moment. DI Lucy Warren.

The killer had turned towards her, advancing in a few steps, but she met him head-on, grappling with him as Brodie clung on to consciousness. They came back towards him, and then Lucy shoved the killer away. Before he could get back to her, she picked up a book and swung it, and despite the aisle being narrow, it connected with the killer's face, breaking his nose. He screamed out and, when his hands covered his face, Lucy kicked him hard in the bollocks.

He collapsed in a heap.

Brodie collapsed on top of him, just as a rush of boots came thumping up. The last thing Brodie heard was Lucy calling his name.

2

EDINBURGH, THREE YEARS LATER

Monday

'Are you nervous?' Ruth Campbell asked.

Liam Brodie looked down at her face and smiled. 'You asked the same thing on this day exactly one year ago and the answer is still the same: I'd rip the bastard's head off if I could.'

'That's a no, then.' She smiled at him.

'That's a no.'

She pulled him closer and hugged him before gently pushing him away and brushing toast crumbs off his tie. 'You should eat eggs for breakfast,' she said to him. 'No carbs.'

'It's much easier to toss a couple of slices of bread into the toaster.'

She smiled and shook her head.

'Anyway, how are you dealing with all of this?' he asked her.

She gave him the same look she had given him the last time he asked her. 'I hate having to go and talk to him. I deal with people who have addictions, who are feeling grief taking over their lives and others who just need somebody to talk to, to help them get through life. I don't need to be talking to somebody who killed women. However, as a subject, he's fascinating. My boss told me we could learn about human behaviour from Kane, so that's why I go.'

He put his hands on her shoulders. 'My boss wouldn't have asked if he knew you couldn't handle it.'

'I know, Liam. Gabriel Kane is such a bastard, and I have to let him think he's gaining the upper hand.'

He dropped his hands. 'I told you before, if you want out, then just say the word and I'll tell Cross to shove it.'

She nodded.

Detective Superintendent Rob Cross had spoken with Ruth three years ago, when Kane had said he would talk only to her. Quid pro quo: if they ever wanted to get some of Kane's victims back.

Meeting after meeting took place, bouncing ideas back and forth, and the chief constable herself had stepped in and told Cross to make it happen.

Brodie picked up his coffee from the kitchen countertop and finished what was left.

'I have to go and brush my teeth,' he said. He went through to the bathroom and took his brush from the glass on the sink. Ruth had slowly started leaving more and more of her things here over the past three years: the transition between staying overnight and moving in with him.

He started brushing his teeth and looked at the grey hairs starting to appear in his hair. Stress, Ruth had said. He had scoffed at that, telling her that thick hair ran in his family, and he would rather have that than go bald early.

It was three years to the day since Dr Gabriel Kane had stabbed him. 'I was trying to kill you, Liam,' he had said later on. 'Nothing personal. I just wanted to escape. And if it wasn't for the help of your DI, I would have achieved it.'

The man had locked eyes with him when he had spoken the words, a smile playing on his lips, but the depth of the evil in his eyes seemed to go on forever.

Kane's stature wasn't what Brodie would have called big, but what he didn't have in size, he more than made up for in cunning and tenacity.

That first time Brodie had spoken to him in the psychiatric hospital had been the first time since that night in the book depository. He had wanted to tell Kane, to shout in his face with only inches between them, 'If I hadn't moved the way I did, I would have died. You fucking missed! And now I'm still here, breathing God's fresh air, and you're in a cage, going to spend the rest of your life in it.'

He had kept quiet instead. And, of course, the cage was a room with a table in it. Screwed to the floor. A bed was in one corner of the room, and a table and chair near it, also screwed to the floor.

Three years later and Kane was in a room that would have put some hotels to shame. He had worked his way up the earning ladder, as it were.

He had revealed two more bodies. Helpless victims. Women he had overpowered and strangled before burying them. Revealing the first victim's location on the first anniversary of the attack. The next one on the second anniversary. The reveal planned months in advance, but not the destination.

Kane had said he would give them back to the family in return for some special considerations, carefully negotiated by the chief executive of the hospital.

That's when Brodie had met Ruth for the first time, just after Kane had first been incarcerated. She had been called in to talk with Kane. As a forensic psychiatrist, it had been her job to talk with Kane long before he would be taken out so he could show where the body was hidden.

That was when Brodie had started working with her, although it was DI Lucy Warren who had initially spoken with Kane. Then Kane had demanded that Brodie be brought on board or the whole thing would be called off.

The bigwigs had almost pissed themselves, the chief herself saying – and Brodie remembered her face when she had said it in front of him – 'Fuck that for a game of soldiers.'

Then the minister for justice had got involved and suddenly Brodie was a pawn in Kane's little game. He had got to know Ruth Campbell better, little by little, first over a coffee in a café on Morningside Road, poring over notes, sharing opinions, Lucy Warren with them at first, but then she had seen what was happening between her boss and the psychiatrist.

'I'll leave you two alone,' she had said one evening, smiling as she got up from the table and leaving. But before she did, a look passed between her and Ruth. A look that said she didn't want to be a third wheel.

'You don't have to go,' Brodie said. 'I'll give you a lift home.'

'I have my own car, remember? Thanks anyway, boss.'

Ruth had carried on, poring over the notes as though nothing had happened. Then she had invited him along to her flat, for a coffee that tasted better than this place. And it was free.

'I hate the way Kane thinks he's getting one over on us,' Brodie said now.

'He has to think that way, remember? If he doesn't then he might not reveal the location of the next victim.'

'He'll do it just to have his little day out into the country.'

Brodie's phone rang.

'Hello?' He listened for a moment. 'Can't you put her off?'

Ruth didn't hear the other side of the conversation.

'Right. Tell her no direct contact with Kane. I mean it. Reiterate it, or it will be the last time.' He nodded a few times. 'Okay, Lucy, thanks.' He cut the call and put his phone back in his pocket. 'That was Lucy, if you hadn't guessed already.'

'I didn't have to guess; you said her name out loud and I don't have hearing problems.' She smiled at him.

'That... woman from the cable TV news station who writes to Kane asked him if she could tag along today, and now he not only agreed, but made it a condition.'

'We've done so well to keep the press at bay, but it was bound to happen one day.'

'I told you, he's getting some power back and he's manipulating us.'

Ruth shook her head. 'He's not. I spoke to the reporter. Her name's Catherine Wheeler. I agreed to talk to her.'

'What? Why didn't you say anything?'

'It was the clinical director's idea. Kane brought up Catherine's name, and Director Lake thought it over and asked me to liaise with Catherine, just to feel her out, as it were.'

'Have you seen this woman on TV?' he asked. 'She's all smiles and false teeth but she's like a shark.'

'She's not, she's very nice.'

'Just don't go swimming with her.' He looked out of his living room window. His flat was down at Western Harbour in Newhaven, one of the blocks of new flats. His place looked out over the water, across the Firth of Forth to Fife. He mentally pictured where his stepson would be, geographically, and thought about how he was doing in Kelty.

Eric was twenty-seven now, and had multiple sclerosis. He had first come into Brodie's life when he was a toddler, as Brodie started dating his mother, and he had become his stepson the day he married Fiona, and their bond had grown over the years, so much so that he regarded Eric as his son.

Now Eric was living with Chrissie in Kelty, near his grandmother, Fiona's mother. The old woman was getting on now, and was happy to see her grandson every day.

'I'll give Eric a call later,' he said out loud, more to himself than to Ruth.

'He'll like that,' she said, picking up her own coffee mug and taking it through to the kitchen. 'I like it here,' she said, coming back into the room. Brodie was still standing looking out over the sea, watching as a plane came in for its final approach to Edinburgh Airport, gliding in over the Forth, lining up with the runway.

'We should get away for a wee while,' he said as she put her arm around his waist.

'I'd like that. A little bit of sun and getting burnt in places that don't normally see the light of day.'

'I'm only wearing swim shorts,' he said. 'I don't need to be flaunting my boyish good looks on a foreign beach.'

'True. We wouldn't want there to be an international crisis.'

'I knew you'd understand.' He touched the small scar that ran along his chin where a knife had caressed his jaw. A souvenir he always carried with him, a reminder of the first time a psycho with a blade had tried to kill him. When it was still raw, it had made him feel self-conscious, but his late wife, Fiona, always told him it never made a difference to her.

Ruth laughed and he kissed her on top of her head and she let him go.

'Come on, let's get up to the hospital,' she said.

He looked at his watch. 'There's plenty of time. Let's go and get a free roll first.'

3

FIFE

'Aw, come on,' DS Cameron Reid said as they walked towards the pool car, in Fife's HQ. 'Just a wee wager.'

DI Art McKenzie yawned and shook his head. The older he got, the more he thought he wasn't a morning person. Not even nine o'clock yet. Normal people should still be in bed. 'That's sick. This is the boss we're talking about.' He looked at the younger man disapprovingly. The two of them had wagers on anything they could think of, but DCI Alan McRae was his friend outside of work, as well as their boss. He was also missing.

'You know what he's like, Art. Likes a good drink, likes to go out with women. Have a good time. Remember that lassie he met last year on holiday?'

'Calling her a "lassie" is stretching it a bit.' Art shivered at the thought of the woman, who had the morals of an alley cat. She had been younger than Alan, but what she lacked in years, she more than made up for in experience. Twice divorced, with two young kids – fuck trophies, one of the blokes from CID had called them – and a way of skirting the law had just been some of her attributes.

But Alan McRae had been bored sitting around watching TV of an evening. He wanted something more out of life, and that something was going to a singles night at the bowling club.

'What was her name again?' Art asked as Cameron got in behind the wheel.

'Dawn.'

'Oh, aye,' Art said, plonking himself into the passenger seat. 'He was lucky to escape her.' The car door creaked as he slammed it shut.

'Maybe he's just met Miss Right,' Cameron said. 'I mean, he's just been in Tenerife for two weeks. Holiday romances happen all the time. Like Dawn. Maybe he met somebody else and decided he didn't want to come back to this life.'

'Stop talking shite. Alan wouldn't have gone on holiday and not come back to work. At the very outside, he would have told his sister. Daisy's a basket case. She was crying on the phone to me.'

'Fucking heid case, more like,' Cameron said.

'Here, that's enough,' Art said, tutting and shaking his head.

'I mean, he still lived with her, didn't he?'

'He did. But only until he got his own place.'

Cameron laughed. 'He got comfortable, you told me. Maybe he over-stayed his welcome and she turned him into a human version of Miracle-Gro.'

'Don't you go fucking talking like that in front of her. Wee bastard. And get this fucking thing moving. I'm already sweating my arse off.'

Cameron turned the engine on. 'We've seen lots of weird stuff, boss. It's not beyond the realm of possibility.'

'Neither is you getting your fucking jotters. Daisy is good friends with Chief Superintendent Harris. You can explain to him that you were only joking when you're on the carpet. You can laugh all the way to the job centre.' Art rolled the window down. 'You let one go? This car's minging.'

'Have a word with yourself. These cars are bogging. Even a scrapyard would get the boak thinking this thing was going into its crusher.' Cameron looked at the DI. 'Where to first?'

'Lawyer's office. Supposedly he saw Alan,' Art said.

They drove from Glenrothes to the small village of Cupar, and Cameron decided to park in the police station car park there.

The office was tucked down a side street, off the main drag. Cameron parked the car, and they approached the office that had once been a shop.

In the window hung photos of houses for sale in the surrounding area. Art opened the door that had *Duvall & Butler, W.S.* painted in gold on the glass.

A woman sat behind a desk facing them. There was a tall potted plant over to one side of the window that overlooked the street. Art was no botanist, but he thought it looked sick.

Wendy Delgado looked like her hair was blonde and she was just dying the roots brown. She looked like she was at the age where she could still run for a train but there was only a fifty-fifty chance of her catching it.

'Can I help you?' she asked, peering over her glasses.

The office was small and had a stale air about it. Out-of-date magazines lay on a table that sat in front of two dining chairs, in what amounted to a waiting area.

'DI Art McKenzie and DS Cameron Reid,' Art said. 'You called us about a possible sighting of a man who's listed as a missing person.'

'That was him through the back. Maurice,' she replied, looking at them. 'Art, huh? Bit of an old-fashioned name for a young man.'

Art liked the idea that the woman thought he looked young, even though he was three months past his fiftieth birthday, but he would have been more impressed if she were twenty-five with no brown roots. 'My dad was a fan of Art Garfunkel,' he said, feeling like he had to explain himself.

'Lucky he didn't call you Garfunkel.'

Art shrugged. 'Well, my mum was a fan of Lulu, so I guess I got off lightly.'

'Who was your father a fan of?' she asked Cameron.

'Liquor.'

'Licker, huh? I haven't heard of him, but I'm sure that would have got you a leg up with the cheerleading squad.'

'Is he ready now?' Cameron asked, impatience starting to creep into his voice.

'He is. He's probably stalling, hiding fishy papers, or fake account books or maybe even the BB gun he keeps in his top drawer. He thinks I don't know about that gun, but if he ever thinks he's going to bend me over that desk and have his way, the time I'm finished, that desk will be the only drawers that he gets into.'

I don't think you'll have anything to worry about, Art thought but didn't say. Let the woman have her fantasy before she goes home to her two cats.

The intercom buzzed on her desk. 'Wendy, tell me when snitch and snatch are here.'

'They're here now, listening to you.'

'Aww, shite,' he said, his voice sounding further away as if he'd jumped back from the machine. 'You were supposed to give me a heads-up.'

Wendy took her finger off the button. 'He'll have me driving the getaway car next. Maybe he should try paying me more than a freckled kid in McDonald's. You can go through. And call him by his first name. That always winds him up.'

'Thanks,' Art said, opening the door to Maurice Duvall's office. He and Cameron walked in.

The older man was sitting behind his desk, waving a hand in front of his face. 'The landlord doesn't allow smoking in the office, but he hasn't got an ex-wife to look after. The maintenance is killing me, so I have the odd ciggie.'

'We won't tell if you don't,' Art said.

Duvall was going bald, so he had shaved his hair as close to the skull as it would go without it making him look like an inmate. His belly wasn't as big as it once was but still had a long way to go.

'How can I help you?' he asked, indicating the police officers should sit on the old, scabby chairs on the opposite side to him.

'Mrs Delgado called us and told us about your sighting of DCI Alan McRae.'

'Oh, yeah. I forgot I asked Wendy to do that. She can't remember to pick up toilet roll when I send her to the supermarket, but she can remember to call the police about a man who's been missing for a week. I think she's losing the plot.'

'I heard that!' Wendy shouted from the other room.

'Yeah, we'll be using strips of newspaper by tomorrow, just so you know!' He lowered his voice. 'Probably got her ear to the door, nosy cow,' Duvall said in a lower voice.

'Can you tell us more, Maurice?'

'It's pronounced *Maw-reece.*'

Cameron rolled his eyes at Art. *Of course it is.* 'Can you tell us what you were doing up on the trail?'

'You don't have to ask in that tone. I wasn't standing outside a playground with a raincoat on.'

'Believe it or not, although this is a small town, we do have work to do,' Art said.

'I was walking my dog. I just happened to look over to the start of the trail, and he walked up into the woods.'

'Are you sure it was DCI McRae?' Cameron asked.

'Not a hundred per cent. I mean, it very well could have been,' Duvall said.

'You got a look at his face?' Art said.

'Not exactly.'

'Then what made you think it was McRae?'

'Most people who go up that trail are wearing casual gear. Some of them actually wear the proper gear. You know, hiking boots, and appropriate clothes. This man was wearing a suit. So he stuck out.'

'Did you see where he came from? What kind of car he had, Mr Duvall?' Cameron asked. *Maw-reece.*

'I was in the car park, putting Zeus into the back of the car, when I just happened to look over. He was driving a VW Golf. Dark blue.'

'I don't suppose you got the number plate?' Cameron asked.

'For what reason?' Duvall looked at the younger detective like he was daft.

Art had no reason to doubt that *Maw-reece* was telling the truth but he would have a patrol unit search around the area of the park to see if they could spot Alan's VW Golf. 'Do you normally walk your dog at lunchtime?'

'If I'm not busy eating lunch at my desk... But sometimes, yes.'

'Nice name for a poodle, Zeus,' Art said, pointing to a photo of the dog that sat on a bookcase.

'She likes to think she's a tough guy.'

'Did you see anybody else walk onto the trail after McRae did?' Art asked.

Duvall stared at them for a moment. 'I never actually saw him walk up to the trail. I just saw him in the car park. There were a few cars there. It was a nice day for hiking. Probably some tourists as well as locals.'

Art and Cameron asked a few more questions, but Art sensed they weren't going to get any more useful information out of the older man.

'Well, if there's anything else you can think of, please give us a call at the station,' he said. 'Glenrothes.'

'Oh, I will.' There was no conviction in Duvall's voice. They all stood up and the older man shook hands with Art, but Cameron was funky about such practices and passed. *Piss fingers* he had once told Art, citing the reason he didn't eat bar nuts.

'Just one more question,' Art said. 'The name Butler on the window. Where does he work?'

'He doesn't. Not any more. He's a silent partner.'

They closed the office door. Wendy Delgado was pretending not to notice them as she played solitaire on her old computer.

'He's been bumping gums with Mrs Howard, the femme fatale who owns the cupcake store over on Crossgate,' Wendy said, in a low voice.

Art looked at her like she'd had a swig of Johnnie Walker while they had been in the office. 'By *bumping gums*, I take it you mean he had her bent over the desk with his BB gun out?'

'Not his desk, in his car. I'm not sure if the gun came into play. Why do you think he goes to the trail at lunchtime? They find a nice quiet spot in his car and go at it. With *Fifi* in the front no less. That's animal abuse.'

'I thought it sounded funny, a poodle called *Zeus*,' Cameron said.

'Are you sure about this?' Art asked.

Wendy looked at him like she wasn't sure if he meant the dog's name or Duvall's illicit affair with the cupcake lady. 'My friend saw them when she was walking her dog. The windows were steamed up and the car was rockin', so she didn't go knockin'. And he drives an old people carrier. Mrs Howard has no scruples.' She looked at Cameron. 'What car do you drive?'

'A Ford Mondeo. You can sit in the back if you like, but I'd have to hand-cuff you first.'

'Well then, cheeky chops, if that's how you play, who am I to argue?' She grinned at him.

Cameron, realising his remark had backfired, took his notebook out to cover the red that was slowly creeping up his face. 'Mrs Howard you say?' He scribbled the name down.

'How often does he go there?' Art kept his voice equally low.

'Every day. Although at his age, I'm sure the windows don't get steamed up every day. Maybe they play gin rummy or something. He'd better watch his heart though. His doc says he needs to cut back on red meat and smoking. If you ask me, I think he's had one too many of Mrs Howard's cupcakes. Duvall, not his doc.'

'You've been very helpful, Mrs Delgado,' Cameron said, putting his notebook away. It hadn't helped to cover his red face.

'Anytime, honey. My husband's long gone, so if you ever fancy going line dancing... or something... call me.'

'I'm married, but thanks,' Cameron said.

She was laughing as they left the office.

'Jesus, I could flip a burger on my face,' Cameron moaned as they walked over to the cupcake shop.

'She's a live wire, alright,' Art said. 'Let's go and see Mrs Howard.'

'I hope to God she's not got a mouth on her.'

'Of course she has. She's been bumping gums with *Maw-reece*, remember?'

Cameron made a face as they crossed the street.

4

EDINBURGH

Brodie's mother, Isobel, owned a little café down on Edinburgh's Shore, a street that ran parallel to the Water of Leith, a river that ran out to the sea. It was creatively called Isobel's. She and Brodie's father – Dougal, a retired bus driver – ran the place.

Brodie parked his car around the corner, and he and Ruth walked around. It was at the corner of the street and had some tables and chairs outside.

'I'm going to try and eat healthy,' Brodie said, as they went inside.

'No, you're not. I mean, it's not like your parents serve salads.' Ruth smiled and nudged him.

'I know. Who am I kidding?'

Inside, Isobel beamed a smile at her son. There were a few customers sitting, drinking coffee and eating bacon rolls.

'If you're here to help, you're too late,' Dougal Brodie said, coming out of the back from the kitchen. 'I've already done the dishes.'

'Damn, I knew we should have come earlier,' Brodie said.

'Hi, Ruth,' Isobel said. 'Get yourselves a table and I'll rustle up some rolls and coffee.'

'Thanks, Ma,' Brodie said.

'How are you, Ruth, love?' Dougal said, coming round the counter to give Ruth a peck on the cheek. 'He behaving himself?'

'Oh, give over,' Brodie said. 'She's my princess. I take care of her, alright.'

'That's what I expect to hear, young man.'

Brodie shook his head. 'He'll be telling me to go to my room, next.'

'Don't you knock it, son,' Dougal said. 'I taught you a valuable lesson.'

'I waited until he had gone to bed then sneaked out of my bedroom to go drinking with my pals,' Brodie said.

'That will be right.' Dougal gave his son a mock stern look. He turned to Ruth. 'He probably drank my bloody whisky, too.'

'I was more of a lager man,' Brodie said.

'Get yourselves a seat.' He watched them sit. 'Today's the day, isn't it?'

'Aye. We're heading up there after this,' Brodie said to Dougal.

'That bastard. Just give me ten minutes and a pair of pliers and he'll tell me where the rest of them are buried.'

'As much as I'd like to, unfortunately, we have laws to think about.' Brodie locked eyes with his father for a moment.

'The law's a farce, son. I know you have to uphold it. But Kane stabbed you and almost killed you. That's something I'll never forget. And if he knows what's good for him, he'll stay locked up.' He smiled at Ruth. 'Tea as usual?'

'Thank you, Dougal.'

'Coming right up.' The older man left and went back through the kitchen door.

'He was in the army,' Brodie explained. 'Before he was a bus driver.'

'I know. You've told me many times.' Ruth put a hand on his. 'He's just being a protective father. Let him vent.'

'As long as that's all he's doing.'

Moira, Brodie's sister, came out with two plates with a bacon roll on each.

'Hey, sis, what are you doing here? The Western General getting rid of nurses now?'

'I always take a week off work around this time, and this year is no different,' Moira said. She was five years younger than Brodie's forty-seven and was slim built with medium-length blonde hair pulled back into a ponytail.

'Didn't you go to Spain this time last year?' Ruth asked.

'Yes, I did. I didn't fancy going this year. I'm saving money now I'm getting divorced.'

'Are you sure you and Roger are finished for good?' Brodie asked.

'Oh, yes. The skinny bastard was cheating on me. He denied it at first, but then he admitted it. I'm settling into my new flat on Leith Walk and loving every minute of it.'

'A chance to go out boozing with your pals again,' Brodie said, grinning, taking a bite of the roll.

'I still went out with them. Roger went to his model railway club. At least I thought it was a model railway club.'

Dougal came in with two mugs, one tea, one coffee.

'Thanks. Both of you,' Ruth said. She looked at Dougal. 'Let me pay for it this time.'

'Your money's no good here,' Dougal said. 'I mean it; the last time you tried passing some euros.' He chuckled as Isobel lightly slapped him on the arm.

'You're fine, honey. This is on the house. While we still can.'

Brodie had bitten a chunk out of the roll then stopped to look at his mother. 'What do you mean?' He washed down the soft roll with coffee.

'The restaurant next door went under. Now there's a new place opening up. We could be next.'

'Oh, Bel, don't be daft,' Dougal said.

'It's true. You never know what's around the corner.'

Brodie smiled at his mother. 'Don't be daft, Ma. You'll be fine.'

'We have a plan B, if that ever happens,' she said.

'And what's that?' Brodie asked.

'We'd sell up and go live in Spain,' Dougal said.

'That sounds like a plan,' Ruth said.

'It is,' Brodie said. 'He just said it's plan B.' He grinned at her.

'Ignore him, Ruth,' Dougal said.

'Why don't you sit down?' Brodie asked. 'I thought you said the dishes were done?'

'Lots to do, son.'

'Do you really think that it's going to happen?' Ruth asked, biting into her roll.

'Edinburgh's changing beyond all recognition. Who knows when they'll put all of this down and start again?' He smiled a sad smile. 'Anyway, I'll call you later. Maybe get a pint one night?'

'Count on it, Dad.'

Brodie watched as his father walked back into the kitchen, as strong as he had ever seemed, albeit a little softer around the edges. He was still a hard man, though, with a different sense of right and wrong compared to Brodie. Dougal had once told his son that he could never have joined the police after leaving the army. They had trained him to use all sorts of weapons, taught him how to fight, and he would feel handicapped coming on to civvy street and dealing with these bastards who thought they were tough.

'I have to keep an eye on my customers,' Isobel said. 'Maybe we could get together for our dinner one Saturday?' she said, looking hopeful.

'Of course we will,' Ruth said. 'Our treat.'

'I'll keep you to that,' she said, and smiled as she went behind the counter.

They finished up and left the café.

* * *

The Reader sat in the café in Sandport Place, directly across from Isobel's. He had been about to go in when the detective walked up, so he had diverted to the coffee place across the street. He chose a table at the window where he could keep an eye on the front of the other café. He had more than enough patience to sit and wait and drink his coffee, reading a newspaper, or at least pretending to.

After a while, the man and woman left. The Reader would have gone out and bumped into the man, just to see his face up close, if he had been alone. The woman posed the problem.

DCI Liam Brodie wouldn't recognise him, of course.

That would come later.

But by then, it would be too late.

5

FIFE

It was obvious that Mrs Howard didn't sample her own cupcakes, if the older woman behind the counter was indeed the proprietor. She was slim, with a pretty face framed by blonde hair.

'Help you?' a younger woman said, smiling at them.

'Police. We'd like to speak to Mrs Howard.' Art looked at blondie and saw the smile slip, confirming this was Mrs Howard indeed.

'That's me,' blondie said.

The younger woman looked at Art and Cameron. 'It is. She really is Mrs Howard.'

'I believe you,' Art said, shifting his gaze towards Mrs Howard. 'Is there somewhere we could talk in private?'

Her cheeks turned a little red and she nodded. 'Through the back.'

The assistant looked at them all in turn, wondering if she should come through too, but Mrs Howard looked at her. 'Keep an eye on the shop, Francine,' she said.

Francine looked as if she was going to argue at first, but then thought better of it. Jobs weren't thick on the ground in Cupar, and this was better than sweeping streets.

Art wasn't a breakfast person, but the smell of the cupcakes was starting to make him hungry.

The door opened and a woman came in, holding a toddler's hand.

'Do you want a cupcake, Joey?' the mother asked.

The little boy smiled and nodded and pointed to one of the glass-fronted cabinets.

Yes, Mummy, I'd like to get my high blood-sugar level kicked off at an early age, Art imagined the boy saying.

He gently nudged Cameron, who took the hint and followed Mrs Howard through a door marked *Staff only.*

There was a short corridor that led to an office. If Art expected to hear and smell a bakery going full tilt, he was sadly disappointed.

'We bake the cakes off-site,' she said, as if reading his mind. 'Please, come into my office.'

Art had one last look through the back where stacks of boxes were, presumably for delivering cakes, if that was your thing. A roller door was on the back wall, large enough for a small van to reverse through.

The office was surprisingly large and a window looked out onto the back of the property.

Two uncomfortable-looking medium-backed chairs sat against a wall, looking like they'd been whipped from a function room in a drunken dare. They were probably brought out to sit in front of the desk either during a job interview or a dressing-down, Art thought.

'Don't just stand there, grab a fucking chair,' he whispered to Cameron. The younger detective grabbed one and dragged it over, then the second one for himself. Art always checked strange chairs for suspicious marks and stains, but neither chair looked to be guilty, and they were free of dust, so he sat down, Cameron right next to him. 'It's a big room,' Art whispered again, throwing his colleague a look to tell him that, although he liked him, he didn't like him that much.

Cameron scooted over.

'Thank you for agreeing to speak to us, Mrs Howard,' Art said. 'I'm DI McKenzie, this is DS Reid.'

Cameron nodded and took his notebook out.

'Call me Katherine,' Mrs Howard said, as if she expected the men to tell her to call them by their first names.

'We're here to talk about you and Mr Duvall,' Art said, ignoring her request.

Mrs Howard took in a deep breath and Art watched her face. He'd been on the other side of many an interview table in the station where people looked exactly like Mrs Howard was looking right now: like she was deciding whether she was going to lie or not.

'I don't know what you mean,' she said.

A look passed between Art and Cameron. They'd heard this before: the interviewee starting off by saying they don't know what the police are talking about.

'Let me get right down to this,' Art said, his tone changing. 'It's about your relationship with Maurice Duvall.' He couldn't say *Maw-reece* in front of this woman.

'Maurice?' Neither could she, apparently. 'We're just friends.'

'Friends?' Cameron said. 'We heard differently.'

'Did you now? From that nosy old cow, no doubt.' There was a sharper edge to her voice now.

'We heard that you and Mr Duvall are having a sexual relationship,' Art said.

Mrs Howard put a hand to her mouth, and her eyes went wide. 'What?' she said after her hand was back down on the table. 'Me and Maurice? That's ridiculous. We've been friends since school. Sometimes we walk our dogs up at East Lomond Hill trail. Beside the big masts. Nothing else. And yes, we sit in his car with the dogs and have a wee cuppa if it's cold outside. That Wendy should mind her own business.'

Art nodded. 'Okay, I agree. But we're more interested in whether you spotted DCI McRae, who has been listed as a missing person. Maurice seems to think you spotted him at the trail.'

She shook her head, her anger not quite willing to let go yet. 'It was a guy in a suit. Maurice just mentioned it because it seemed so out of place.'

'You didn't see his face?'

'No. He could have been anybody. But I saw him get into a car.'

Art perked up at this. 'Can you give us a description?'

'It was a blue Volvo.'

'Do you know the model?' Cameron asked, not holding out much hope.

'An XC40. I could tell by the shape. My mum has one, and before you ask, it wasn't her. Hers is silver. And, no, I didn't get the number plate. Fifi was jumping around with Henry in the back at the time the suit got in the car. And that isn't a euphemism for anything else, although that Delgado woman would have you think otherwise.' She looked at them in turn. 'Henry's my poodle.'

'Did you see if he went off in the car?' Cameron asked. 'Or if there was a blue VW Golf there?'

'The car didn't move. I think the suit got out of a VW before he got into the Volvo. It was still there when Maurice pulled out of the space. He had to go back to his office, and I was coming back here to the shop to do some paperwork.'

'How did Wendy Delgado know you and Maurice went up to the trail?'

'I have no idea. But she had made a snide comment to Maurice before.'

'Bumping gums,' Cameron said.

'What?' Mrs Howard said.

'It's an expression she used.'

Mrs Howard shook her head. 'Manky old cow. I'm surprised she didn't make a pass at you.'

Cameron looked at his notebook again, not wanting to make eye contact with Art.

'I don't think we're her type,' Art said.

'You've got a pulse, haven't you?' she said.

Art resisted making a face, not one like Mrs Howard had just made, doing an impression of Fifi about to launch some dog vomit in the back of Maurice's car, but it would have been close had he not reined it in.

They wrapped up the interview and she promised she would be in touch if she remembered anything else about the little Volvo.

Outside, a warm air was blowing as they walked back over to the police station.

'Why would the boss be meeting somebody up at a trail?' Cameron asked.

'I don't know. It might not have been him. If it was, maybe he was meeting a woman. I had a drink with him on a Friday in the bowling club and he always liked a good time with women. Maybe he met one who was married and they were meeting in secret. I wish we could figure out where he went.'

'Maybe he wanted to start a new life,' Cameron said. 'Some people do, you know. Live off the grid.'

'Nah. Not Alan. He wasn't into chopping down trees for firewood or drinking his own piss.'

'I said living off the grid, not living on an island with cannibals chasing after him,' Cameron said.

'Both have the same appeal, if you ask me,' Art said. 'Anyway, that's not his style. He wouldn't just up sticks and leave. Talking about piss, I need one now,' he said, going into the police station. Cameron wondered if Fifi and Henry liked a cupcake before they started shagging on the back seat of *Maw-reece* Duvall's car. Somehow he thought Wendy Delgado would know about it if they did.

6

EDINBURGH

'I like your sister,' Ruth said after they had left the café and were walking to the car. 'Her and I should go out more often.'

'You've only seen one side of her. She's calmed down a lot but she could drink a bottle of vodka for breakfast.'

'What? No.'

'You know what I mean. If drinking was a national sport, she'd win gold every time. Her and that group of women she used to go out with. They lived for partying and clubbing.'

'She doesn't give that impression.'

Brodie stopped as they reached the car. 'She's calmed down a bit over the last few years, but she was wild.'

They drove up to Morningside and the Royal Edinburgh Hospital. Ruth worked across the road normally, in the occupational unit, which was a wide umbrella for all the departments it sheltered. Hers were substance abuse and grief clinics.

Not dealing with serial killers.

* * *

This, the third anniversary of the attack – a date that lingered in his mind every day, he had told her – Ruth sensed a slight change in him. Like something was different. There was an edge to today's trip out in a prison van.

No visitors were allowed into the secure unit of the Royal Edinburgh Hospital while Dr Gabriel Kane was on the move.

Two armed response units bookended the prison van, while two more marked patrol cars were also in attendance, one at each end.

A patrol car blocked off the entrance to the car park when Brodie pulled up. A young uniformed officer recognised him and let him through. There were Uniforms everywhere, some of them armed.

The hospital was on lockdown, all the patients in their rooms now. Inside, the air was crackling with a mixture of anticipation and stress and, Brodie thought, fear.

Fear that something was going to go wrong. Fear that maybe Kane was going to sneeze or maybe cough and a gun-happy trigger finger would blow his head off.

Detective Superintendent Rob Cross was pacing back and forth, issuing orders that had already been ordered to officers who were nodding their heads and wishing they could have one last coffee before they hit the trail.

'You're late,' he said to Brodie when he saw him walking along the corridor with Ruth by his side.

'Fifteen minutes early,' Brodie said. Cross was almost the same height as Brodie, but was broad-shouldered, like he had played rugby somewhere down the line.

'That's what I mean,' he said, locking eyes with Brodie. 'You're usually half an hour early.' He looked at Ruth. 'Hello, doctor.'

'Morning, Rob. We stopped off for a roll at Isobel's place before coming up here.' She smiled at him. 'I hope that was okay.'

'Aye, of course it was.' Cross knew that he couldn't stop Ruth from doing that, and he was grateful that she had once again been on board with coming along on what he jokingly called the Helter Skelter Tour. 'How are Isobel and Dougal?'

'They're keeping well. Serving delicious food as always. In fact, if I weren't watching my figure, I would eat there more often.'

'Watching your figure? I thought you had him for that?' He nodded sideways at the big man.

'Sometimes it's a two-person job,' Brodie said.

'I hear you.' Cross looked at his watch. 'Great way to start the week, isn't it? Monday's are for easing into the week, not holding this nutcase's hand.'

'A necessary evil,' Brodie said.

'Right then, let's get up. We're twenty minutes past the time we said we'd be up. Lucy's up there, probably chewing her fingernails off to stop her from stabbing that arrogant bastard.' DI Lucy Warren, the woman who had saved Brodie's life.

'Keeping him on his toes?' Brodie said.

'Psychology; he knows that although he's the one who's showing us where the victim is, we're still in charge. I told him earlier in the week that if he starts fucking us around, I'll call it off, and he'll be lucky if he's wiping his arse with sandpaper when I'm finished.'

'And his reply was?' Brodie asked.

Cross shook his head. 'Nothing. He just smiled that psycho smile of his.'

'He knows he can call your bluff,' Ruth said.

'Aye. He knows that if I cancelled, all hell would break loose. The chief constable would have my balls in a jar in her office.'

'That's not something I can unsee,' Brodie remarked. 'Speaking of which, is the TV news crew present?'

'They are. They're upstairs doing a quick interview with Kane.' Cross raised a hand when he noticed Brodie was about to complain. 'The chief herself gave the go-ahead after Wheeler pulled a few strings. Someone knows someone else who is acquainted with the justice minister, and we were instructed to make it happen.'

'Is Lake up there?' Simon Lake, hospital director.

'Of course he is. He was bugging one of the make-up lassies to make sure they took care of him so he would look good on the six o'clock news. I hope if Kane goes off his nut with a sharpened toothbrush, he lets Lake have it first.'

'Please don't joke like that, Rob,' Ruth said.

'Wishful thinking,' Cross said. 'That man's a pain in my arse. He's acting as if he's running the show, as though this wouldn't have happened without his go-ahead. He fails to see that there are people well above my pay grade making these decisions, who make him look like a canteen lady.' He glanced at his watch again and signalled to a man in black fatigues. The armed unit commander.

'Sir.'

'Chief Inspector Williams, are your team members ready for escort duty?' Cross asked.

'All ready, sir, yes.' Williams looked around at the four-man unit as if to check they hadn't legged it in the time it took him to come over and talk to Cross.

'Right. Let's go up and get Dr Death. Get your team ready, commander.'

They trooped over to the lift and crammed in. On the top floor, there were heavy doors with reinforced glass. They walked along to the first one, were let through and stood in what amounted to a holding area while an operator in a control room opened the next door electronically.

'Let the fun begin,' Brodie said as the second door was unlocked.

7

FIFE

DI Art McKenzie sat back in the passenger seat, quite happy to let his colleague do the driving today.

'Mr Mister, or Johnny Hates Jazz?' Cameron said from the driver's seat. Art must have looked like he was dozing off, and Cameron hated driving when Art was getting some shut-eye. He said it made him feel like a chauffeur. Art told him if he was his chauffeur, he'd fire his arse out the door.

'Johnny Hates Jazz,' Art replied without any hesitation.

'Really? What about Mr Mister's "Broken Wings"?'

Art looked over at him. 'Their one hit? Nah. I like "Shattered Dreams".'

'Good choice. My Morag couldn't stand me playing eighties music.'

'That's when the rot set in,' Art said, turning to look out of the windscreen.

'Nothing to do with me not doing my own ironing, then?'

'Trust me, if you're not together on a music level, there's nothing else left. The rest of it is just padding.'

'Liking eighties music and refusing to iron my own shirts. Wow. I was fucked from the start,' Cameron said.

Art looked at him. 'Why didn't you iron your own shirts?'

'I tried. I was shite at it. Morag said just because she worked from home didn't mean to say she was my personal housekeeper. So I ended up paying somebody to iron them.'

'You weren't... entertaining this woman, were you?' Art asked.

'What? No, of course not. I mean, I was pleasant with her, but I didn't try anything on. Besides, she was almost the same age as my mother.'

'Aye, I can see that would be a disastrous move, right enough.'

'We just stopped communicating.'

'Her words or yours?' Art asked.

'Hers, of course. I communicated to her every day when I asked her how her day went. Her answer? "Oh, just the same as every day." What the fuck does that mean? You were shagging the postie?'

'You don't think she was, do you?'

Cameron shook his head. 'He's an old bloke. Ready to retire. Complains about his back all the time and smokes like a chimney. He's honking from his cigarette smoke.'

'You smell that through the letter box?'

'Not quite. But if we get a parcel or something that needs to be signed for. The old bastard has BO as well. If Morag was sleeping with him, then that would really crash my ego.'

'Left here,' Art said. 'Where the sign is pointing for Arncrouch.'

'You sounded just like Morag there,' Cameron said, turning left at the *Give Way* sign.

'You didn't hear me telling you to iron your own fucking shirt, did you? I'm just telling you because you seem distracted.'

'She used to give me directions because she thought I was a dozy bastard.'

'That too.'

The sun was out, and Art was beginning to feel the heat in the car, so he rolled down the window, feeling the wind jump into the car. Up ahead, the road was blocked off with police vehicles and a silver Volvo XC90.

'Sherlock's here,' Art said, nodding to the SUV. Ronald 'Sherlock' Holmes, one of the pathologists from Dunfermline.

Cameron pulled in behind the last marked police car. A Uniform was standing in the middle of the road. A big bulldozer of a man, with hands like shovels and a face that only a dog could love. He made The Rock look like a pimply Boy Scout. He was from the Highlands, where he no doubt knocked down trees for a living, without the aid of machinery.

'Cameron, ya fuckin' baw bag,' PC Don McCoy said, all thoughts of respect for colleagues of a higher rank gone out the window. 'And yourself, Arthur. How's things this morning?'

'Fuck me,' Art said under his breath. Another twat full-naming him. But what could he say to the big bastard? He'd tried telling the man before, when they were raiding a pub one night, but McCoy was so busy throwing somebody through a window that he didn't hear Art.

'Don, ya big fucking hairy twat,' Cameron said, grinning at him. 'Why are you standing in the middle of the road like a John Deere on steroids?'

'Fuckin' somethin' goin' on in that fuckin' hoose,' McCoy said, nodding over his shoulder. 'I'm guessing that's why you pair are here?'

'No, we're just passing through, Donald, and we heard this wee village is nice this time of year,' Art said with a deadpan face, full-naming the big bastard.

McCoy's brow furrowed for a second before he started laughing. 'Oh ho, ya bastard, ye nearly had me goin' there! Fuckin' passin' through. Good one.'

The smile suddenly left his face and Art's heart skipped a beat for a moment: he thought the other man had suddenly taken offence. Then they heard the sound of a car approaching.

'Go ahead, lads, I have to deal with this.'

Art and Cameron looked round to see an old man approaching in his car. They heard McCoy using the words 'fanny', 'closed' and 'get t'fuck', strung together in a sentence informing the unfortunate driver that police presence was ahead and please come back later.

'Come on, before he suggests we go for a pint,' Art said, moving forward, Cameron hot on his heels.

'Aye, I wouldn't like to be in the boozer with him when he has one too many.'

'One too many what? Fucking kegs?' Art said. Another Uniform was standing at the front door of the cottage, a female whom they recognised, and who wasn't on the comedy circuit.

'Morning, sir,' she said, and they nodded to her.

'See? That's how it's done,' Art said as they walked into the dim hallway.

'I'll let you tell McCoy that, will I?' Cameron suggested, and he was answered with where he could shove that suggestion.

There were white-suited forensic techs walking about, one with a camera.

'Have you ever wondered why there aren't any forensic techs who are serial killers?' Cameron asked.

'Surprisingly, I don't lay awake at night thinking about that stuff. Obviously you've got too much time on your hands. Get your mother to teach you how to knit. Or iron a shirt.'

'I'm just saying. They would know all the tricks on how to get away with murder.'

'You're giving me the fucking fear now, talking like that. Next thing you know, you'll be talking about how a young detective can get away with murdering his older colleague.'

'I have thought about that.'

Art looked at him. 'Walk in front of me, ya wee bastard.'

Cameron stepped in front, grinning.

A Uniform pointed along another hallway. 'It's along there, sir.'

The room, potential crime scene or the body, Art wasn't sure which one the man meant, but it was maybe all three.

Ronald Holmes was suited up, on his knees, looking down into the hole the chimney had made. Dust was on his knees and other parts of the suit. The hood was pulled up and a mask pulled down.

'No need to get on your knees when I come into the room, Sherlock,' Art said.

'Aye, you wish,' Sherlock said. He was a few years younger than Art and had an affable personality. He smiled at Cameron. 'Give's a hand up here, Cam, my bloody knees have locked.'

'No problem. I know you older boys need a hand from us young ones now and again.' He smiled, stepped forward, and reached out an arm. Sherlock grabbed it, and Cameron hauled him to his feet.

'Bloody hell,' Sherlock said. 'You know the knees were never designed to be knelt on? It's an unnatural position that us as human beings invented.'

'What have we got down there?' Art asked.

'Skeletal remains. Decades old, I would say, but we'll have somebody come in and have a wee look at them, for the record. The clothes are degraded but mostly intact. It was also wrapped in a plastic sheet. It looks like a child.'

'A child?' Cameron asked. A cold fear ran down his spine as he thought of his own two children. He hated not seeing them every day, and now knowing this skeleton was a child made him want to see his kids and give them a big hug. He fought his emotions for a moment before composing himself.

Sherlock nodded. 'Part of the chimney has landed on it, so I can't tell if it's a boy or a girl, but it looks like the size of maybe a seven- or eight-year-old. The chimney landed in the middle, tearing through the plastic. Right now, though, it's just a guess, but definitely a child.'

'I'm assuming foul play?' Art said, his voice low. Children dying always had an effect on him.

'I'm not sure yet. I want to take the plastic wrapping off carefully. The forensics crew will have to dig it out and, after I get it on the table, I'll call you with my findings,' Sherlock said.

'Thanks, doc.'

Art and Cameron left the room and walked back the way they came. 'Let's go and talk to the men who found it and called it in,' Art said. He knew that if DCI Alan McRae had been here, he would have been leading the investigation. 'I want to go and have a word with Daisy, Alan's sister. I spoke to her on the phone, but I want to speak to her face to face.'

'Fine by me.'

Outside, they watched as the mortuary van stopped at the end of the street and started reversing back towards the door of the cottage.

'Come on, Cam, let's get out of here before we get blocked in or something,' Art said, and they waited until the black van was stopped before walking round it and heading back to their car.

They heard McCoy before they saw him.

'Now, ya baw-heided cunt!'

'Oh, Christ,' Art said. 'I hope that's not the chief constable doing her rounds.'

'I don't think McCoy would care,' Cameron said. 'He's off his nut.'

They rounded the corner to see McCoy with a red face like his head was about to explode, a woman sitting behind the wheel, her window down and her mouth open.

'Don't make eye contact with him, for fuck's sake,' Art said, as they speed-walked to their car.

McCoy turned round to them. 'See ye later, lads!' he shouted.

The woman turned to look at them. 'Do you know this man?'

'Nope,' Art said. He jumped in, Cameron right beside him and Art got the engine running. They took off, with McCoy waving goodbye to them.

'Fucking arsehole's waving now. All we need is somebody calling Standards,' Art said.

'Deny everything,' Cameron said.

'Way ahead of you, brother.'

8

EDINBURGH

'Are you not riding with me in the cramped prison van that shouldn't be allowed to carry stray dogs, never mind human beings?' Gabriel Kane said as he shuffled out of the hospital, wearing a brightly coloured boiler suit as he was considered a flight risk, shackled in chains, flanked by two heavily built uniformed officers who weren't armed. No firearms to be next to Kane at any given time. That was what the sharpshooters were for.

'I've never been in the back of one of those things, and I don't intend to start now,' Brodie said.

'I have to say, that young ginger-haired hooligan with the rifle over there looks like he might be having too much fun,' Kane said, nodding in the direction of one of the snipers.

'Make you nervous?' Brodie asked. 'Maybe you could talk to your therapist about your life choices.'

'You may mock, Liam, but if he starts shooting then he might miss me and hit you.'

Brodie took a few steps back. 'Let's give him a better shot then, shall we?'

'Laugh if you must, but you know how gingers can be. They've been known to go off their head. He might start cracking off a few just for fun.

Not all lunatics are like me, you know. Just ask Ruth; some of them wear uniforms.'

'I'll bear that in mind next time I'm in Tesco.'

Kane was ushered into the van, and put into one of the single cells, while there were other armed officers in the other cells.

'Toodle-pip,' Kane said as the door was shut on him. Then the back door of the van was closed and locked. The engine was already running with two of the prison transporting crew in the cab, ready to follow the escort vehicles.

'He's a fascinating man,' Catherine Wheeler said, walking up to Brodie. 'I had a very nice chat with him. Maybe *we* could have a chat later? Over dinner?'

'Sorry, I'm busy,' Brodie said. He looked around to see if Ruth had heard and she was standing with raised eyebrows; maybe the woman she thought was a nice person wasn't so nice after all.

'Come on, Trudi,' a man standing close by said to her. 'We want to be following the convoy.'

'I'm coming, Ricky,' Catherine said, and Brodie could see the flash of anger as her TV persona slipped for a second. 'Liam Brodie, this is Ricky Brent, my producer. The man with the camera is Travis.'

'How you?' Ricky said, staring at Brodie. It was obvious that – apart from not being able to string a full sentence together – he was holding out for being asked to dinner by Wheeler, and wasn't pleased that this detective, who hadn't even met Wheeler before, was being invited out tonight.

'Busy,' Brodie said. The press weren't his favourite species of human being, and the TV crowd were one step above bottom feeders.

'Let's get the car started,' he said to Ruth, who stepped around the TV crew and walked beside Brodie.

'Hold up,' Rob Cross said, rushing to catch up with Brodie and Ruth. 'I'd like to cadge a lift with you. That nutbag has got me all wired up. I'm glad that we don't carry guns. Sometimes I'd be tempted. You know he called me a fat bastard?' Cross said, stepping in line with Brodie.

'You? That's ridiculous. What was he thinking?'

'Sometimes I can't tell if you're taking the piss out of me or not,' Cross said, opening the back door of Brodie's car and plonking himself in as Ruth got in the front.

'Should Ruth and I sit on the same side of the car to counterbalance you, sir?' Brodie said with a straight face, bending to look in. 'Wouldn't want the car tipping over.'

'You're hilarious.'

Lucy jogged across the car park. 'You mind if I join you all?' she asked, poking her head in.

'Not at all. Jump in the back,' Brodie said.

'I'd rather just sit,' she said with a grin, getting in.

Ruth laughed as Brodie got behind the wheel.

'I don't know how you do it, Ruthie,' Cross said, 'talking to Kane all the time.'

'I only have to do it once in a while. When he asks for me. Otherwise, he has his own psychiatrist.' She smiled at Cross. 'I'm sure you have to talk to a lot worse on a daily basis.'

'And that's just the high heid yins,' Lucy said.

'Belt up,' Brodie said as he started the car.

'Beg your pardon?' Cross said.

Brodie grabbed his seat belt and stretched it out after clicking it in. 'Seat belt.'

'I knew that.'

They followed the convoy of police vehicles out of the hospital and a battery of flashes greeted them as press photographers snapped their photos, before jumping into their cars.

The route had been well planned, and police patrol vehicles were already blocking the roads to the north of Edinburgh. No press would get near Kane.

'It's inevitable that some of those paparazzi arseholes with lenses bigger than their dicks will get a shot of Kane,' Cross said, tempted to give them the vickies as they passed, but he stopped himself. All he needed was a video of him mouthing 'go fuck yourself' to appear on the news.

'You need to get tinted windows on this thing,' Cross said.

'I told him that,' Ruth said, turning to look at him.

'You also suggested a set of furry dice to hang from the rear-view mirror,' Brodie reminded her.

'I was pulling your leg,' she said, looking back at Brodie again.

'You know what gets me?' Cross said. 'He won't tell us who she is until we find her,' he said, answering his own question. 'Same as last time and the time before that. Then he gloats.'

'You have to understand that he's playing a game and he wants us to know he's in charge,' Ruth said. 'He's in this game right now, and when he takes us to where she is, that game is over.'

'And he gets his little perk, in accordance with the justice minister,' Brodie said.

They made good time with the motorcycle outriders.

The cemetery was old, the place unkempt with an abandoned look. The council didn't waste their money on keeping the weeds and overgrown grass at bay.

Brodie followed the van as Kane gave his instructions to the Uniform inside the back of the van. They drove down the driveway that had been overtaken by weeds.

'I don't like this,' Cross said, looking out the windows.

'The armed team are already here and they'll be taking up positions when we stop,' Brodie said.

When they got out of the car, he could hear the police helicopter over-head. A truck came in behind the convoy, pulling a trailer with a Bobcat: a small tracked digger with a bucket on the front.

'Imagine coming in here after dark,' Lucy said, looking around. They were in a smaller, older part of the cemetery, separated from the main part by a high stone wall that was covered in ivy.

'No thanks,' Cross said, pulling a face, like he'd just stepped in something.

They watched as Kane was brought through the archway. He was smiling despite being shackled.

'She's in here somewhere,' he said, locking eyes with Brodie.

'Your lawyer has possession of the papers with the agreement on them,' Brodie said. 'We can't renege on the deal. You'll get Netflix. And the other thing.'

'Alright, then. Why are we standing around when there's work to be done? Oh, and I can tell you for a fact that you're going to need the Bobcat. I know you brought it along, just on the off chance that I wasn't talking nonsense and was going to give you the runaround, but tell the driver to start it up.'

Lucy nodded to Brodie and walked away, skirting Kane, not so much in case he lunged at her, but the other way round.

Brodie looked around, at the gravestone outlines in the wall. Many of the gravestones now lay on the ground where they had fallen or were pulled over. It was the council's policy to have the groundskeepers knock over loose headstones, so it looked like a battlefield of fallen warriors.

The driver approached, gave Kane a look that suggested he might find a suitable orifice to ram a shovel if the older man should even think about having a go, then got on with measuring the width of the archway. He crouched down, his jeans slipping, giving the world a view of his arse crack.

The men turned while Lucy wasn't quite as quick.

'Look away, look away,' Cross said to her. 'You'll go blind.'

'Does nothing for me, sir,' she said.

'It'll fit,' the Bobcat driver said to nobody in particular, and walked back to the trailer to unhitch the piece of equipment.

Lucy came back through and they stood around, Brodie looking at the small machine with more admiration than was really called for, thinking that most of the men there would have admitted to wanting a go on it after the driver was finished.

The driver steered the Bobcat expertly through the archway and stopped, waiting to be told what gravestone to lift.

'Well?' Cross demanded. 'What fucking gravestone?'

Kane tutted and shook his head the same way he would show his disapproval to a young boy. 'There are ladies present,' he said.

'Just get a move on,' Cross said.

Kane looked around as if he couldn't remember which one, then looked over to his right, lifting an index finger within the constraints of the shackles and moving it up and down, as if counting.

'The first one there. Big white one. Fell off the wall. With my help, of course. And a bloody big sledgehammer and a crowbar.' He looked at Brodie. 'See the ivy there? It's—'

'Right, we don't need to listen to any more of your drivel,' Cross said. 'You heard the man; first one there. Tip it over sideways then pull back.'

The driver nodded, and turned the Bobcat to the right, churning up the overgrown driveway, flattening the tall grass and chewing up the ground whenever he had to move it from the straight and narrow.

The Bobcat driver angled the machine so he could get the bucket underneath the stone and then he gently lifted it. It was made to look easy, something they couldn't have managed manually, and Brodie imagined Kane on top of the wall, sheltered from view from the top floor of the flats opposite, whose view was ruined by tall trees inside the cemetery. He could see in his mind's eye the doctor banging away with the sledgehammer until there was enough room for the crowbar, then a resounding thud as it toppled over onto the ground.

'Fuck me,' Cross said, and Ruth let out a gasp as they all looked at what had been hidden for years under the gravestone.

9

FIFE

Art McKenzie had called ahead to make sure that Daisy McRae was home. It was coming up for lunchtime and he was starting to feel hungry. Maybe Daisy would be in the mood to rustle up some sandwiches. No, probably not.

It never failed to amaze him just how alike Alan and Daisy were, like twins without being twins. Their eyes, their mouths, their laugh. Alan had once told him that they were seventeen months apart – Daisy had popped out of their mother's birth canal first, a story that made Art gag every time Alan felt like repeating it.

'Thompson Twins or Duran Duran?' Art asked as Cameron got back in behind the wheel.

Cameron started the engine and squinted his eyes, as if giving this question a really good go, like he was taking a spelling test in school and hoping the bell would go soon as he knew he was fucked. 'Duran Duran.'

'What?' Art said, tugging his seat belt just a little bit harder than was necessary. 'Away you go.'

'Aye. And the *Wedding Album*... album, from 1993. "Come Undone", though. I prefer that to "Ordinary World".'

'That's it, it's official: Cameron Reid talks pish.'

Cameron laughed and pulled away from the bowling club car park.

'Let's hear it for the Thompson Twins. All three of them.' He turned left.
'Shouldn't it have been the Thompson Triplets?'

'They were named after the Twins in the Tintin series, as you bloody well know. Don't be winding me up now.'

Cameron laughed again. 'What's your favourite Thompson Twins track?'

Art thought about it. '"Nothing in Common".'

Cameron nodded. They were both eighties aficionados, and their conversations would sometimes turn to that subject. Art told his younger colleague that they regularly had an eighties night at the club where the DJ would give it laldy with the records, especially after a few beers. One night he was so pished, he fell over onto his turntables, everything crashing to the floor. Although Art thought they might just be for show and the DJ was using a streaming service to play the music. It was hilarious nonetheless.

'Good choice,' Cameron said. 'Why that song?'

'It was on the soundtrack to a Tom Hanks movie way back in 1986.'

'What was the movie called?'

'*Nothing in Common.*' Art rolled his eyes and looked at his colleague like he should have known that.

'Never heard of it.'

'It's probably in somebody's VHS collection.'

Daisy was wringing her hands, like she was an unscrupulous medium about to take them to the cleaners. The house was a two-minute drive from the bowling club. It was a one-storey detached modern bungalow with a driveway at one side, big enough for two cars.

One car was there, a little red hatchback, but Alan's VW Golf was missing.

'Come away in, Art,' she said to them as they walked up the pathway to the front door. 'You too, Cameron,' she said to the younger detective, as if he had been going to hover about outside.

The sun was overhead and the air felt sticky now. Inside, it was much cooler, and Daisy led them into the living room, which was at the back of the house.

'Have you found him?' she asked, dispensing with any niceties.

They stood around in the living room, Art once again looking at the prints of the countryside and horses and trees hanging on the wall, anything so he didn't have to look Daisy in the eyes. Then he plucked up the courage.

He sucked in a breath and his answer came out like a sigh. 'No. But he was spotted somewhere unusual before he went on holiday.'

'Where? It wasn't in that lingerie shop again, was it? 'Cause I told him about that.'

Art could feel his cheeks starting to burn. Daisy was in her late fifties, but Alan had told him that his sister had never married. She was a civil servant, drank at the bowling club and had taken her brother in when he got divorced three years ago. Alan had got his feet under the table, as it were, and was in no hurry to move out, and Daisy hadn't been in any hurry to get him to leave.

'No, nothing like that. I'm sure he was just in there buying a Christmas present,' Art said.

'Not for me!' Daisy said, clutching an imaginary string of pearls on her chest.

'No, no, I meant for a girlfriend, or something.' *Shite.* Art admonished himself. What would the *or something* be? A mannequin he secretly kept in his wardrobe?

'He was seen up at the trail, outside Cupar, before he left for Tenerife,' Cameron said, jumping in.

Daisy looked puzzled. 'Up there? Alan doesn't go hiking.'

'We think he was meeting somebody, Daisy. Somebody who owns a little Volvo XC40. A blue one. Do you know anybody who owns such a car?' Art asked.

Daisy was silent for a moment as they all stood in her living room, waiting for the mother ship to beam them up. Then she looked at Art. 'Yes, I do.'

10

EDINBURGH

A uniformed officer turned towards a gravestone, bent his head around it and threw up, making retching noises that would put a cat to shame if they were both in a furball-throwing competition.

'Fuck me,' he said, forgetting for a moment he had an audience. He looked up to see other Uniforms watching him, while the detectives looked down at what was once a recognisable human being. Watching a puking probationer was no new thing for them.

The form that had been lying under the gravestone was dressed in female clothes, but gender identity would have to wait until it was on a stainless steel table in the mortuary. Brodie for the moment assumed it was a woman, partly because Gabriel Kane had said it was, but Brodie had long ago learned never to assume anything. Like the bastard was telling them the truth.

She wore a summer dress, faded yellow with some indistinguishable flowers on it. Long ago, it might have looked pretty, but now it resembled a dirty rag with only a hint of its original colour. Dark hair was at the top of the form, but any facial features had been ruined by the massive weight that had fallen on top of it. Arms and legs protruded from the dirty clothing, barely recognisable as human limbs.

The thing that Brodie was staring at was the black book that had been crushed into her chest. A Bible. A gold cross was embossed on the front cover. No other marking was needed to explain what it was.

'Why the Bible?' Brodie asked Kane, who stood transfixed, looking like he was reliving every second of killing her. Stains were on the dress, mixed in with the dirt. Not that the front of the gravestone had dirt on it when it had been tipped over. It was marble and was still in remarkable condition. But Brodie saw that a very shallow grave had been dug into the original grave so, when the stone came down, it would be lying flat, just like the other stones around it.

'She was a religious woman. I thought it fitting,' Kane said. He looked away from the corpse and smiled at Brodie. 'Quid pro quo, Liam. You have your victim, now I want to go home.'

Brodie was starting to feel the heat get to him. Claustrophobia circling the wagons. He wanted to loosen his tie but Cross frowned upon that sort of hooligan behaviour.

'Did you hear what I said, Liam?' Kane said.

Brodie slowly looked at Kane and he fought to keep his voice steady. To keep the rage caged inside of him. 'I heard you. You'll go when I say you can go, Dr Kane.'

'Gabriel.' Kane smiled.

'Have you forgotten something?' Brodie said.

'Have I? I'm not sure.' Kane smiled, keeping the game going for as long as he wanted it to. Then he laughed. 'Marianne Taylor.' He locked eyes with Brodie. 'We'll talk further.'

Brodie remained silent. The deal was finished now. Kane would get whatever it was he wanted. And since he had all he needed, this time he had requested access to Netflix, and a book of poetry. The condition where Brodie and Kane were on first-name terms was over. For the time being. Kane always had a way of coming round full circle.

'Right, get that piece of shite out of here and get the forensics team in here,' Cross said.

Kane kept looking at Brodie, but the big detective saw the older man's smile slip.

'I do hope that remark wasn't addressed to me, detective superintendent?' Kane said. He kept his eyes focused on Brodie.

Cross stepped across to Kane and stood in front of him. 'Get a bit of fun out of doing that, did you?' He moved his head sideways towards the corpse.

'You know, I might tire of revealing where my victims are buried. I might just stop. Unless you start showing me respect.'

Brodie watched Cross's face slowly change. His boss never lost his cool, not that Brodie could remember. The crow's feet were a little more pronounced now, the wrinkles on his forehead a little bit deeper, but years of working with the lowest of the low had conditioned him to remain calm. 'This little relationship we've got going on is like a seesaw; I step off and you fall flat on your arse. I make one phone call, and all the nice things you have in there, all the little privileges and niceties, will be gone in a heartbeat. I'm the spokesman on the ground, and I'm the one who the big brass talk to about you. I need a little respect from you, doctor. If I call you a piece of shite now and again, well, you're going to have to get on board with my little eccentricities. Do you understand what I'm saying?'

Kane smiled, like they'd been telling each other dirty jokes. 'Why, of course, Mr Cross, sir. My apologies, sir. I won't speak out of turn again, sir.'

Brodie knew the doctor was taking the piss out of Cross while making it look like he was being subservient, and no doubt Cross knew it too, but Kane was attempting to let the detective superintendent save face.

Cross nodded to the guards and they took Kane back to the van.

'This bloody place stinks,' Cross said, walking over to Brodie and Lucy. 'And I don't mean the dead body. This place honks of rotting vegetation.'

'It's not taken care of, that's probably why, sir,' Lucy said.

'Or maybe it's just that fucker,' Cross said, nodding through the archway where Kane was taken. 'I have another idea of how we could get him to tell us where his victims are buried; it involves a car battery and pair of jump leads.'

'That might also involve you losing your pension too, sir,' Brodie said.

'Sometimes I think, fuck it, Liam. Walk away from all of this.'

Brodie stood, looking his boss in the eyes. 'You're not walking away from this. Not when you've put so many years into this job. You're going to get what you deserve from this.'

Cross smiled a wry smile. 'Kane thinks I should get what I deserve, too, but I think you and him are on a different track.'

'Fuck him, sir. Let's just concentrate on getting this lady back to her family so they can give her a decent burial. If she has any family, that is.'

'I know that's the main thing,' Cross said, 'but he's such a smug bastard.'

'He is,' Lucy said. 'He couldn't stand to forget who his victim was. That wouldn't fit in with his narcissistic personality. Now he thinks he has the upper hand.'

'He always will, as long as there are other victims out there,' Brodie said. He had one last look over at the victim as the pathologist walked in. Then he walked back to his car.

11

FIFE

'This is your local?' Cameron said as Art pulled into the small car park just along the road from the Windygates bowling club.

'You say it like I drink in a brothel, or something,' Art replied. 'I do live here, after all.'

'I know, but... a bowling club? I never saw you as a bowler, boss.'

'Social membership. It's somewhere I can go for a quiet pint. Somewhere I'm not judged for being a copper.' Said in the same tone he would use if the patrons thought he was a nonce.

'Fair enough.'

They walked the short distance to the club entrance. Inside, the lunchtime bowlers were gearing up to have a couple of beers and a bite to eat before going outside.

'I don't know how they do it, some of them,' Art said, nodding to a couple of bowlers in their suits. 'Go out on the green half-pished and throw the bowl about.'

'It must take a certain amount of skill not to create a divot, right enough.'

'That's golf.' Art looked at his colleague as they walked up to the bar. 'You don't play a lot of sports, do you?'

'I played table tennis in school. Does that count?'

'Did you win any trophies?' Art asked.

'No.'

'Then close but no cigar.'

The bar manager approached them. He was older than Art, heavier with dark eyes, like he had seen his way around the world and had decided to drop anchor in this little village north of nowhere.

'Art. Bit early for you, isn't it? Well, on a weekday, anyway. Didn't you have enough last night?' He chuckled. 'This your colleague? The one you were telling me about?'

'No, this is somebody else. Dick, this is DS Cameron Reid. Cameron, Dick Drever, bar manager.'

'How do?' Dick said, grinning at Cameron. 'I won't tell if you don't. The usual?'

'No thanks, Dick. I don't drink on duty,' Art said.

'Since whe... I mean, I didn't realise you were on duty,' Dick said, when he saw Art briefly shake his head.

'We're actually here in connection with the disappearance of DCI Alan McRae.'

'Al? Fuck me, where's he disappeared to?'

'If we knew that, we wouldn't be here,' Cameron said. 'Have you seen him recently?'

Dick's smile slipped a little bit. Then he focused on Art. 'The last time I saw him was a few weeks ago, when he was in with you. He was going on holiday, wasn't he? Tenerife or something. I told him the Canaries were better in the winter. When you're freezing your nuts off over here, you can be over there getting a nice tan.'

'He did go to Tenerife, and came back but he didn't go back to his sister's house and hasn't been seen since.'

'I can ask around, Art, see if anybody's heard anything,' Dick said.

'Thanks, pal.' He looked at Cameron. 'Fancy a wee scran? It is lunchtime, after all.'

'Sure. You got a menu?' he asked Dick.

'Just what's on the chalkboard there. Take a seat and Rita will be over to take your orders. Pint, Art?'

Fuck's sake, Art thought, making eye contact with the bar manager, who, by rights, should have been slapping himself on the forehead as he remembered Art didn't drink on duty. Attention span of a fucking golden Lab. 'I'll just have a Coke, Dick. What are you having?' he asked Cameron.

'I'll have a pint and a nip,' Cameron said.

'Coke for him, too,' Art said. They read the board while Dick poured two watery drinks from the spray gun into glasses with some ice. 'Cheers,' Art said, paying for them, and they found a table in a corner where Art could keep an eye on the front door. Old habits, he told Cameron for the millionth time.

Then Rita came over to take their orders. She hadn't seen Alan McRae either.

12

EDINBURGH

It was late afternoon by the time they had the debriefing. Det Supt Cross was in a meeting with his boss. They were having a Zoom meeting with one of the assistant chief constables, who was turning so red with anger that he looked like smoke was about to start blowing out of every orifice. Brodie and Ruth stayed at the hospital to have a session with Kane, just like the two previous years.

Catherine Wheeler was after an interview with Brodie, who told her that she had more chance of getting an interview with Jack the Ripper.

'I wonder if she kisses her mother with that mouth,' he had said to Ruth after Wheeler objected.

Gabriel Kane was sitting in his usual chair, waiting for Ruth. Two attendants were present with him, and Brodie acknowledged them as he and Ruth came into the room. They both left, telling Brodie they would be just outside the door.

'I've always liked this room,' Kane said. 'Even though the prints on the walls are fixed in place and would have to be taken down by a joiner. The books too; pieces of wood with book covers on them. Plastic plants. All designed to give off a certain ambience while being impossible for a madman to use as a weapon.' He smiled at Ruth. 'Are there any personal touches in here, Ruth?'

'Just him,' she replied, nodding at Brodie.

Kane smiled. 'You're a lucky lady. I wouldn't have pegged you for dating such a rugged man, but it takes all sorts.'

She sat down on a chair opposite Kane, and Brodie sat on another one close to her but closer to Kane, putting himself in the firing line. Normally, one of the attendants would have been sitting close by, but Brodie had told them that wouldn't be necessary.

'We kept our end of the bargain, Kane,' Brodie said to him. 'Now it's your turn.'

Kane looked at the policeman and kept the smile fixed in place. 'Now, now, what are the rules?'

Brodie looked at the doctor. The older man had just turned sixty but kept himself fit. His face showed lines at the side of his ice-cold blue eyes and his hair was getting greyer every year, but there was still a sharpness to him, like he was assessing every word Brodie spoke, every move he made.

'First-name terms.' Brodie spoke the words evenly, not letting any anger or emotion creep in.

'Did you have a mental breakdown or something? Your synapses not quite firing on all cylinders?' Still the smile, but it had an air of smugness now. Maybe because he had been taken out of the orange jumpsuit and was now back in his regular clothes. Back in his own environment, where he had an element of control.

'I forgot,' Brodie said.

'My guess is, you know that I know you're lying, so you deliberately used my last name, hoping it would get under my skin. So I would let myself get riled by the provocation, but no such thing is going to happen. You're annoyed by today's outcome, not at finding the body, but knowing that I was indeed responsible for another woman's death.'

'It must have made you feel proud today,' Brodie said. 'Exchanging a woman's life for a book of poetry and a subscription service.' He looked at Ruth for a moment, and she very slightly shook her head. Brodie was charging in and Kane would close down if they didn't handle him carefully.

'It did. It made me feel proud that I killed a woman and she was just listed as a missing person and nobody could obviously find her. Nobody had a clue.' He smiled.

'Why don't you start by telling us about Marianne, Gabriel?' Ruth said.

Kane's smile was even wider now. 'See? Ruth knows how to play the game. You could pick up a few cues from her. But then again, you aren't a psychiatrist like we are.'

Brodie ignored the jibe.

Kane dismissed him with a slow movement of his eyes as he turned to Ruth. 'Marianne and I got to know each other very well. She was reserved, had never married, no kids. She told me she had just turned forty. She was perfect for me. We were only friends though. There was never any sexual relationship with my victims. DNA is bad enough, but doing other things to them? Not my style. I just liked killing them.'

'Who was she?' Ruth asked. 'One of your students?'

'No. Marianne was somebody I met in a coffee shop. One of those anonymous places you find on every street corner nowadays. She was reading a book and I started talking to her about it.' He chuckled. 'I then apologised. I told her I know what it's like when you're trying to read and somebody interrupts you. Do you read, Liam?' he asked, not moving his head to look at the detective at first. Then he slowly turned to look at him, as if he already knew the answer.

'I do.'

Kane's eyebrows rose up. 'Byron? Keats? Whitman? Or maybe one of the Brontë sisters?'

'I'm more of a thriller reader.'

'Of course you are. Men attacking other men. I can see why you enjoy such books.'

'You were the one who attacked me, remember?' Brodie said. 'With a knife. Trying to kill me. Is there any such scene in a Walt Whitman poem?'

Kane didn't answer. He carried on. 'Do you know the first edition of *Leaves of Grass* was printed in Brooklyn by two Scottish immigrants?'

'I can't say I do.' The book of Whitman poetry was the book Kane had requested in return for giving up the victim.

'See? You learn something new every day.'

'I thought we were going to learn all about a murder victim.'

'And you shall.' He looked at the small side table with the plastic bottle of water sitting on it. 'What, no glass?' he said with a small laugh. He slowly grabbed the plastic bottle, broke the seal and had a drink from it, wiping his mouth with the back of his hand. He put the bottle back. That was all he was permitted to have; no hot liquids, nothing with additives, just plain water.

'What made Marianne a victim for you?' Ruth asked.

Kane looked at her face, a slight smile playing around his lips. 'The same reason you would be, Ruth, if circumstances were different. She was attractive, but it was her intelligence that attracted me to her. The fact that she was sitting in a coffee shop reading poetry.'

'How long were you friends with Marianne before you killed her?' Brodie asked.

Kane rolled his eyes towards the ceiling, as if the answer lay there. Then back to Brodie. 'A few weeks. Long enough to get her to trust me, but not long enough for her to get to know me so well. Don't you remember these answers from a year ago? That has been my MO all these years. I do wish you would keep up, Liam.'

'I just wanted to see if your story changes, year after year,' Brodie answered.

'Why would it? You think I'm a pathological liar? If I am, I'm a damn good one.'

'I'm the one who can't keep up with everything,' Brodie said, trying to show inferiority to the doctor, to make him feel like he was so far above the detective that he was looking down on him, metaphorically.

'I know it must be hard for somebody like you.'

There was a knock at the door. They all looked. Brodie was expecting to see one of the orderlies coming in. They were told that they weren't to disturb them, unless it was an emergency.

It was a woman.

'Ah. DI Warren,' Kane said, breaking a smile.

Lucy ignored him. 'I'm sorry, sir, but can I have a word?' She was holding a buff-coloured folder.

Brodie got up, keeping his eye on Kane, but the doctor stayed where he was, making no attempt to move.

Brodie closed the door behind him as he and Lucy stepped into the corridor. The two orderlies were standing further down. It was agreed with the hospital that, when they were debriefing, Cross and Lucy would work in one of the offices.

'What's wrong, Lucy?'

'The boss asked me to bring this folder. It contains the dental records we requested.'

Brodie took the folder and opened it, reading the contents. 'Are we sure this is her?'

'Yes. The friend who reported her missing informed us that she had personally taken Marianne to the dentist since Marianne did not drive. This is the accurate account. We've started the deep dive into her.'

Brodie nodded. 'Thanks.' He watched as the DI turned and left, then he went back into the room. He passed the folder to Ruth before sitting down.

'I think I was correct in guessing you're a pathological liar, Kane,' he said.

Kane wasn't smiling as he looked at Brodie. Ruth read the contents of the folder before closing it and keeping a hold of it.

'Care to share?' Kane asked.

Brodie looked at him, and knew this game had just got a lot tougher.

'The body we found under the gravestone today?'

'What about it?' Kane said, no sign of a smile now, sensing that something was wrong.

'It's not Marianne Taylor.'

13

EDINBURGH

The Reader stood in his library and took a deep breath through his nose. The scent of the books was intoxicating. He could feel the aroma of the paper travelling through his lungs and into every pore of his body. He loved books. Lived for them, ever since he was a young teenager and his father had been handy with a belt. He had started reading after finding the small book exchange. You bought a book, took it back when you'd read it and he'd give you two-thirds of what you paid for it and then he'd sell it again.

He had been a voracious reader back then. And of course, there was the local library, but they only held so much stock. Sometimes he'd buy a book and keep it, and read it more than once.

Now he was holding the paperback in his hand, the one he got from the café in Leith.

The one belonging to the filthy cop. He wouldn't take this one back because if it sat there, they'd have his DNA. The old man in there was a book lover. He'd told The Reader this one day when they were talking. The Reader had been probed about his line of work: was he retired? No. What did he do for a living? Stock market. Investing. Entrepreneur. It was all true, but very vague. It wasn't always that way. He led a very different life, one of privilege some might say, but he had got there through hard work and determination.

He had met his wife, Nancy, through a mutual friend. At a dinner party at the friend's house, just like millions of other people met their other halves at such a function. It hadn't been a blind date, as there were several other single people there, as well as married couples, not including the hosts.

He hadn't been seated next to her at the dinner, but diagonally across, and he had caught her looking at him a few times. He'd looked back, catching her staring at him, and she had smiled cheekily and given a small laugh into her glass before looking away.

The woman who was sitting to his left loved herself, and proceeded to tell him how she had been a model years ago. The Reader thought it could very well have been modelling socks. She had the kind of voice that would scrape ice off a windscreen on a winter morning.

Dinner dragged, and might have tempted him to take his own life had it not been for the old colonel sitting on his right. Drunk, brash, amusing him with anecdotes from his days in the army, Colonel Murray – Mustard to his friends – had been a hoot. But looking to his right had kept his eyes away from Nancy. He had reached over to grab one of the wine bottles occasionally so he could look over at her. Twice she was chatting with a dashing young man to her right and wasn't looking over at him.

'Shot his bloody bollocks off, he did,' Colonel Mustard said, and The Reader had looked away and hadn't a clue whose bollocks had been detached from their rightful owner.

'Sounds like fun,' he said.

The colonel looked at him with a stern face for a moment, before bursting into laughter. 'It was! I've never had so much fun.' He downed the contents of his glass. The Reader didn't know what the liquid was, but it was having its effects on the older man. 'Of course, they don't let me have a gun nowadays, more's the pity,' he added, solving the mystery of who had been the one pulling the trigger. The Reader hadn't asked who had been on the receiving end, friend or foe.

The house was large, detached, old, cost a fortune to run but was private, the hostess had told him as they were in the vast library after dinner. Colonel Mustard had been poured into the back of a taxi after having mistaken a large potted bush outside the front door for the outside bathroom.

He didn't know it then but, Nancy, the woman who would be his wife, had gently persuaded him to leave at that point. The house was at the end of a long drive so there were no prying eyes, nobody hiding behind net curtains and no dog walker passing by with a mobile phone and a sense of indignation.

The colonel's wife – who, The Reader assumed, didn't have the nickname Miss Scarlet – had stood while the taxi driver helped the old boy into the back after the promise of a big tip, even though he suspected he would be throwing a bucket of soapy water across the rubber floor shortly.

'I know a place we could go and have a quiet drink,' Nancy said to him as they stood in the small group of people watching the taxi driver wrestle the colonel, like it was a new contact sport and the old boy was giving it everything he had but was losing badly.

'A bar?' The Reader said.

'A café. I feel like a nice cup of tea. It would feel weird if I was sitting in there on my own, reading a book.'

He raised his eyebrows and smiled at her. 'You're a reader?'

She gave a brief laugh. 'Yes. There aren't many of us left, if you ask some people.'

'I'd love to,' he said.

'Read my book?' she said, teasing him.

'That too. But go to this mysterious little café.'

'There's nothing mysterious about it. It's open twenty-four hours and there's always somebody in it through the night.'

He looked at his watch. 'It's almost midnight.'

'The witching hour. Maybe I'll turn into a pumpkin or something.'

'We'd better get a move on, then.'

That night had been wonderful, sitting drinking endless cups of tea until the breakfast cook came in and they ordered a fry-up. Neither of them felt tired, but when the sun came up, they went their separate ways.

The Reader waited a day to call Nancy, and they arranged a proper date. It was the start of something magical. He fell in love with her on the second date and asked her to marry him three months later.

They didn't want to wait long, so they arranged a day for their wedding. It turned out that would be the day of Nancy's funeral.

14

EDINBURGH

Brodie had skipped lunch and now it was halfway between lunch and dinner and he felt his stomach grumbling.

He had to admit, Gabriel Kane had a good poker face. No tics, no eye movement, no sweating, just the briefest hint of a smile that was questioning Brodie's statement.

'You want to do this little dance, Liam? Try to throw me off balance?'

Brodie resisted the urge to look at the camera that was recording this conversation. Det Supt Rob Cross would be watching on a monitor, and Brodie didn't want to look at it.

'Just telling you how it is, Kane,' Brodie said.

'Here we go with last-name using again. I thought we had an agreement?'

'We did; you agreed to tell us who your victim is. That was obviously a blatant lie.'

'Maybe you mistook her for somebody else,' Ruth said, in a tone that was placating, as she would talk to her grandfather who had just pissed the bed.

'Ruth, you really are a sweetheart,' Kane said, shifting his eyes to her, 'but please don't treat me like a fool.'

Christ, he doesn't know, Brodie thought. *He really thinks that's Marianne Taylor.*

'Could you be mistaken, Gabriel?' Brodie said, switching tack now.

'Either beating me with a verbal hose or killing me with kindness. There doesn't seem to be any middle road with you, Liam.'

'That's exactly what it is: meeting you halfway.' Brodie locked eyes with the doctor.

Kane took in a deep breath and let it out slowly. 'How can you be so sure that it's not her?'

'Marianne Taylor had her own teeth. Her friend told us that she was the one who drove Marianne to the dentist. So we know that she was missing, had her own teeth and was never found. The woman we found today had false teeth. Top and bottom. Unless Marianne went to another dentist and had all her teeth pulled, then it's not her. But DNA is being extracted as we speak and Marianne has a sister who lives in Dundee. She's agreed to a swab, then we'll get it to the lab and we'll get a familial DNA result if it's her.' Brodie stared at Kane. 'But we both know that's not her. Why don't you just tell me who it is?'

He watched every line on Kane's face, looked at his eyes, watched the breathing. The old bastard hadn't known it wasn't her.

'I want to go back to my room now, please,' Kane said.

'Just a few more questions,' Brodie said.

'Now!' Kane shouted, the mask slipping.

He was escorted out of the room and back to his own room.

'You aren't playing games with him, Liam, are you?' Ruth asked when it was just the two of them.

He looked at her. 'I wish I was.'

15

FIFE

Art McKenzie and Cameron Reid sat in the rancid pool car, trying not to breath in through their noses. Having the windows wound down had helped a little bit, but it also encouraged flies to have a go at breaking through the smell barrier, and even though they frequently picnicked on puke, the car was too much even for them.

'Do you think if we set it on fire, they would replace it with a new one?' Cameron asked.

'Why don't you try it and find out? What's the worst that can happen? You get to sit and think about it every day when you're in Saughton?'

'Aye, you're right. I'd get treated worse than the prisoners.' He looked at Art. 'I wouldn't shower if I was in there. I'd just keep the same clothes on every day.'

Art shook his head. 'Where the hell do you get your ideas from? I have never, in my entire life, ever heard of a prisoner who kept his clothes on all the time.'

'First time for everything.'

They were sitting across the road from a short, dead-end street, keeping an eye on a one-storey bungalow in Glenrothes. It was a well-respected development, a place where Alan McRae's ex-wife lived. Which was once the marital home.

The little driveway at the side of the house was empty. So were the spaces in front of the double garage on the other side. Art had contacted the station and got a hold of the landline number for Alan's previous address. It rang but nobody answered. Art didn't know if that meant the number was still in use at the residence or whether it had been disconnected and issued to another address.

'Maybe she's renting it out,' Cameron said, looking over his shoulder from the passenger seat into the back, trying to find the source of the smell.

'Maybe she's just away shopping.'

'I bet you a tenner she's done a runner,' Cameron said.

'Ten?' Art looked at his younger colleague. 'Why don't we make it fifty?'

Cameron was still looking for any sign that something had died in the back. 'Fifty? You're on.'

Art started the engine, and Cameron turned to look out the windscreen, seeing the blue Volvo in the distance turn into the street.

'You owe me fifty,' Art said.

'You saw the car coming when I was looking away. Bets are off when you're a cheating bastard,' Cameron said. 'You're meant to lead by example for younger colleagues and those in lower ranks. You have no morals.'

Art grinned. 'I just want to see your wife's reaction when I tell her you lost another bet.'

'Aye, well, what the eye doesn't see, the heart doesn't grieve over. And you're still missing the point. That one was voided simply because you resorted to smoke and mirrors.'

'My arse. I was looking through the windscreen like you were supposed to be doing.'

Cameron buckled his seat belt. 'I wish they would give us a decent motor, something with a nice tune that we could easily weave in and out of the schemes.'

'You just described an ice-cream van.'

He drove a short distance and turned into the street, pulling up to the bungalow and parking outside the front door. They watched as Pat McRae walked into a side door with a bag of groceries in one hand.

'Looks like she hasn't left the country with Lord Lucan after all,' Art said.

They stepped outside into a day that had been warm but was now deceiving them with a biting wind. Art kept his hair short, while Cameron did not, and the wind tousled Cameron's hair as they walked to the front door. Art rang the doorbell.

'Who is it?' Pat asked from the safety of the other side.

'Pat, it's Art and Cameron.'

'Oh, it's you, Arthur.'

Fucking Pat and his mother were the only ones he knew who full-named him. And that annoying bastard, Don McCoy.

The door opened a crack with the chain on, like the little metal links would stop somebody with big boots and determination, and they could just see part of her face.

'Do you want to come in?' she said.

'That would be wonderful.'

'It's just that I'm just out of the shower,' she replied.

'That's the quickest I've ever seen somebody take a shower,' Art said. 'We just saw you come in the side door with a bag of groceries.'

'Bugger,' she whispered, stepping back and sliding the chain. The door opened, and Pat stood looking at them.

It had been a long time since Art had seen Alan's ex-wife. The last time was at the bowling club when she had one too many. 'Just letting my hair down,' she had said before puking in the rose bushes. Art had helped Alan get her inside and then left his friend to deal with the aftermath. 'Stay and have a drink,' Alan had said, and Art had all but told him to fuck off. He didn't mind helping get the drunk wife into the house, but that was where their friendship cut off.

Pat's face had more lines than Art remembered. More crow's feet at the side of her eyes, with bags underneath. Her skin looked saggy and pale.

She stepped back and opened the door wide.

'Cameron,' she said, nodding to him.

'Mrs McRae.'

They trooped in, and Art had a fleeting memory of coming to a New Year's party at this house years ago. He had no recollection of leaving.

'Would you like a drink?' Pat asked.

Art gave Cameron a swift sideways look before telling her that a soft drink would be acceptable.

They followed her into the kitchen, where she grabbed a couple of cans of Coke from the fridge and handed them over. They popped them open and sat at the little table in the corner.

'You must be wondering if I have a man in my life,' she said, sitting down.

The question caught Art off guard momentarily before he quickly composed his answer. 'Nothing to do with us, Pat,' he replied. He thought she could have a platoon of the Scots Guards in here, and it would have nothing to do with him.

'Have you ever... you know... after...' she said, which, to the uninitiated, could raise so many questions. *Have you ever thought about writing to the adult movie star again after you got out of prison?* was one.

'After my wife died? No. There have been some dates, you know, but nothing serious,' he said. Was she stalling for time? He wasn't going to let her, especially since she hadn't asked them what they were there for. Because she knew. 'You know why we're here, Pat.'

She looked down at her hands which were sitting in her lap, twiddling. Then she made eye contact with him. 'Yes. I'd heard Alan was missing. Daisy called me to ask if I'd seen him.'

'And you told her...?'

'I told her the truth. I haven't.'

'That's not quite true, is it, Mrs McRae?' Cameron said.

She looked at him, almost as if she had forgotten he was there. 'I haven't. She told me he's missing, and I'm sorry and all that, but we're divorced. I'm not Alan's keeper. He might have run off with a stripper for all I know.'

'What about the car park up at the trail?' Art asked.

'What about it?' Looking back at him now.

This was how it was going to be, Art thought. Like pulling fucking teeth.

'You were seen talking to Alan in your car, before he went off on holiday.'

'No, I wasn't.'

Flat-out denial. That was how a lot of interviews started out. *I wasn't there. I didn't see anything. It doesn't make you go blind.*

Art didn't mind. It was to be expected. The guilty always started off that way, but Art had been opposite hundreds of people saying the same thing, which had only served to hone his skills in seeing right through them. Sweating, fidgeting, making a funny face without realising it, and eye movements that made them look like they had a mild form of Tourette's. Now that his question was out there, Pat had begun displaying all the symptoms. Alan would have been all over her like a rash.

'What was it you talked about?' Cameron said.

'Even if we did meet up, I don't think that's any of your business,' Pat said, her cheeks starting to flush.

'So you *did* meet up then?' Art said.

Anger and the face changing colour. Art knew she was lying to them, but why? Because they were divorced, and she couldn't care less if he was missing? He desperately wanted to have a look around the house now, but without consent or a search warrant, that wasn't going to be possible. And he doubted that she would fall for the *Can I use your bathroom?* excuse, where the copper would pretend to go for a piss and then start raking about in her knicker drawer. She had been married to a copper, after all.

'If something's happened to him, we need to try and find him, Pat,' Art said, an edge to his voice now.

Her lip began to tremble. 'I know. I truly don't know where he is. I promise you, Arthur. We did meet up there, at the trail. But he left and got back into his own car, and I drove away before he left. I haven't seen him since.'

Art grimaced inside; he hoped the wee bastard sitting next to him wouldn't start full-naming him, or else he'd have to slap him one.

'Obviously, I can't make you tell us what you were discussing up at the trail and why you would need to meet up there,' Art said, 'but it might help.'

Pat sighed. 'Of course.' She looked at them in turn before returning her gaze to Art. 'Alan was scared.' She held up a hand to ward off the next question. 'I don't know what he was scared of, but he was scared. He mentioned something about getting in deeper than he intended. His words, not mine. I've never seen him like that before. He wanted to meet there to reduce the chance of us being seen. He got into my car, and we sat and talked. He told me he was going to Tenerife the following day and hoped things would have cooled down by the time he returned. I swear that's all he said. Then we discussed his work, my work, politics. He left my car and got back into his own.'

'Can you tell me if you're seeing somebody else?' Art asked. 'Somebody who might have found out and who got a bit jealous?'

'I've been seeing somebody,' she said.

'Can you tell us who?' Cameron asked. He'd put the burp-inducing can on the table. The last thing he wanted was to encourage a vurp.

Pat blew out a breath, signalling that she might not get approval when she revealed the name of her latest boyfriend. 'Dick Drever.'

Cameron's eyes went wide and Art could see the younger detective was about to blow out something like, 'You've got to be fucking kidding me.'

Instead, he said, 'I've met Dick.'

Art jumped in. 'We talked to him at the club to see if he had seen Alan.'

'And had he?' Pat asked.

Art shook his head. 'No.'

'Did he find out that you had seen DCI McRae that Friday at the trail?' Cameron asked.

'If he did, he didn't say anything. But you know Dick, not the sharpest pencil in the pencil case.'

'Is this a serious or a casual relationship?' Art asked.

'Casual. I'm not moving in with him, or anything. It's just company, you know? It gets lonely sometimes.'

Art knew exactly what that was like. His wife, Dee, had died of breast cancer two years ago. Surgery hadn't helped as it had metastasised into other parts of her body. He had been with her every day in the hospice until she slipped away.

'I understand,' he said simply.

'I wish Alan had told me what he was scared of, but I don't know.'

'He came back from holiday, we know that much. Border Force

confirmed that to us. After he left the airport... he disappeared into thin air.'

'Who would want to hurt him?' she asked. 'Was he being threatened at work? Was somebody out to get him?'

'Not that we know of,' Art said.

'You know, even though we divorced, I didn't harbour any grudge towards Alan. In fact, he would come round for a coffee and we'd chat and have a laugh. We got on better after the divorce than at the end of our marriage.'

'That's often the way,' Art said as he stood up. Cameron did the same.

'I'm sorry I couldn't be of more help,' Pat said, getting up and coming round the table to hug Art. She ignored Cameron.

'If you can think of anything, Pat, anything at all that might help us locate Alan, please give me a call.'

'I will.'

They went back out to the car and Art started it up. 'Fucking hell,' he said.

'What?' Cameron said.

'You, manky bastard. I could smell that burp a mile away. If that's how fizzy drinks affect you, maybe you should drink tap water.'

'I should have. I will from now on. Fizzy drinks always make me do that.'

'And yet you still took one.'

'Lesson learned, boss.'

Art started the engine. Looked over at Cameron. 'What did you make of Pat?'

'I think she's a lying cow.'

'I said what do you think, not insult her. If Alan heard you say that, he'd shove a boot so far up your arse, your eyes would spin.'

'No disrespect, but I learned to talk like that from you.'

'No, you didn't, ya wee bastard.'

'See?' Cameron had a smug look on his face.

'However, disrespect aside, I agree with you. I think she's hiding something. Alan told her something, and she was sworn to secrecy. And because they're still friends, she's protecting him. But she might be putting him in danger by keeping quiet. If it's not already too late.' He said the last words in a quiet voice, as if voicing them would make them come true.

As the car turned around and left, Pat stood behind the net curtains in the living room. When it had turned out of her street, she turned to the figure standing behind her.

'They've gone,' she said simply.

16

EDINBURGH

Brodie stood at the window of his living room and drank some of the whisky in his glass, feeling the warmth course down into his gut. The lights were on over in Fife, even though it wasn't fully dark yet. Night-time was slowly coming. It had been a long day, and a tiring one, and now the wee dram was helping him relax.

Ruth came up behind him and wrapped her arms around his waist. 'Don't let him get under your skin,' she said.

'I can't help it. It's like some macabre puzzle; he's either taking the piss, or he genuinely thought that was Marianne Taylor. I can't decide what it is.' He turned away from the window to look at her. 'He was a psychiatrist. He knows how to play head games. I thought being a detective had taught me how to play head games with people, but Kane takes it to a whole new level.'

'Let's sit and watch some TV.'

'We can. Let me call Eric first.'

'Okay. I can go to the bedroom, give you some privacy,' Ruth said.

'Don't be daft.' He walked over to the small desk in one corner of the living room, where a MacBook Pro sat, closed and turned off. A small printer sat off to one side, waiting for Brodie to start writing the great Scottish crime novel, that he may or may not have inside him.

He sat on the office chair as Ruth put on the TV, keeping the volume low.

'Eric? It's Dad.'

'Hey, Dad. How's things?'

'Could be better. Could be worse.'

'Is Ruth there?'

'She is.'

'Tell her I said hi,' Eric said.

'Eric says hi.'

Ruth looked around from her show. 'Tell him and Chrissie I said hi.'

'She says hi to you both.'

They chatted, Brodie asking how his gran was. Fiona's mother. The old woman was getting along fine. Still having a wee nightly nip of whisky, purely for 'medicinal purposes'.

'I'm having some medicine now as well,' Brodie said, laughing. 'How's your MS?'

'I had a flare-up last weekend. It was pretty bad. My walking isn't getting any better.'

'You should have called me.'

'I'm not going to call you every time I have a wee flare-up, Dad. I have Chrissie to look after me.'

'I know that. And she's an angel. But I still want to know. Or I'll come across to Kelty and skelp your bloody arse.'

'I'm twenty-seven, Dad. I could take you any time I wanted.'

'Keep telling yourself that, ya wee brat.' They both laughed.

'How's work?' Eric asked. 'I saw that reporter on the TV talking with Kane. That's a new slant on things. Kane didn't give an interview last year.'

'Or the year before,' Brodie said.

'I don't know how you can be in the same company as him and not put your hands round his neck.'

'That's why I'm the copper and you're not.'

'That's true.'

'How's business doing, son?'

'The usual bread-and-butter stuff. Chrissie is so much better with all the physical stuff than I am,' Eric said, with just a hint of bitterness in his voice.

'You're partners. She doesn't mind doing that stuff. She relishes it, you told me.'

'Ach, don't mind me. I'm just feeling sorry for myself. This flare-up is making me tired and narky.'

'Nobody's blaming you for being that way. Chrissie's a saint.'

'You don't have to tell me twice,' Eric said. 'I don't know what I'd do without her.'

'Do you have any interesting jobs on the go?' Brodie asked.

'Nah. Cheating husbands. Three of them just now. A job for a lawyer, following somebody. It pays the bills.'

'That's the main thing, Eric.'

'Are you coming over to see Gran soon? She was asking for you the other day.'

'I will. Soon, I promise.' Brodie felt guilty for not seeing the old woman. He loved her, as she was the remaining family that Brodie still kept in touch with. Fiona's brother hated his guts and they never communicated. They had a falling-out at Fiona's funeral, George blaming Brodie for his sister's death. No matter it was cancer that took her, it was Brodie's fault. Somehow, he had told Brodie that if she hadn't been with him, then she would still be alive.

He hadn't spoken to George since.

'Tell Gran I'll bring in one of her favourite cakes.'

'I will, Dad. But she didn't tell me to bug you about visiting. She knows how busy you are. It's just that she loves seeing you.'

'I know she does. And I love seeing her too.' He loved seeing photos of Fiona sitting on her dresser in the living room. He and Ruth both went now. He had felt awkward, telling the old woman he was seeing somebody else now, but she had laughed and told him not to be daft. He was a police officer, not a monk. Fiona wouldn't have wanted him to live a solitary life. Ruth was welcome anytime, and God bless Ruth, she had spoken to Gran like she had known her for years.

Plus Gran was happy that Eric was still a part of his life. Eric's biological father was nowhere to be found, and Brodie was all the father Eric had ever known.

They chatted about cars for a little while, Eric's favourite subject. He drove a Honda CR-V now, as it was easy to get in and out of, but better health and a pot of money would see him in some imported Japanese Honda sports car.

'I'd best be off, son,' Brodie said, looking over at the TV and seeing that Ruth was watching a DVD.

'Okay, big guy. Love you.'

'Love you too.'

After he disconnected, he sat on the couch beside Ruth.

'How's our boy?' she asked. She always called him their boy now, having immediately connected with him and Chrissie after meeting them for the first time.

'He's having a flare-up. He feels tired and, when this happens, his walking usually gets worse.'

'Poor love.'

'What are you watching?' Brodie said, nodding to the TV. Ruth had stopped playing what she had been watching.

'It's the bookshop again.'

Brodie nodded and sat down beside her, watching the freeze-frame of the interior of the bookshop, like she had been watching a sitcom and there was some funny moment coming up. But there was nothing funny about what was on the screen: Gabriel Kane looking up at the security camera.

Kane's face was frozen, his eyes sharp, a slight smile playing on his lips. There was a book in his hands. The title couldn't be made out at this angle, the camera looking down from the ceiling, half of the frame taken up by a bookcase, the other half by the till and the woman who owned the place, standing in front of the till and behind the counter.

'Run the tape, honey,' he said, sitting back and watching as all the players started moving, as if a director was behind the scenes and had shouted, 'Action!'

Watching the DVD of the CCTV footage was something they did after Kane had taken them to reveal where his victims were. It was taken from the camera in the bookshop, not long before Kane was caught. Going over the footage, dissecting every minute. This was the third time they had watched the film at home, Brodie looking for something that he might have missed the first hundred times he'd watched it in the station.

Kane looked away from the camera as another customer walked by him. A slender woman, blonde, wearing a long raincoat. She approached the counter with her book and put it on the counter. They couldn't make out the title. She had a large bag slung over her right arm, and reached into it, pulling out her purse to pay for the purchase in cash. She lifted the book and put it in her bag before taking her change. Then she walked away to the right, to the exit.

A man, dark-haired, average build. Average height. They could just make out the top of his head as he walked up to the counter, paid for his book and exited stage right as had the woman in front of him.

Kane ignored them and looked at the book, flipping through the pages. They had never traced the woman in the bookshop, despite a request in the newspaper for her to come forward.

Then the title of the book could be made out as Kane held it in one hand while he widened the gap between two other books that had moved closer to each other when Kane had pulled the book out. *Leaves of Grass*. Walt Whitman. The same book he had requested earlier that day, his reward for being a good boy and taking them to where he had buried a corpse.

Why hadn't he bought that book? Did he already have a copy? Maybe it was lost after his arrest and he merely wanted another one. No. Brodie knew better. Everything that Kane did was calculated. He left nothing to chance.

They watched the footage again. There had always been something that nagged away in the back of Brodie's brain after he had watched it over and over.

He had asked for a copy after the trial and had been given one. Kane in the bookshop. The owner behind the counter. Two customers as well as Kane. A man and a woman. Nobody came forward. It was a simple scenario, yet Brodie knew he was missing something.

'I think I'll have a cold beer,' he said. 'You want one?'

'No thanks, love,' Ruth said.

Brodie got up and went through to the kitchen and took a bottle of Stella from the fridge and sat back down.

'You look tired,' Ruth said to him.

'I am. It's been a long, stressful day.'

'I know. I was there.' She smiled at him and gave his hand a squeeze. Then they switched the DVD player off and watched some regular TV. Brodie fell asleep after the beer. He woke later, when it was dark outside and the lights in Fife were more noticeable now. Somewhere over there was Eric. He missed his son living at home, but knew he was in good hands.

Brodie went to bed thinking about a woman who had taken the place of another woman called Marianne Taylor.

17

FIFE

Monday evening. While Brodie was watching a DVD, drinking whisky on his couch in his apartment in Leith, DI Art McKenzie was with DS Cameron Reid in the Windygates bowling club.

'Just play it cool,' Art told the younger man. 'Rules for tonight: no dancing on any tables...'

'That was one time.'

'...no vomiting on the green, but if you're that pished you need to puke, I'm not going to be a happy camper.'

'Of course I'm going to take it easy. Blend in, you said,' Cameron said.

'Dick Drever knows us. He met you at lunchtime, remember? We're not going to draw attention to ourselves, is what I meant. Just two coppers in for a pint after a long day.'

'Right. Not sitting like we're undercover. Which we are.' Cameron drank some of his pint.

'Not officially. I invited you along here tonight to have a drink since you said you liked it here when we were going about our inquiries earlier.'

'I never said that.' Cameron looked at him. 'I said somebody could improve the décor in here by setting fire to the place.'

'A little bit louder, if you don't mind. I don't think they heard you up in Dundee.'

'I'm just saying.'

'Well, don't just fucking say. They may be bowlers in here, but some of them are nutters.'

Cameron looked over at a group of men sitting at a table, playing dominoes. Old men, who may have been able to handle themselves a long time ago, and the meaning of 'getting wired in' for them meant getting wired into the Hun.

'Here's Drever coming over,' Art said.

'You two couldn't keep away, eh?' Drever said, smiling, standing at their table. He was holding three empty pint glasses by his fingers.

'Aye, I wanted to show Cameron what a good time we have in here.'

Drever looked around. 'Regular Vegas casino, this place.' He looked back at Art. 'Any sign of Al?'

Art shook his head. 'Nothing.' He sipped at his pint. 'How's April?' He sat holding his pint glass, looking up at the big bar manager.

Drever looked down at him. 'She's keeping well. Same old, same old.'

'Last week, one of the boys was saying that her mother's ill. At death's door, he said. I'm sorry to hear that.'

'Aye, but she's lived a good life. April is away staying with her.'

Is that why you're shagging Alan's ex-wife? 'Well, when you speak with her, tell her I send my best.'

'Will do, Art. Thanks for that.' Drever walked away, picked up more pint glasses and went behind the bar.

'He's married? And sleeping with Alan's ex?' Cameron said.

'It happens...' Art said.

'Aye, but it just seems... personal. Like she's still married to Alan, if that makes sense.'

Art looked at him. 'It does. That was remarkably lucid. Have you taken some pills or been sniffing glue again?'

'I think this lager's been watered down. How's that for lucid?'

Art tutted. 'Burn the place down. Lager's watered. What next? You think Alan's been taken by aliens? Having a truncheon shoved up his arse?'

Cameron was watching the TV and turned to Art. 'What was that?'

Art turned to look at him. 'I said, you think he's getting it shoved up his arse?'

They both looked up to see a man stopping at their table. Wearing a dog collar.

'Hello, vicar,' Art said.

'Arthur. I didn't see you at church on Sunday. Were you under the weather?'

Art had forgotten about this old codger calling him Arthur as well, despite telling him numerous times to shorten it to Art. Senile old sod. 'I was a bit... under the weather, yes.' Lying on his couch nursing a massive hangover. Saturday night had been karaoke night and the last thing Art remembered was dancing with a younger woman to Eric Clapton's 'Wonderful Tonight'. A little bit of arse grabbing may also have been involved, and he was sure he hadn't invited her home.

'I hope you're feeling better now,' the vicar said. 'I'm having a wee refreshment myself. Keeps the cold out. I generally only have one, but sometimes I'll have more than one.' He stood looking at Art.

'Oh. Aye. Would you like another one?'

The vicar smiled. 'Oh, I really shouldn't. But why not, since you're offering?'

Art waved at Drever and indicated that he was buying the vicar a nip. Drever nodded.

'Dick's getting it for you, vicar,' Art said.

'Oh, that's very good of you, Arthur.' He turned around and made his way to the bar.

'Drunken old sod,' Art said. 'It's not even fucking cold outside.' He looked at Cameron. 'I notice you didn't jump in to buy him a drink.'

'He's not my vicar.'

Art shook his head. 'As I was saying, Drever didn't let the grass grow under his feet before having it away with Alan's wife.'

'Ex-wife,' Cameron corrected him.

'Aye, but he never showed any interest in her before now, but as soon as Alan's missing, he jumps in there.'

'How do you know it's not been going on for a while?' Cameron asked.

'True, but he has to be careful not to get caught. His wife would not be best pleased. I heard she's handy cutting up sausages with a butcher's knife.'

Cameron looked up at the TV again.

'You alright, son?' Art asked. 'You seem distracted.'

Cameron looked at his boss. 'It's Morag.' His wife.

'Is she okay?' Art said, putting his pint on the table.

'She's fine. But we've split up. I'm back living with my mother again.'

'Why didn't you say something earlier?'

'I thought we could patch our marriage up, but things just went sideways.'

'Sorry to hear that, pal. Honestly. Morag's a great girl.'

'Just don't tell Drever, or else he'll be along to my house with his slippers and dressing gown.'

'How's the kids taking it?' Art asked.

'They're six and four. They think Daddy's working away somewhere.'

'Like on the oil rigs? Or the circus?'

Cameron looked at Art to see if he was taking the piss. 'Something like that.'

'You're going to be driven nuts, staying with your maw again.'

'I could always move in with you.' Cameron supped his pint and stared off at the TV again.

'That's all we would need at the station, to have people think we're a couple.'

Cameron looked at Art. 'We're a what?'

'I said, we're a fucking couple.'

Art turned to see the vicar standing at the side of their table. 'I just wanted to say, I hope I see you at church next Sunday,' he said.

'I'll be there,' Art said, not quite making eye contact with the man of the cloth.

'I think you need it,' the vicar said in a low voice as he walked away.

Art shook his head and looked at Cameron. 'Go to fucking church. Aye, watch me.'

'Sunday, Arthur,' the vicar said, his back still to them as he walked further away.

Art shrank down a bit in his seat, holding his pint up to his mouth for a few seconds, hiding behind it. Nothing wrong with the old bastard's hearing, he thought to himself.

'Same again, Arthur?' Cameron said.

'Don't you fucking start. But yes.'

Art watched the vicar leave as Cameron got up and went to the bar. He felt sorry for his younger colleague. He would give anything to have his wife back. He would never get that chance but he hoped there was still a chance for Cameron.

And for Alan.

18

EDINBURGH

Tuesday

Brodie slept longer than he intended. Ruth didn't, but she hadn't been drinking the night before. He showered, shaved and had coffee while sitting at the small dining table, watching TV. The morning news reported on Kane's little jolly from the hospital, but none of the segments featured DVD or photos of the cemetery.

That evening, the interview with Kane was going to be aired. Brodie ran the contents of the DVD through his mind again, picking away at it, frame by frame almost. He'd watched it dozens of times, each time stopping it when Kane put the book back on the shelf. The other customers. The woman going to the counter. The man standing behind her. Both of them paying for their book and leaving.

He made a mental note to go to the bookshop later on. It was still there, the last time he looked. But it wouldn't surprise him if the place had been turned into a café selling expensive coffee or the building torn down for student housing.

He would call up first.

The day had started off sunny with a forecast for rain in the afternoon. This being Scotland, that would probably follow with snow in the evening.

'You feeling okay this morning?' Ruth said, coming into the living room and picking up the TV remote.

'I'm fine.'

'Not hungover?' She smiled at him.

'I'm not one of your patients,' he said, and immediately regretted it. 'I'm sorry. I apologise. That was uncalled for.'

'You don't have to apologise, Liam. You're under a lot of stress. I'll just make you beg for sex the next time you're feeling horny.'

She wasn't smiling now, he noticed. Just a little smirk playing around on her lips. 'Yeah, right. Just wait until you're begging for me, and maybe I'll say no to you,' he said.

'I would have you eating out of my hand.'

He looked at her and drank some coffee. 'I give in.'

'See?' She laughed at him and channel-hopped until she found a rerun of *Frasier*. 'I love Eddie on this show,' she said, pointing to the little dog.

He nodded in agreement, and they watched the show for a few minutes before Brodie cut in. 'You've watched the DVD with me plenty of times.'

She hit the mute button. 'Yes.'

'Do you ever get the feeling that there's something on that DVD that's staring us in the face and we can't quite grasp it? Like trying to hold a wriggling, wet fish.'

She looked at him and nodded. 'Yes. Every time. It all looks innocent enough, but there's something there. Almost like Kane's looking at the camera, taunting the police to find him.'

'It's a little bookshop, the owner, Sylvia Green, is the only one who works there, and those three were the only customers that day.' The DVD was from two weeks before Kane was arrested. Two weeks before Brodie was stabbed, three years ago.

'You interviewed her, Liam?' Ruth said, shifting forward quickly on the couch. 'The owner?'

He nodded. 'Of course.'

'And she told you she's the only one who worked there at the time?'

'Yes.'

'She's lying to you.' Ruth grabbed the DVD player remote and turned it on. The disc was still in from the night before. 'Come and sit next to me. I'll show you why.'

He sat down, Frasier and his father's dog gone for the moment.

Ruth started the DVD from the beginning and let it play, and then, when Kane looked up at the camera, she paused it. The female customer was at the counter, talking to the owner. The man was behind. The camera showed part of the owner, just the right-hand side of her as she faced the woman. The bookcase was right up to the counter where the owner was standing.

'There!' Ruth suddenly shouted, and Brodie jerked. 'Did you see it?'

'See what?' he asked.

'Nope. It is just there for a fleeting second. If you blink, you miss it. Let me rewind.' She rewound the DVD and tried frame by frame, making Brodie wish he had pulled the trigger on buying the old VCR on eBay. He was sure it wouldn't have taken this long to find whatever it was Ruth was looking for. 'Here, watch this,' she said, and the DVD moved slowly this time.

'What am I looking for?' Brodie said, trying to keep the agitation out of his voice.

'The owner's right arm. She's standing looking at the customer and then she reaches under the counter for a bag to put the book in. As she moves, ever so slightly, it creates a gap between her arm and the end of the book-case, giving us a glimpse of what's behind her.'

Brodie stared intently, and watched as the owner's arm moved slightly, showing yellow. Ruth paused the DVD. Then played it again, still moving slowly, and when the owner moved again, the yellow was gone.

'Look closely,' Ruth said. 'The yellow has a pattern on it. Like it's a dress. Like the one the victim was wearing in the cemetery.'

'Jesus,' Brodie said. 'There was somebody else there that day.' He looked at Ruth. 'The owner kept that quiet.'

'I wonder why?'

'She's got something to hide.'

Brodie got up off the couch and called DI Lucy Warren.

19

EDINBURGH

The bookshop was in Newington, down a little side street. It had once been a science-fiction bookshop but had turned into just a general bookshop years before.

Brodie parked outside the Greenmantle pub on double yellows, put his hazards on and placed the police sign on the dash.

'You read?' he asked Lucy Warren as she was about to get out of the car, looking over her left shoulder to watch for traffic entering the tight one-way street.

'I read magazines,' she said, getting out.

Brodie looked over the roof of the car at her. 'You don't read books?'

She closed the car door. 'I have done. But who's got time these days to read books?'

'I have. Michael Connelly is one of the best. Not to mention James Patterson.'

'They're all detective novels, aren't they?' she said, coming round the car.

'Thrillers. You should try them. Or are you one of those closet romance readers? The books where all the guys have their shirts off, and they all look the same.'

She laughed. 'I don't think so.'

Inside, the bookshop was stuffy. A little bell above the door announced their arrival. Brodie could smell the books as soon as he entered.

Rows of bookshelves ran away from them off to the right. At right angles to the others, there was a shelf that ran from floor to ceiling, the one where Gabriel Kane had stood. There were no customers in, and Brodie wondered how the place made any money.

Brodie walked up to the shelf, to roughly where the book had been put back on the shelf.

'It's still here,' Sylvia Green said, standing and staring at them. '*Leaves of Grass*. The one that Kane was fiddling with. If people want it, I tell them it's not for sale.'

Brodie looked but couldn't see it.

'It's not up there any more,' she said when she saw him eyeballing the shelf. 'Somebody would steal it in a heartbeat. The book that famous serial killer Dr Gabriel Kane was playing with? It would go for a song.'

'You're not interested in selling it, Mrs Green?' Brodie said as he and Lucy approached the counter. It didn't look like anything had changed since he was last here, and he felt that he could describe the whole place to a T since he had looked at the DVD so many times.

'I'm waiting for the day when I can't afford electricity then I can sell it and pay the bill.'

'Listen, Sylvia,' Lucy said, 'you don't mind if I call you Sylvia, do you?' She carried on without waiting for an answer. 'We're here just to ask you a quick question.'

'The question is not about Kane,' Brodie said. 'It's about the assistant who was working the day Kane was in here.'

'What assistant? I don't have an assistant. As you can see.' She swept an arm theatrically around, turning to the area behind the counter which was large. Several bookcases were behind there, one with books on it with rubber bands round them with bits of paper as if people had ordered them.

'What are those?' Lucy asked, nodding to the books with the slips of paper.

'I have regular customers who are looking for certain books. I look out for them and, if I get a copy, I put it aside with their name on it and give them a call.'

Brodie nodded to the door behind the counter. It suddenly opened and a few seconds later a woman came out holding two mugs.

'Here we are, tea,' the woman said. Then she stopped. 'Oh, I'm sorry. I didn't mean to interrupt. I'll just put these down here.'

The woman put the mugs down on a table at the back.

Sylvia Green sighed and let her breath out slowly. 'Detectives Brodie and Warren, this is a friend of mine, Karen Blair.'

'Work here, do you?' Lucy asked.

'Just part-time—'

'No, she doesn't,' Sylvia said.

'No,' Karen said, her face turning red, like she had gone onstage and forgotten her lines.

'Come on, Sylvia,' Brodie said, 'we're not here from Revenue and Customs. We don't care that your assistant is working off the books.'

'I just need help sometimes,' Sylvia said. 'I have MS. I struggle.'

Brodie nodded. Eric wasn't a complainer, but he had lots of issues and would call him just to vent. If this woman was telling the truth, he felt for her.

'We just need to know who was in here working with you the night Gabriel Kane was here,' he said.

Sylvia looked sheepish for a moment. 'Will I get in trouble?' she asked.

'Not if I put in a good word with the procurator fiscal's office. You could be charged with withholding information. Which carries up to two years in prison.' Brodie was just spouting numbers now, hoping for a reaction. He got one from her friend Karen, who gasped and clutched her chest like she was about to drop down.

'I think I just peed,' she said, scooting off through the back again.

'I didn't employ her full-time. She was a friend of mine. Lived on her own and didn't have many other friends. We got talking one day, and I told her that I could do with a hand in the bookshop. You know, just working the till, filling shelves. Sometimes easy tasks like that are a pain. Literally. I would go and have a seat in the back for a little while just until I felt better.'

'I understand,' Lucy said. 'Can you tell us her name?'

Sylvia nodded. 'Ivy Jack.'

'When was the last time you saw her?'

'Oh, let me think; it was a very long time ago. She just stopped coming around, and I lost touch with her. She wouldn't return my calls, and I ended up getting a new assistant.'

'You didn't have a falling-out or anything?' Brodie asked.

Sylvia shook her head. 'No, nothing like that. I think she was a bit shaken up to see that Kane was in here when she was working.'

'Did Kane have any interaction with Ivy?' Lucy asked.

'Yes. She spoke to him. That DVD I gave you from my security camera? It shows Kane looking at the Walt Whitman book. Then it shows him leaving. I told you that was the only time he was in here. I lied. He came in again, but I was in the back and Ivy served him. She was pleased to see him. When I came out of the back, they were laughing and joking. She felt comfortable with him because... she knew him.'

Brodie felt the adrenaline kicking in. 'Knew him from where?'

'I really shouldn't say,' Sylvia answered. 'I'm scared. You have to understand that.'

'Dr Kane is in a psychiatric unit,' Brodie assured her. 'He's not going anywhere. You're safe.'

Sylvia snapped her head at him. 'Just like those other women were safe?'

'Kane wasn't behind bars then.'

She looked at him, the sudden flash of anger dissipating. 'She was in therapy. She was one of his patients. Why do you think he came here? Because he knew Ivy.'

Brodie looked at Lucy before looking back at Sylvia. 'What did he buy?' Brodie asked.

Sylvia looked at them both before answering. 'A Bible.'

'I'm going to need her details,' Brodie said. 'Where she lives.'

Sylvia wrote an address down on a slip of paper and handed it over. 'That's the last known address I have for her. When she didn't come back, I went to check on her, but there was no sign of her. One of her neighbours said he hadn't seen her in a long time. It was like she had disappeared off the face of the earth.'

Brodie slipped it into his pocket. 'You told us at the time that you didn't know the other two people who were on the DVD, who were in at the same time as Kane. Is that true?'

'Look, you have to understand, I'm a one-woman business. I didn't want to attract any more people in here than was necessary, like the Revenue people.'

'You lied about them,' Lucy said.

'Only about me not knowing them. Well, I didn't know them, per se. They were regular customers. I knew them just to say hello to and to talk about books. I didn't know anything about them personally.'

'Who was the woman?' Brodie asked.

'She would come in every couple of weeks and buy a couple of books. But her name was Marianne. I heard her talking with Kane before she came up to the counter.'

'What did she say? Can you remember?' Lucy asked.

'Nothing specific. He just said to her, that's a good one.'

'Do you remember the book she bought?' Brodie said.

'It was a cookbook. She told me she was having somebody round for the first time and she wasn't a good cook, but she liked a few of the recipes in there, so she bought it.'

'What about the man behind her?' Lucy asked. 'Do you know his name?'

Sylvia shook her head. 'No, I swear. I never really spoke to him. He was quiet.'

'Do you remember the book *he* bought that day?' Brodie asked.

Sylvia nodded. 'It was the other copy we had.'

'The other copy of what?'

She was silent for a moment before answering. '*Leaves of Grass.*'

20

EDINBURGH

Brodie pulled into the hospital car park, Lucy riding shotgun.

'You think I should give some of them a go?' Lucy asked Brodie.

Brodie looked at her, puzzled. 'Give what a go? Weight-loss tablets?'

She shook her head and looked at him with wide eyes. 'Where did that come from? Do you think I need to lose weight?'

'No, of course not,' he said, realising he'd put his foot in it. 'I just threw that out there.'

'Bloody hell. I mean, I know I have a little junk in the trunk, as the Americans say, but I go to the gym. I run. Watch what I eat. Are you saying I'm fat?'

'Of course not,' Brodie said, trying to put the pin back in the hand grenade. 'I wasn't sure what you were talking about.'

'Thrillers. Books. What you were talking about earlier.' She took her seat belt off and looked down at her stomach.

'You're the only person who can pick up a conversation an hour later as if we're still talking about it.'

'I was thinking about what you said.' She opened the door and stepped out into the sunshine. Brodie gave thought to waiting until she had slammed the door shut, and then driving away at high speed. Changing his name and living somewhere by the sea.

The door slammed and he winced. 'Is that door closed?' he asked, sarcastically.

'What did you say?' Lucy asked as he got out.

'Nothing. Thinking out loud about what you said about the books.'

'And?' she said, pulling on sunglasses.

'And I think you should. Broaden your horizons,' Brodie said.

'So now I'm uneducated as well as fat?' Lucy said, walking round to his side of the car.

'No, I'm not saying that.'

She grinned. 'Just yanking your chain. I knew you wouldn't have the balls to call me fat.'

Brodie made a face and shook his head. 'While we're at it, you could do with a fucking haircut.'

Lucy laughed. 'So could you. Fatso.'

They walked across to where Det Supt Rob Cross was standing next to his car. He was smoking a cigarette. 'Look at this,' Cross said, holding out the cigarette. 'Fucking smoking again. That bastard in there. He's bringing so much heat down on me from up top. I should stub one out on the bastard's eyeball.'

'I thought there was no smoking in the hospital grounds?' Brodie asked.

'There's a nutcase in there who toppled a gravestone on top of a woman. I think they've got more to worry about than me smoking in the car park. Besides, just let them fucking try. I'm in the mood to deal with them.'

'What does your wife have to say about your smoking again, sir?' Lucy asked.

'Let's just say, I didn't broadcast it to her this morning. I'll email her later. Let her chew out some spotty wee office boy before she gets home, then we can sit down with a glass of wine, and she'll say I have to stop, and I'll agree and tomorrow I'll buy an extra packet of mints.'

'Mints don't cover the smell of smoke,' Brodie said. 'And yes, I'm talking from experience.'

'Don't piss on my parade,' Cross said, taking another drag. 'I'd forgotten how good these things taste.'

'We'll have that written on your tombstone,' Brodie said.

'Here lies Robert Cross. Anybody got a light?' Cross chuckled. 'You know, there's a hundred per cent chance that all non-smokers are going to die.'

'Can't argue with that logic,' Brodie said.

Cross nipped the ciggie and put it in the packet beside the unsmoked ones. 'Right, fill me in before we go up and see Dr Jekyll.'

'I thought he was the sane one?' Lucy said. 'Mr Hyde was the nutcase.'

Cross conceded the point. 'Aye, you're right.'

They entered into the secure reception area.

'Anybody would think you've been reading,' Brodie said.

'I know things,' Lucy said. 'You don't have to read to be smart. Or a smart-arse.'

Brodie filled Cross in about Ivy Jack working in the bookshop at the time Kane was captured on the CCTV.

'You think that's her?' he asked. 'The one under the gravestone?'

Brodie shrugged. 'Kane bought a Bible from the bookshop. And it was a Bible we found on the victim.'

'Right. I'll hold Kane down and you stomp on his bollocks if he doesn't talk.'

'Old-school technique?' Lucy asked.

Cross grinned. 'I wish. We would often talk about how we would interrogate those bastards, each of us trying to outdo the other with as gruesome a fate as we could imagine. And still it would be nothing to how their victims felt. Nobody advocates for them, Lucy. When you're in the job long enough, you'll hit the wall, mentally.'

'Every day,' she replied, side-eyeing Brodie.

He mouthed, *Fuck off,* and she stuck her tongue out at him.

Inside, the hospital was cool and had the universal smell of all hospitals, whether they were for ill or mentally ill patients. Maybe they bought the disinfectant in bulk, Brodie thought. This place reminded him of his granny dying when he was a boy, back in the old Royal Infirmary down by the Meadows. He recalled having to stand with his mother just inside the ward doors with everybody else until they were given permission to go in, then he would sit with a couple of toy cars, or a colouring book, waiting for the bell to go, telling them it was time to leave. Then it would be like a football match just got out. In his eyes, the wards were huge, with many beds in them. Maybe it was just his perspective when he was young, but now they had all been made into apartments, and the new Royal had four beds to a ward.

'Earth to Brodie,' Cross said. 'You still with us, captain?'

'Sorry, I was miles away,' Brodie said.

'I'm smoking. You're going fucking doolally,' Cross said. 'All we need now is for Lucy to pull an axe out and start saying, "Here's Johnny," and that would complete the picture.' He popped a Polo mint and offered them around. Lucy shook her head, and Brodie took one.

'They're not too bad,' Cross said, 'considering I found them in the car park.'

Brodie made a face. 'Fuck's sake.'

Cross grinned. 'I'm kidding. I found them in a suit pocket. But I picked the lint off.'

'You're a laugh a minute, if you don't mind me saying, boss,' Brodie said as they stopped at the lift.

Cross looked at him. 'I do mind you fucking saying. A bit of respect for your superior officer. Cheeky bastard.'

Brodie grinned and hit the call button several times, the universally known trick that would make the lift come down faster.

Upstairs, the hospital director, Simon Lake, was waiting for them.

'The board have been giving me grief over this,' he complained. 'They're being bombarded by the press looking for a statement. The press officer is about to take her own life. At the very least, she's threatened to quit.'

'Oh, boo-fucking-hoo,' Cross said. 'You know who else was getting grief? The woman we found dead under a fucking gravestone yesterday. Get one of those poncy board members to give her family a call and tell them how stressed they are. Listen, son, if you want to, give any of those tossers my number and I'll gladly speak to them.'

Lake shrugged. 'Don't shoot the messenger. I couldn't give a monkey's about them. I passed it on, now I don't give a crap. I'm just biding my time here.'

'Good for you, son. I don't blame you. Now, let's go and see Dr Crippen.'

'Still can't call him by his real name?' Lake said, smiling.

'He doesn't deserve it. Plus, it's better than what I really want to call him. The swear jar is overflowing as we speak.'

They went through the security doors and into the therapy room, where each of the detectives took a chair.

'Call if you need me. We should do this again soon. It's been fun,' Lake said.

'Don't let the door bang your arse on the way out, doc,' Cross said.

Lake grinned as he left the room.

'Must be fucking nice, not giving a shite about your job,' Cross said. 'I think he must be vaping something dodgy.'

'There are cameras in here, sir,' Lucy said. 'He'll hear what you're saying.'

'Good.' Cross held up a middle finger.

'Are you sure there are cameras in here?' Brodie asked.

'This is not a room where psychiatrists talk to patients. It's more of an interview room,' Lucy said.

'Is that a fact?' Cross said. 'Or are you just blowing smoke out your arse again?'

'I heard Lake saying that ages ago.'

'He also said he didn't stand outside a primary school with a bag of sweeties. Pick which one you want to believe.' Cross looked around. 'Do you think they would notice if I smoked in here?'

'No, but I would,' Gabriel Kane said as he was escorted into the room by two orderlies.

Cross whipped his head round. 'Fucking creeping about. Still, that's your thing, isn't it? Sneaking up on people,' Cross said.

'Dry wit as usual, I see,' Kane said, taking a seat.

'You can wait outside,' Brodie said to the orderlies, who nodded and left.

'Trust me, there was no humour intended,' Cross said.

'Offence taken,' Kane said, settling back and crossing his legs.

'I couldn't give a fu—'

'Anyway,' Lucy jumped in before any fists were thrown, 'we'd like to talk to you about your victim, the one we found yesterday.'

'What about her?' Kane said.

'We already told you it wasn't Marianne Taylor,' Brodie said.

'Yes, you did, Liam,' Kane said, locking eyes with the DCI, scepticism in his voice.

'What do you know about Ivy Jack?' he asked.

There was a shift in Kane's demeanour, a slight hardening of the eyes, narrowing as he maintained eye contact. He didn't look away as he answered. He was too good at this game to do that. Brodie would have seen that as a sign of guilt, according to the body-language class he had taken.

Instead, Kane smiled after he'd recovered, which only took a split second. It was enough for Brodie to notice. 'Nice woman. Very chatty. Sylvia shouldn't have kept her hidden through the back so much. Ivy had such a nice personality.'

'Had?' Cross said. 'She isn't of this world any more?'

Kane slowly turned to look at him. 'You know she isn't.'

'Is that who we found yesterday?' Brodie asked.

Kane shifted his gaze once again. 'You tell me.'

'That day you were in the bookshop in Newington, Ivy was working. We saw her on the camera. Did you interact with her the day she went missing?' Lucy said.

'I interacted with Ivy on quite a few occasions. She was one of my patients, which you no doubt already know. She was very funny. To be honest, I think she had a thing for me. I could tell. Sexual transference, it's called, when a patient redirects romantic feelings to a therapist.' He stared at Lucy and smiled.

'Don't worry, doctor, I certainly don't have a thing for you.'

'Of course you don't.'

'Let's just stick to Ivy,' Brodie said, jumping in. 'Did you kill her?'

'That's not how we play this game, DCI Brodie. That would be a crude way of having this conversation. I mean, it *is* a conversation, isn't it? It's not one of those sessions when you threaten me and throw me around the room after you've switched the cameras off?'

'You'd soon know if he threw you around the room,' Cross said. 'You'd be talking in a high voice.'

'Your penchant for violence, detective, is mind-boggling. It would seem that you would have been better suited to policing in a different era. Maybe you were transported from the 1970s? Where using physical force with prisoners was, if not quite tolerated, then a blind eye was certainly turned.'

'Blah blah,' Cross said. 'Stop trying to change the subject.'

'Do you realise that I could simply stand up, knock on that door, and the orderlies would take me back to my room?' Kane said with a smile.

'And that would be the last time you enjoyed a room with a window. You wouldn't be able to look out into the outside world, albeit a limited one through bulletproof glass, but a view nonetheless,' Brodie said. 'Det Supt Cross there would make a phone call, right up the chain of command, and up there, somebody would make a phone call and within an hour you would be moved to a room without a view, without any TV, or subscription services. Oh, and without your books. There would be no keeping your books in your room, or borrowing any from the mobile library.'

Cross looked at Kane with a smile. 'You're free to leave any time you want, Gabriel.' *Use his first name, throw him off.*

The three detectives waited for an answer or a movement. Kane went for the former.

'I was just saying, that's all. Of course I'm not going to get up.' He smiled as if this had all been a joke. 'Where were we? Oh, yes, Ivy Jack. As I said, we got on well when she was working in the shop, and I got to know her innermost feelings when we were in session and I saw her as a perfect target.' He kept the smile but slightly narrowed his eyes. Brodie had no doubt the man would slice Cross's throat given half the chance. 'Anyway, I took Ivy out on a few dates and we got to know each other.'

Brodie sat forward. 'Why don't you tell us the truth? There was no dating, no taking her out or having a laugh, was there? You just killed her.'

Kane's smile vanished as if it had been wiped away. 'There *was* laughter and joking around in the shop, but you're right, I clearly embellished it to humanise the story more. I waited for her one day when she finished her shift and followed her home. Ivy wasn't old, but she wasn't young either. She was at the perfect age, not naïve but trusting. One day, she was at the bus stop, alone, in the rain. I stopped my car and offered her a lift, making an excuse of having to go somewhere, but I could drop her off if she wanted to come with me. Then we could get a coffee. She seemed pleased by that. I drove to a quiet park, telling her that my dog walker was sick and I was there to get my dog. She was excited to see the fictitious animal. We got out and walked over to the treeline and I made sure that nobody else was around, which they weren't as it was still raining, and not a large park. I stabbed her in the ribs, ramming the knife up high and hard. She gasped and looked at me but by then it was all over. I walked back to my car and drove it over, put her in the boot and drove her down to the cemetery. I placed the Bible on her chest before toppling the gravestone.'

'Where did she live?' Lucy.

'Comiston.'

'What day of the week did you pick her up?' Brodie.

'Wednesday.'

'What car did you drive?' Cross.

'Same one I drove when you arrested me. Where is that, by the way?' Kane asked.

'What was she wearing?' Brodie.

'Same as what she was wearing yesterday when you discovered her lying in the cemetery: a yellow dress.'

'What about Marianne Taylor?' Brodie asked. 'She went missing around the same time as Ivy. Did you kill them around the same time?'

'Not far apart. I talked to Marianne. She was a regular in there, just like me. I followed her and found out where she lived.'

'Where *did* she live?' Cross.

'Leith Walk,' Kane answered.

'Who did she live with?' Lucy.

'By herself.'

'Were you in her flat?' Brodie.

'Nope. I stood across the road and waited.'

'Waited for what?' Cross.

'To see if she would come out again.'

'And did she?' Lucy.

'Of course she did.'

'Where did you kill her?' Cross.

Kane looked at them all for a second. 'You know the rules. I gave you a victim on the anniversary of Liam's stabbing. Come back next year and I'll show you where she is.'

Brodie laughed. 'I don't think so, Gabriel. When you identified Mari-anne Taylor in the cemetery and got it wrong, you piqued our interest. Now we're not going to let it go.'

'You may have to, Liam. That's the way we play this game.'

'How about we change the rules?'

'How about we don't?'

Brodie nodded over to Cross, who took out his phone and dialled a number. 'Hello. This is Det Supt Rob Cross. Put me through to the assistant chief, please.' Cross waited a moment. 'Hello, ma'am. Sorry to bother you, but I need you to make a phone call to the chief. We need Dr Gabriel Kane moved to solitary confinement, and all his privileges removed, with imme-diate effect.' He listened again.

'Wait,' Kane said, tutting. 'I'll tell you what you want to know.'

'Ma'am, there's been a development. Sorry for the inconvenience. I'll update you later. Thank you.' Cross hung up. 'She knows what you're like and she's getting pissed off with this lark, Dr Kane.'

'The thing is, and I promise you that I'm not pulling your chain, but my mind is actually a little fuzzy. I'll have to go away and think about this, Liam.' Kane stood up. 'I'm feeling a little unwell. I'd like to be seen by the doctor and then retire to my room. It will help me think a little more clearly. I'll be in touch, gentlemen. Lady.'

Kane walked forward and stood a few feet from the door, facing it. Brodie got up and knocked on the door and, a second later, it opened.

'Dr Kane needs medical attention,' he told the orderlies. 'Make sure he sees the doctor.'

One of the men nodded, and then Kane was gone, the door closed behind him.

'What the fuck do you make of that?' Cross said, taking his cigarettes out and toying with the packet.

'I told you yesterday, he didn't know that was possibly Ivy Jack in there. If it is indeed her. For some reason, he was convinced it was Marianne Taylor,' Brodie said. 'We'll check the details, but I think he got the details wrong. Or he's yanking our chain.'

'Do you think he's killed so many women that he can't remember who was buried where?' Lucy said.

'That's a possibility. But he got all the answers correct about Marianne. I've no doubt he killed her. But he was a bit more vague about Ivy.'

'Maybe it was because they were both in the bookshop at the same time, Ivy working and Marianne as a customer.'

'Now we just have to find out where Marianne is buried,' Brodie said.

21

FIFE

Tuesday morning for Art and Cameron had been mostly paperwork relating to the cottage where the bones were found. Now, Art suggested they go and talk to Pat McRae, Alan's ex. Cameron was just as eager to get out into the fresh air, away from the stale smell in the station.

Pat McRae's car wasn't in the driveway when Art pulled up.

'Maybe she saw us coming and booted it off,' Cameron said.

'Not laughing at the idea of us driving around in an ice-cream truck now, are you?' Cameron said. 'We could have lured her out with a ninety-nine.'

'Aye, you're right. And if she asked for two, we would have known Drever was in there.'

'With his boxers round his ankles.'

Art looked at him. 'One step too far.'

Cameron grinned. 'What? We already know she's seeing him. I don't suppose he comes round just for a Mr Whippy. Or maybe he does.'

'Let's just go and knock on her door before you turn her into the neighbourhood hoor.' Art turned the engine off and they stepped out into the warmth. There were clouds in the sky but no immediate threat of rain.

Art walked up to the front door and rang the bell. Cameron stepped up and banged a fist on it a couple of times.

'Easy, Christ,' Art said. 'We're just here to see if she knows any more than she told us yesterday, not drag her out in handcuffs.'

'Sorry. I just didn't like the way she was lying to us yesterday.'

'Maybe she had reason to,' Art said, ringing the bell again. He stood on his tiptoes and raised a hand to the glass in the door, peering through one of the five glass panels that formed a semicircle. Flowers were shaped into the glass, distorting the view, but he focused on a plain piece and looked into the hallway.

'She there?' Cameron asked.

'Aye, walking about naked.' Art flattened his feet and turned to look at his friend. 'No, she's not there.'

'You could have just said that,' Cameron said. 'Instead of voicing some fantasy—'

'Go and look through the garage window,' Art said, cutting him off. 'See if her car's in there.'

Cameron walked along the little pathway that ran in front of the house, a shortcut to the garage for times when they didn't put the cars inside. Although Art suspected that Pat always parked in the little side driveway that was next to the kitchen door. Safer and quicker. He was looking over at the neighbour's house when Cameron shouted, jerking him out of his thoughts.

'Art! Fuck's sake, get the door in! She's in the garage.'

'What?' Art answered, confused.

Cameron ran back. 'There's a hose leading from the exhaust into the car.'

Art grabbed the door handle but the door was locked.

Cameron stepped back and kicked the door just at the lock. His foot bounced off the uPVC. 'Fuck,' he said, grabbing his knee.

'Round the back!' Art shouted, and took off running, followed by Cameron, who was running as best he could. He saw Art round the corner of the house and disappear into the back garden. When he got there, Art was holding up a fair-sized plant pot, about to throw it at the French doors. 'You sure the hose is coming from the exhaust?' Art asked. 'I mean, she's not washing her car or something?'

'Aye, I'm fucking sure!' Cameron shouted, and Art launched the pot through the glass. As it was going through the air, Art turned away and Cameron thought it was going to bounce off the double glazing, but no, the glass exploded into tiny pieces and then Art was through. Cameron was ignoring the pain as he followed his boss through into the kitchen and then along the hallway towards the front door, when he stopped at another door that could have been a closet but was the door into the garage.

Inside, the fumes were thick but not thick enough that Art couldn't see Pat sitting behind the wheel. He covered his mouth and ran over to the switch that activated the electric door opener and the garage door trundled up.

Cameron opened the car door and grabbed a hold of Pat, pulling her from the car as Art got on the phone, calling for an ambulance, turning the engine off.

Outside in the fresh air, they felt for a pulse and found nothing.

'Christ, Pat, what have you done?' Art said as Cameron went to work with the CPR.

The ambulance arrived a few minutes later and the paramedics took over. Then they got her onto a stretcher as a patrol car turned up. Along with Detective Superintendent Chris Breck.

'Aw fuck,' Art said, turning to face Cameron.

'What happened here, Arthur?' Breck said, walking up to them.

Cameron nodded and said a quick, 'Sir.'

Breck nodded back.

Art turned to face the big boss. Big in rank, big in stature. Breck was six-five and looked like he ate dumbbells for breakfast. Hair cut short, mirroring his years in the Royal Marines.

'We were coming back to have a word with Alan's ex-wife, Patricia,' Art said. 'There was no answer, so I asked Cameron to have a look through the glass in the garage door and he saw the hosepipe there running into the car with the engine running.'

'Jesus. That's never a good sign,' Breck said, and Art didn't know if the boss was being sarcastic or what. 'What then? You managed to get the door open?'

'We ran round the back and tanned the French doors in,' Cameron said. 'Then we got into the house and found the garage door and got inside.'

'Cameron got her out of the car while I got the garage door open and we got her outside and tried CPR while we waited for the ambulance that I'd called,' Art said.

'I don't think she's going to make it,' Breck said. 'One of the paramedics looked at me and shook his head. But that's for a man in a white coat to decide, one who'll get a big bonus for calling the time of death.'

'By the amount of exhaust fumes that were in there, I'd say she was in there for a wee while.'

Breck turned to the Uniforms who were standing a few feet away. 'You two, keep any onlookers from getting closer. Tell them fuck all.'

'Yes, sir,' the female said. The other one looked around as if expecting to see a horde of villagers with pitchforks, but saw only an old couple at the end of the road standing gawping, holding a carrier bag of shopping each.

'Just keep your eyes peeled,' Breck said. He turned back to Art and Cameron. 'Let's go and have a look inside.' They walked towards the open garage door. 'Why didn't you try kicking the front door in?' Breck asked.

Art gave a quick sideways glance at Cameron before answering. 'These uPVC doors have hooks that grab the frame when you lock them, so we thought it was quicker to run round the back.'

'Thanks for giving me a lesson on how a uPVC door works, Arthur. Like I'm a big, dumb ox or something.'

'Time was of the essence, sir,' Cameron said.

'Besides, we might have broken a leg, the strength of these doors,' Art said.

'Christ, don't talk like that. We're short enough with Alan being fuck-knows-where. He better have a good fucking excuse when he comes back.'

Art was pleased that Breck thought this was a temporary thing with McRae, just like he did. Unlike Cameron, who thought McRae was getting ready to be fitted with a wooden overcoat.

Breck walked towards the open garage door, and stood looking at the little Volvo. 'What would make her take her own life?' He looked at both men.

'I have no idea,' Art answered. 'She and Alan were still friends. It's not as if he was bothering her.'

'That you know of. What goes on behind closed doors, and all that. Maybe it was friends with benefits,' Breck said.

'It wasn't like that, sir. Alan would have told me over a pint. But he liked to play the field. Besides, Pat was seeing the bar manager at the bowling club where Alan and I had a drink.'

'Was she now?' Breck nodded as he walked inside, careful not to touch anything. The hose was on the floor but it had been inside the passenger window. 'Did you notice anything in the house, when you were busy ransacking the place?'

'Hardly ransacking, sir,' Cameron said.

'I was just being facetious, sergeant. I meant did you notice any suicide note?'

'We were busy running through the house to get to here,' Art said. His tone implied the *dumb fuck* but the words weren't spoken.

'Right, then, let's get in and see if we can find one,' Breck said, leading the way with his hands in his trouser pockets.

Art and Cameron walked behind, touching nothing. When they got to the living room, Art stopped at one of the chairs.

'I think she was murdered,' he said.

'Explain,' Breck said.

'The curtains are drawn. There's a lamp on and a cup of tea, half finished. There's a magazine open but placed on the chair, like she got up to answer the door. Alan told me once that every evening, when he wasn't out for a pint at the weekend, he and Pat would sit and have a cup of tea. They would watch TV together. What with the lamp being on, it looks like she might have kept the tradition on, even though they weren't married any more.' He dipped his small finger in the tea. 'Cold.'

Breck nodded. 'Like maybe somebody rang the doorbell and she got up to see who was there.' He looked at Art. 'Maybe she thought it was Alan, or her boyfriend.'

'Exactly. She answered the door and let her killer in.'

'If she doesn't make it, and I would bet my pension on her not making it, then we'll make sure a post-mortem is done. Maybe it will reveal something.'

'Like she was coerced into the car,' Cameron said.

'We're not going to jump to conclusions. Have a look around,' Breck said. 'We have probable cause to search, so don't let anybody give you any grief about this. If they have a beef, get them to call me.'

Art and Cameron split up to have a look around. The shattered glass in the kitchen from the French doors notwithstanding, the house was neat. A few bills sitting in a letter holder on the counter near the kettle.

He knew how Pat must have felt, being divorced and on her own. His wife had died and now Art lived alone. He felt loneliness grip him hard at times, but every time he thought about finding somebody else to start a new life with, the guilt kicked in. He enjoyed women's company, even a couple of the single ones in the bowling club, but just the thought of dating again put his head into a tailspin. Obviously that was why Pat had felt desperate enough to start dating Dick Drever.

He made a mental note to have the Uniforms get a joiner out to board up the French doors after forensics had been through the place.

He went into the bathroom and looked for any signs that Drever stayed over: razor, men's deodorant, an extra toothbrush. One towel hanging on a towel heater. A range of women's cosmetics and hair mousse. A hairbrush with blonde hair in it. Pat's colour. The bathroom smelled like somebody had showered here recently, a damp smell. But there was no sign that Drever stopped the night.

Next, into Pat's bedroom. Her bed had been turned down for the night, ready for her to slip into. A digital clock sat on the bedside cabinet next to a lamp. In the space underneath the top was a pile of magazines, a paperback sitting on top. Art crouched down so far but felt his knees creak.

There was a little drawer above the magazines. He pulled on a glove and opened it. Inside was the usual disarray that a woman might have in there: tweezers, nail file, mints, a roll of antacids, a pair of reading glasses.

A quick look through a set of drawers and the wardrobe with nothing jumping out at him.

'Find anything?' Cameron said, coming into the room.

Art looked at him. 'Nothing out of the ordinary.' He shook his head. 'What the fuck, Cam? There was no indication of her wanting to top herself. What would make her do it if it wasn't murder?'

'We need to talk to Drever, see where he was last night.'

Cameron nodded in agreement.

They heard Breck talking and they found him in the living room with his phone.

'Right. We're going to the mortuary in Kirkcaldy. That was Sherlock Holmes on the phone. About the skeleton that was found under the floor-boards. He's ruling it a homicide. And I just called Accident and Emergency. They just pronounced Pat McRae dead a few minutes ago. Now we have to pull our finger out and find out if she was helped on her way, and from what we saw in the living room, the light and stuff, it could go either way. The procurator fiscal's going to need more. Pat might just have decided to do it there and then.'

'The death can surely be ruled as suspicious,' Art said.

'You know better than that, Arthur; what suspicions do we have right now? Unless you come back and tell me her boyfriend confessed, then there's nothing really to go on.'

Art knew the boss was talking sense, but felt there was more to it. 'At least we can go and talk to Drever tonight.'

'Don't go pointing any fingers. For all we know, McRae had a breakdown, came here and killed his ex.'

Art let that set in for a moment. 'You're right, boss.'

As Breck led the way out into the sunshine, Art kept his mouth shut until he and Cameron were in the car.

'Are you thinking what I'm thinking?' he asked Cameron.

'That Alan McRae is a fucking lunatic and how did we miss the warning signs?' Cameron said.

'Clearly not,' Art said, tutting. 'Remember, Alan was seen getting into Pat's car up at the trail. She told us he was scared of something. What if he got himself into some sort of shite that he couldn't get out of? And dragged Pat into it?'

'I wonder what kind of trouble?' Cameron said.

'Let's hope we find him and he can tell us.' Art thought that if Pat was murdered, then they might never get the chance to question Alan.

22

EDINBURGH

Ivy Jack hadn't been married. But she had a sister. And they didn't live in Comiston like Gabriel Kane had told them.

The afternoon heat was giving Brodie a tanking. He didn't like too much heat, preferring a more moderate temperature.

'If we ever wondered if Kane was a lying bastard, then we just had it confirmed,' Lucy said as they pulled up outside the large detached house in a quiet cul-de-sac in Liberton. A Victorian build, it had been split into three apartments.

Alice Jack lived on the ground floor, right-hand side.

'Can I help you?' she asked, answering the door. There was no caution, Brodie thought.

They showed their IDs. 'DCI Liam Brodie, DI Lucy Warren,' he said, and her eyes went wide. 'Are you Ms Alice Jack?'

She took in a deep breath as if he'd just asked her an inappropriate question regarding the colour of her underwear and her cheeks flushed. 'Yes. Is it about Ivy?'

'May we come inside, Ms Jack?' Lucy asked.

'Yes, yes, of course.' She stood back and held the door open. She was a tall woman, closer to six feet than not, but skinny, dressed in an old-fashioned skirt that had folds in it and which looked like she was waiting to go on-set where she was the matriarch of a Highland dynasty. The blouse was white with pearl buttons and a thin gold chain was around her neck.

The house was well kept and smelled of old money. The carpet was thick and plush underfoot. Several doors led off the hallway, which was square and was lit by a small lamp sitting on a table.

'Please come through to the living room,' she said, taking the lead and walking ahead.

A couple of leather couches made up the seating arrangements, with a couple of wooden dining chairs waiting in reserve should a small party of people decide to pop in unannounced.

'Please take a seat,' Alice said, rushing over to one of the couches like musical chairs was about to start.

They sat opposite. Brodie was surprised to see that the TV wasn't the size of a football pitch but something that was borderline antique. At the very least, it had probably acquired classic status.

'We don't watch much TV,' Alice said, seeing Brodie looking at the screen.

A black cat walked into the room, looked at Brodie and miaowed at him, walking right over and rubbing against him.

'That's Dutchess,' Alice said. 'Dutchess, that's Liam and Lucy. They're here to talk to Mummy.'

The cat purred as Brodie ran his fingers down the cat's back near her tail. She arched up a bit, obviously enjoying the physical attention.

'Is this about Ivy?' Alice asked again.

Brodie stopped playing with the cat, and Dutchess moved over to Lucy. 'Yes, it is.'

'Have you found her?'

'Ms Jack—'

'Alice.'

'Alice, I'm sorry to tell you this, but we found a body, and we believe it may be Ivy. But we're going to need your help.'

'Oh, God. She's dead.' Alice put her hand up to her mouth and started crying. Lucy got up and walked over to her, careful not to stand on or get tripped up by Dutchess, and she sat down beside the crying woman, putting an arm around her shoulder.

'I'm so sorry, Alice,' she said, and the woman put her head against Lucy.

Brodie took the time to look around the room. Photos were on a sideboard, all of them of two women together, obviously on different days, in different places. He could now see what Ivy looked like, pre-gravestone days. A pretty if not attractive woman, she looked pleasant, with a nice smile.

There was an open box of hankies on a side table next to Brodie, and Lucy indicated with her head for him to get it. He pulled one out and she shook her head slightly; *the box!*

He balled up the hanky, shoved it into his suit pocket and handed the box over.

'Here, take a hanky, Alice,' Lucy said.

Alice pulled away and tore a couple out of the box and dabbed at her eyes as she sniffed. 'What... how did she die?'

Brodie knew he couldn't tell her right at that moment. That would come later, when Alice was in a better place to be told the truth, but this wasn't it. 'I can't reveal that at the moment due to the investigation,' he said. 'However, we would like to get a DNA sample from you, if we could.'

'DNA? Can't you identify her?'

'No, we can't, not through normal channels.'

Alice stared wide-eyed at them. 'That means she's been dead a while, doesn't it?'

Lucy looked at Brodie, who answered, 'I'm afraid it does.'

'Can you tell me where she was found?' Alice asked.

'Again, this is just the start of the investigation, so I'm not at liberty.'

Alice nodded and looked down at the carpet before glancing at them both in turn. 'She was murdered, wasn't she?' She smiled a bitter smile. 'What other reason is there to investigate? Somebody took her life.'

Brodie locked eyes with her. 'Yes, we believe she was murdered. That's why we need your help with the DNA. We have to be sure it's her, first of all. Did your sister have false teeth?'

Alice nodded. 'Yes. Top and bottom.'

'Let's go back to the beginning,' Brodie said. 'The last time you saw her. I know you made a missing persons report, but think back to that night.

Was there anything unusual going on? Had anybody contacted Ivy? Did she say she was going on a date, perhaps?'

'Oh, no. We never married. We were companions for each other. Men didn't enter into the equation. Not that we are... were... you know...'

Brodie nodded. Two sisters who enjoyed each other's company and who were satisfied with that lifestyle. He'd seen it before.

'She worked in the bookshop in Newington,' Lucy said, 'but if you don't mind me saying, you don't look like either of you needed to work.'

'We don't need money. Ivy just wanted to do something to occupy her time, and she knew Sylvia. When she found out Sylvia needed some help in the shop, she took the job. I have my volunteer work.'

'She must have come into contact with quite a few people in the bookshop,' Lucy said.

'There were regulars, believe it or not. Sylvia, the owner, would go to estate sales just to pick up books. She found some rare ones and would call the collectors she had noted. There were plenty of regular customers, and she always had a good word for them.'

'Tell me about the last day you saw her,' Brodie said gently.

Alice nodded and took a deep breath before speaking. 'She didn't work there every day. Just three days a week, supposedly: Monday, Wednesday and Friday. It was a Friday the last time I saw her. We were going to have a bite to eat that night and then go see a film along Dundee Street. I can't remember which one now. I wish I could remember, but the name escapes me. Ivy would remember. She was good with things like that. Anyway, she left to catch the bus at the end of our street. It took her to outside the old Odeon picture house, the one we used to go to before it closed down. I said I would catch a bus there in the late afternoon and meet her in the shop. When I went to the shop, Sylvia told me Ivy wasn't there. She didn't work on a Friday. I told her she was mistaken. Ivy had worked there on a Friday for a long time. Sylvia said, no, it was just on Monday and Wednesday.'

'If she wasn't going to work on Fridays, where would she be going that you didn't know about?' Brodie asked.

'I have no idea.'

Brodie could see the lie in her face. She was keeping something from them. 'If there's anything you can tell us to help solve Ivy's murder, now's the time, Alice.' Brodie leaned forward.

'Well, I wasn't sure if Ivy had had a breakdown or something. That she might have gone somewhere to be alone and didn't want to tell me at first, when she didn't come back after the weekend, that's when I reported her missing. The police took the report, of course, but nothing came of it. She was an adult; she could do what she wanted. They did the barest minimum to find her, then filed it away and forgot about it. But as time went on and she hadn't come back, I kept her mail for her. Every single piece, except the junk mail. I still have it all.'

'Did any of it make you think she was coming back?' Lucy asked.

'I'll go and get the pile and show you.' She stood up and left the room. She returned a few minutes later. She handed Brodie a pile of letters with ribbon tied around them. She undid the ribbon, flipped through them and pulled a couple out.

Brodie looked at them. There was a printed address on the front from the sender. The Astley Ainslie Hospital.

'She was seeing a psychiatrist,' Alice said.

'Have you opened these?' Brodie said, looking at the back to see if there were any signs that a kettle had been used to steam them open. They didn't appear to have been.

'No.'

'How do you know she was seeing a psychiatrist?' Brodie asked.

'The Astley is where people go to speak to a psychiatrist, isn't it?'

Brodie looked at Lucy, almost as if he was suggesting that she had intimate knowledge of the place. 'I think they deal with a lot of psychological problems there.' He knew Gabriel Kane worked there and that's where he would have seen Ivy. He kept that from Alice for now.

'Ivy was a troubled woman. It all happened after the accident.'

'What accident?' Lucy asked.

Alice drew in a breath and blew it out softly. 'We were out with our friends, me and Ivy. Sylvia, Marianne and two other friends. The summer of 2020, almost five years to the day. I drove that night. I wasn't going to drink that night when we all went out. We went to a pub in the countryside, near Penicuik, and it was great fun. I had one drink, then I got the taste and had a few. Not as much as the others but enough to put me over the limit. We were coming down Lasswade Road, I got to the traffic lights and didn't see it had changed to red. We were having a laugh and carrying on. You have to understand.'

'What happened next?'

'I went blazing through the red light. Two minutes' drive from home. It happened just around the corner at the intersection with Mount Vernon Road. I hit two cyclists. I'm ashamed to say one of them died, and the other was badly injured. I paid my dues to society, but Ivy was beyond furious. We had to get rid of the car because she couldn't drive. And the fact that I took somebody's life – well, you would think I'd set fire to an orphanage the way she went on. I still feel horrendous to this day, but I can't change things.'

'Marianne who?' Brodie asked, the name of Kane's supposed victim ringing in his ears.

'Taylor. I haven't spoken to them in a long time. We didn't keep in touch after the accident. Everybody was too scared. It was a horrific night. We didn't drift apart, more like we ignored each other.'

'Can I ask what the outcome of your court appearance was?' Lucy asked.

'I got two years' probation and was banned from driving for six years. I have to resit my driving test if I want my licence back. I don't know if I do.'

He nodded, not wanting to judge the woman. No amount of admonishment now would bring back the dead cyclist. 'Would you mind if we opened these?' he asked Alice.

'Not at all. Since she's not going to be opening them herself.' Her lips quivered as she spoke and she fought to regain control.

He slid a finger into the seal of the envelope and ran it along, tearing it until it was open. He took the letter out, opened it and read it.

'It's a reminder for Ivy to keep her appointments. She missed one. It's dated after the day she disappeared.'

'Does it say who she was seeing?' Alice wondered.

Brodie shook his head. 'No. I don't think it would anyway. That's private.' The lie came easily.

'I just wondered if there would be anybody who would tell me why she went there.' Alice looked at him. 'She didn't tell me. I had no idea she was going there. As I said, I thought she was working on a Friday.'

'Can I take this? And the other one?' Brodie said.

'Of course.'

'And if I could get Lucy to swab the inside of your cheek for the DNA, that would be great.'

Lucy pulled a bag out of her pocket like a magician and did the thing with the cotton swab and the test tube.

'Promise me you'll catch whoever did this,' Alice said.

Brodie didn't have the heart to tell her they already had.

23

FIFE

Late afternoon and the air was hot outside Queen Margaret Hospital in Dunfermline. Art shivered as they walked through the corridor to get to the lift. His parents had died in here, his father first, then his mother a few years later. His father had had a stroke and Art had said goodbye to him in a bed upstairs. Then his mother had died of breast cancer.

'You're quiet,' Cameron said.

'Just thinking about my folks who both died in here.' He looked at the younger man as they waited on the lift to take them down to the basement level. 'Coming to the mortuary does that. Makes me think about death.'

'Aye, that poor kid,' Cameron said as the lift doors opened and they stepped in. 'I try not to dwell on it, but having my own two kids makes me feel nauseous when we have to attend the death of a child.'

'Me too, son, and I don't have any kids. There are some evil bastards walking about this earth, and we only get to capture a small percentage of them.'

The mortuary corridor was cold, but at least it was well lit. They walked along to Sherlock's office, but he wasn't in.

'He's through in the post-mortem suite,' one of the assistants told them.

'Thanks,' Art said, shivering. 'I'm either feeling the effects of the temperature down here, or somebody walked over my grave.'

'Don't start getting all creepy when there are dead people down here,' Cameron complained as they went into the suite.

Det Supt Breck was already there, having driven in his own car.

For a pathologist, Sherlock Holmes had no right to be so cheery, Art thought. Maybe the man liked a wee drink between cutting up cadavers. He knew he would.

'Gentlemen,' he said, smiling across the table at the detectives. 'This is Doctor Eva Cruz, from New York City. She's doing an exchange with Edinburgh University.'

She smiled at them. 'It's Eva.' She looked like she was sixteen but was probably in her early forties. Dark hair, cut short. She wore no make-up but didn't need it. She looked like she hit the gym frequently.

'Hi, Eva,' Art said, getting a look from Breck in the process.

'Eva,' Cameron said, nodding to her.

'I called Doctor Cruz in to have a look at our victim,' Sherlock said, gently lifting the white sheet back from the skeleton underneath.

Breck looked down at the brown bones that he could see in the tears of the clothes, at the skull grinning at them. It had been cleaned up, probably with a paintbrush to take most of the dirt off, but there were remnants of skin still clinging on, looking like well-tanned leather.

'Small person or child?' Breck asked.

'Child,' Eva said. 'A little boy, in the age range of between six and eight.' She delivered the line with professionalism, but there was an underlying hint of sadness.

'We were very careful removing him from under the floor,' Sherlock said. 'The ropes are still attached to his wrists, his arms behind his back. There's a large hole in the back of his skull.'

'Fuck me,' Breck said, then looked at Eva. 'Pardon the French.'

'That's okay. I'm fluent myself.' She looked down at the boy. 'It looks like he was beaten at some point in his life, too. He had a broken arm that healed. Broken ribs. Broken collarbone. There was also a fragment of a bar of soap.'

'Like it was a punishment,' Breck said. 'Like how your mother used to tell you she would wash out your mouth with soap for swearing, or something.'

'You sound like you're talking from experience,' Eva said with a smile.

'Aye. My mother was very strict. That's why she's going in a fucking home.'

'Can you tell how long he's been dead?' Art asked.

'A long time. Decades. Whoever killed him put him under those floorboards a very long time ago.'

'Any other ID in the pockets?' Art asked.

'Nothing,' Sherlock said.

Breck nodded. 'Right. I need a DCI to take the lead on this. I'll make a call upstairs and see what they come up with.'

'Righty-o,' Sherlock said.

'I'm sure Alan will be back soon,' Art said as they rode the lift upstairs.

Breck looked at him. 'Meantime, we need a DCI running this show. Especially if we find out Pat McRae was helped along. Deal with it, Arthur.'

Art nodded. 'Yes, sir.'

24

EDINBURGH

End of the working day and Detective Superintendent Rob Cross stood leaning against the window in his office, his arms crossed and getting ready to have a coin toss. 'Heads I jump, tails I smoke a cigarette. Call in the air.'

'Heads,' Brodie said.

'Oh, you'd like that, eh?' Cross tossed the coin. He caught it, looked at it then put it back in his pocket. 'You'll never know, will you?' He took out a cigarette and lit it. 'Where are we with Kane?'

Brodie and Lucy were in Cross's office, Brodie sitting in a chair while Lucy made a coffee for herself.

'He's either confused or he's lying,' Brodie said. 'I'm not sure which one yet.'

'Lucy?' Cross asked.

She turned to look at him. 'Same. If you want my opinion, and you just asked for it, then I would say he was guessing. Kane's as sharp as a tack. He doesn't make mistakes.' She finished pouring creamer into the disposable cup and switched the kettle off, then turned back to the two men. 'He genuinely thought it was Marianne Taylor under the gravestone. You could tell by the look on his face.'

'You think he killed so many women that he got confused by them all?'

Cross said. 'The press will have a fucking field day with that. They think he killed six women and find out he killed two hundred or something.'

'We might never find out the true number,' Brodie said. 'But I think he's making out he was some gentle guy who was friends with them before he killed them. Stopping to give one a lift in the rain. Christ, if they only knew. And that's something else he hasn't told us: where he killed them.'

Cross shook his head and sat down in his office chair while Lucy sat next to Brodie.

'Did you not make me one?' Brodie asked her.

'I did, and now I'm drinking it. Cheers, boss.' She sipped at the mug.

'Can't get the staff nowadays.'

Cross blew out the smoke. 'Just so you know, if one of the bigwigs comes in, I'll blame one of you for smoking, just before you're demoted to lollipop man. Or woman. I haven't decided yet.'

'Learn those leadership skills on a managerial course, sir?' Brodie said.

'I watched a YouTube video.' More smoke. More cursing. He pointed a finger at Brodie while holding the cigarette between it and his middle finger. 'Kane better start getting his act together. I got chewed out by one of the assistant chiefs about Kane dicking around, and if I'm going to get it in the neck, so is he. A monkey in the zoo will have more privileges than him.'

'As Lucy said, Kane's sharp. To be honest, I don't think he made a mistake,' Brodie said. 'I think he's just yanking our chains. But I don't want to wait until the fourth anniversary of him stabbing me to find somebody else.'

The phone on Cross's desk rang. He quickly opened a drawer and stubbed the cigarette out on what Brodie hoped was an ashtray. 'Hello?' Cross listened and spoke a few times before hanging up. 'You've worked in Fife before, Liam.' It was a statement, not a question.

'I have.'

'Good. You'll know your way about then. They have a DCI in Glenrothes who's listed as a missing person. There's also a skeleton been found under floorboards in a house somewhere. They need a senior officer in charge. You're it.'

'What about this thing with Kane?' Brodie asked.

'Lucy will be able to handle it.'

'When do they need me?' Brodie asked.

'First thing tomorrow morning. You can pop in and see Eric while you're over there.'

'Glenrothes HQ, you said?'

'Nine sharp.' He tutted. 'I wasted a ciggie for nothing. Lucky I didn't set my fucking drawer on fire.'

'I'm going to miss the fun and games,' Brodie said.

25

EDINBURGH

Sylvia Green had told her friend, Karen Blair, that she wouldn't be in tomorrow. She had a date and she would be out late. Karen was only too happy to take over the duties of opening the shop and running it. Karen's husband had left this earth with the same amount of money he had come into it with, absolutely zero. Like everybody else who dies. The money he left behind was another story. It was enough to keep Karen comfortable, so she only had to work part-time. 'Just for something to do,' she had told Sylvia.

Now that that was sorted, she could relax. Sylvia didn't get dolled up very often, so this was a treat for her. Peter, her date, was married; he had told her. He had been coming into the shop off and on for years now, and they had always hit it off. Then one day, he told her that his marriage was over and that he had moved in with his mother, just as a temporary measure. He was working with an estate agent to secure a rental place until he found the right property to buy. The divorce was going to wipe him out, he said.

She hadn't been sure at first, thinking that maybe she would have to spend a fortune on him, but no, he had been the perfect gentleman, not letting her put her hand in her pocket once.

He was good fun, witty and charming, and Sylvia thought she felt something a little more than friendship stirring. This afternoon had been perfect; they'd had a walk along Portobello Beach, eating an ice cream and enjoying the views over to Fife. Of course, they couldn't walk too far, what with Peter having to use the walking stick to get about, but it was far enough.

Then they had taken the bus along to Leith. The air was salty and a nice cool breeze came in off the sea.

'That's a historic boat,' Peter said, nodding to the *Ocean Mist*, permanently berthed at Shore, sitting in the Water of Leith.

'Really? It looks amazing.'

'Maybe we could come down for a drink one night,' he said, smiling at her.

She looked at him, the short-cut beard neatly trimmed, knowing his blue eyes were watching her from behind the sunglasses. He even suited the Panama hat he wore.

'I'd love that. Maybe I could even meet your mother.'

The smile slipped a little bit and he was silent for a moment. 'That might not be possible. You see, I'm separated from my wife, but we haven't been to a lawyer yet. If she finds out I've been out and about with a woman, my wife could use that against me. But rest assured, we will after I've signed papers.'

'That would be great, Peter.'

'Maybe I could meet the group of friends you told me about,' he said.

'Group of friends?' she said, a puzzled look on her face.

'Yes. The ones you were going on about the other night when you were a bit tipsy.'

'I... I can't quite remember who I was talking about.'

He smiled at her. 'You mentioned some friends. Let me see.' He pretended to think about it. 'Marianne. Ivy. Alice. And some others, I can't quite remember either.'

'Ah. Yes. I haven't seen Marianne in ages. A long time. She was a customer whom I got to know well, then she started coming out with my friends and me. Ivy is Alice's sister. She's a missing person, Peter. She went out one day and didn't come back. I miss her so much. As we all do.'

'What would make her take off, if you don't mind me asking?' he said.

'Something happened. Something terrible. We were out drinking one night and a terrible accident happened.'

'Oh my goodness. That's awful. What about the other friend?'

Sylvia shook her head. 'We don't see her now.' She touched his arm. 'If you don't mind, I don't want to talk about it any more.'

'That's fine.'

The Reader turned to her and smiled. He was used to her calling him Peter, because that was what he had told her his name was, years ago. First a customer, now more as they had got to know each other. He had made her start to fall in love with him, with his charm, good looks and splashing a bit of cash. He had never worn a beard before, but had grown it so he wouldn't be recognisable. The red glasses helped, and the hat he wore, although he had to take that off now and again.

He had worked at it over time, and it had worked like a charm, and now here they were, on their fourth date and he hadn't made a move on her, except for kissing her at her doorstep. And he wouldn't.

'Look, I know this is an imposition, but would you accompany me somewhere?'

'To the ends of the earth?' she said, laughing.

'Not quite as far. But my sister died two years ago today, and I would like to take flowers and put them on her grave. I do it every year.'

'Oh, Peter, I'm so sorry. Of course we can go.'

'It will mean a bit of a hike. After we get off the bus.' The Reader smiled inwardly; he thought Sylvia must think he was a tightwad, getting a bus everywhere, but he had told her he didn't have a car at the moment. The truth was, he didn't want anybody to see him with her in his car. 'First though, let's grab a cuppa. There's a flower shop nearby and we can get a little bunch. It doesn't have to be a huge thing. My sister loved flowers. She would have appreciated any flowers she got.'

He tried to make the tears come into his eyes, at least make them look glassy, but nothing came. He felt like laughing, but that would have been strange.

'That would be nice,' Sylvia said. 'Anywhere in particular?'

'There's a nice little place along here. Called Isobel's. I'm a regular there.'

'Really? I thought you lived in Stockbridge?'

Shit. He did tell her that, didn't he? 'Sorry, I meant to say that was the marital home. My mother actually lives here on the Shore.' Technically, the street was just called Shore, but everybody he knew called it *the* Shore.

They crossed Commercial Street and continued walking along the Shore.

'Which one?' Sylvia asked.

'Hmm?'

'Which flat does your mother live in?'

'In one of the new ones.' He pointed to a block of flats that looked modern compared to the others on either side.

He felt a stab of anger now, wanting to pull out a knife and just stick her with it. If she thought his mother really did live here – God rest her soul – then what was to stop her from just appearing at the door one night? Then he laughed inside. There would be zero chance of that, after today. She wouldn't be popping in on anybody ever again.

He stopped outside Isobel's. 'This is it.'

'They know you in here?' Sylvia said, smiling. 'Maybe I'll ask them all about your secrets.' She giggled like a fucking schoolgirl.

That was another annoying thing about this bitch: she'd suddenly started wanting to hold hands in the street. But he went along with it. It would be ending shortly.

They stepped into the café and the woman was behind the counter, on her own. Was the husband behind the scenes through the back? No way to tell and he wasn't going to ask.

'Hello there,' Isobel said, smiling at them.

'Hello,' Sylvia said.

'What can I get for you?'

'Two coffees, please.'

'Coming right up.'

The Reader was looking at the paperbacks on the bookcase. Sylvia stood beside him, the books attracting her.

'Doesn't this just give you a buzz, standing in front of a bookcase?' she said.

He looked at her and smiled. 'It does. And it's a book exchange; bring one, take one.'

'What a great idea.' They looked at the titles for a few minutes until the coffee was made.

'I'll get this,' Sylvia said, 'since you bought the ice cream.' She walked up to the counter and paid for the coffees. 'I love the idea of the book exchange,' she said. 'I own a little bookshop on the southside.'

'That's great. Our book exchange has been a big hit,' Isobel said.

They sat at a table by the window. There was a bowl with single-serve creamers in it, and packets of sugar. Sylvia took three packets, shook them and poured them in. That was another thing he hated: she kept a sugar plantation on demand single-handedly. It was a wonder she didn't have false teeth. Give it time, he thought.

They chatted about Leith and how it was a wonderful place to be brought up.

'Where were you brought up?' he asked Sylvia, although he knew everything there was to know about her.

'Gilmerton. It was a great community.'

He tuned her out while pretending to listen and smiling. Now she lived in a flat in Marchmont, a million miles away from Gilmerton. Her parents were dead, she had no siblings, never been married but didn't discount it.

He stifled a yawn and looked out the window at the Water of Leith. He loved it down here. A friend of his had lived in the block of flats he had pointed out, the one where his fictitious mother lived in. The old woman had departed this world years ago, but she had actually lived in Lorne Street, further up Leith.

'...going?'

He realised his mind had wandered just a little too far. 'I'm sorry, I was miles away.'

She smiled. 'Is my conversation that boring?'

'No, of course not. I was just thinking about my sister.'

'I'm sorry.' She reached a hand out and put it over his, and put on that little sad smile that people do when they're trying to show empathy but silently thanking God that it wasn't them on the receiving end of what-ever disaster had struck. That phoney look of sympathy they gave, just before they told you that if you ever needed anything, just call. Which they didn't mean and the thought of getting such a phone call made them shudder.

'Thank you,' he said, looking into her eyes, and imagining shoving a fork into one of them. He slipped his hand out. 'I need to use the facilities,' he said, getting up and going into the gents.

When he was in the toilet, Sylvia got up and took a paperback out of her bag and walked up to the bookcase. 'This is a great thriller,' she said to Isobel. 'I finished it on the bus.'

'Well, help yourself, sweetheart. There's a John Sandford there, his latest in paperback.'

'Oh, nice. I haven't read that one. Thank you.'

The Reader came back out and Sylvia waved at Isobel as they left the café.

'The new John Sandford was in there,' Sylvia said, waving it in front of him.

'Great. I'll need to read it after you.'

'Absolutely.' She put it in her bag.

After grabbing a little bunch of flowers and sitting on the bus, listening to Sylvia drone on about things he wasn't interested in but had to pretend to, he made it to the bus stop without taking his own life. They stepped out into the heat, the sky empty and blue.

The walk was a fair distance, but he promised her they would get a taxi into Stockbridge where he knew a great little coffee shop.

'My dogs are barking,' she said when they got to the cemetery gates.

He looked at her like she was daft. 'What?' he said.

'My dogs are barking.' She laughed. 'My feet are killing me. Haven't you heard that expression before?'

He felt an explosion of anger inside. He hated it when people talked shite. 'That's a new one on me, Sylvia.'

Her smile dropped. 'I'm sorry, here I am, laughing, and we're going to your sister's grave.'

'Don't worry about it. Honestly. My sister would have loved you.'

'Really?' Sylvia said.

'Of course.' If she had been alive. And not made up.

They walked through to the other side of the cemetery, to the old part. Through the archway and into what was almost a jungle.

They walked a short distance and The Reader stopped. At the outline of a gravestone. A big, heavy one that looked like it had been flipped over by a Bobcat.

'You know what that is?' he asked, pointing to the bare dirt.

Sylvia wasn't smiling any more. 'Is that where your sister is buried?'

'No. My sister isn't dead.'

'What... what are you talking about?'

He could see the fear on her face now.

'You remember Nancy, don't you?'

He watched as Sylvia started to panic. He could see it on her face.

'No... I don't know anybody called Nancy.'

'Of course you do. Think hard.'

Sylvia shook her head. 'I want to go now, Peter.'

'My name's not Peter.' He told her his real name. Watched as her eyes went wide as realisation kicked in.

'That was where Ivy Jack lay. With that huge gravestone on top of her. I dug the ground out a bit so she wouldn't be noticed. See that gravestone shape in the wall? That was where the marker lived until I brought it down on her. She wasn't dead when it hit her. But she was after.' He looked and saw that Sylvia had peed herself, the front of her jeans darker than the rest.

'I'm going now,' she said, starting to turn away, but then The Reader punched her on the side of the face, knocking her down.

She moaned as he dragged her in front of a tall, heavy headstone.

'I didn't have time to prepare like I did for Ivy, but you have to work with the tools you have, am I right?'

He kicked her bag to one side and the paperback peeked out. He smiled and picked it up.

'This will do nicely.'

Sylvia lay on the dry grass and flinched as he put the paperback on her chest. He disappeared round the back of the large gravestone and she thought for a moment that he had gone, until she looked up and saw the large stone toppling. She just started to scream when the weight cut it off.

The Reader stood and looked down at the back of the stone. There was no sign of Sylvia now. For all intents and purposes, she had disappeared.

He walked along past more toppled gravestones. They weren't an unusual sight in this cemetery. Nobody would blink an eye on seeing these stones lying on their front.

He looked at the headstones, their inscriptions underneath. The temporary resting places of Ivy Jack and Marianne Taylor. And now Sylvia Green. They had recovered Ivy, but they didn't know the whereabouts of Marianne yet. No doubt they would, one day. Maybe, maybe not, he thought, considering Ivy had lain under a stone without anybody finding her until it had been pointed out to the police.

He stood looking at the black polished headstone. Read the names from top to bottom.

Albert Simpson.

Below, his wife Olive Simpson.

Below that, their daughter Nancy Simpson.

His wife-to-be. His beautiful fiancée, Nancy, her life snuffed out before he had a chance to marry her. He could feel himself shaking as the sobs started to overwhelm him. The one woman he had ever loved enough to spend the rest of his life with. Gone, buried in the ground. Waiting for him.

Now, those other women were lying alongside her. Where they belonged.

26

BACK THEN

Nancy's eyes lit up when The Reader stood watching her rip the wrapping paper off the bike. Of course she knew what it was by the shape, but not the colour, or any of the specs.

'It's beautiful!' she said, taking in the purple and white bodywork.

'We will soon be going on our bike tour of the Highlands,' he replied. 'But I think we should get some practice in on them first.'

'I agree,' Nancy said, smiling.

'I got us helmets, and lights and all the kit we'll need.'

'When you said touring, you did mean we would drive up there first, then cycle around?'

He laughed then, not sure if she was serious or not. 'Of course, honey. I'm not as young as I used to be, but I can give it some stuff on the bike in the gym.' He held up a hand. 'I know it's not the same; we'll have hills to climb, but since we're both gym members, we're halfway there. If we go out every night, we can build up to the tour.'

She hugged him then, pulling him in close, smiling, her eyes shining. 'This is going to be so much fun.'

'I know a honeymoon in Aruba would be more fun, but I would rather go there when it's miserable here.'

'Do they have midges in Aruba?' Nancy asked with a laugh.

'I hope not!'

He held on to her then, not knowing what was about to happen, or how his life was going to change forever. But in that moment, he had never been happier.

It wasn't going to last long.

27

FIFE

'I still don't think we should rush in here like we're about to lynch him,' Cameron said as Art pulled into the small car park of Windygates bowling club.

'We're just here to inform the bastard that she's dead, and if he starts giving us lip, then we tell him that we know he was seeing her. Watch his reaction. Then we can boot him in the nuts.'

Cameron stretched after they got out of the car.

'You look like a half-shut knife,' Art said.

'It's that old, shitey bed my mother has in her spare room. I think it came off the ark. Hardly any padding, the springs creak every time I move.'

They started heading for the club. 'Why don't you just patch things up with Morag? Get back to your own scratcher.'

'I wish. But it wasn't my fault in the first place.'

'And there lies the problem; you have a lot to learn about marriage, son.'

'Like what?'

'Like always accepting everything is your fault. Even if it's theirs. Sometimes you just have to keep your head below the edge of the trench. Happy wife, happy life.'

'Maybe,' Cameron said with a shrug.

'Maybe nothing. That's the key to a successful marriage.'

'Worked for you, did it?'

Art stopped and looked at him. 'Aye, it did. I would still be married to my wife.'

Cameron blew out a breath. 'Aye, sorry, pal. You're right. I'll try to talk to her.'

'Good lad.' He opened the door and they walked into the bowling club.

There was the usual crowd in, watching TV, playing dominoes. All they needed was a stripper and that would be the entertainment trifecta complete.

They walked up to the bar, Art glad to see the vicar wasn't in, unless he was skulking about in the gents, lecturing somebody on the perils of drinking or something else. Do as I say, don't do as I do.

Dick Drever was nowhere to be seen, and in his place was a woman Art knew usually served at night. 'Bastard's probably hiding now,' Art said.

'I'd go into hiding too if I was serving that watered-down pish,' Cameron said, his eyes going to the TV again as a football match played out.

'Jesus, here we go again. What next? The barmaid's an old dug?'

Kim, the barmaid, turned to look at Art, glaring at him.

'At the Malt and Shovel in Glenrothes,' he said to her, feeling his cheeks burn.

'You want a drink?' she asked, not quite ready to burst out a smile.

'No, actually, we want a word with Dick,' Art said.

'So do we. He never turned up for his shift.'

'We saw him last night, but only for a wee while. Did he say if he wasn't coming in today?'

'I couldn't tell you. I don't work Monday nights, and I don't socialise in this dump in my free time.'

'Is there any way you can find out?' Art asked, keeping his voice even.

'Ask one of those old coffin dodgers over there. They're never out of the place.'

'Keeps you in a job, though, eh?' Art said, walking away.

'What's her problem?' Cameron asked.

'She's just a bad-tempered old cow.' He quickly turned round to make sure she hadn't heard him, but she had turned away and had picked up the phone behind the bar.

One of the aforementioned old coffin dodgers was named Bert Doogan.

Art nudged Cameron and nodded towards a table where some old men were playing dominoes. 'Bert Doogan. Doolally, everybody calls him.'

'To his face?'

'Behind his back, obviously.'

'What do you call me behind my back?' Cameron asked.

'Wouldn't you like to know?'

'Which one's Doolally?' Cameron asked.

'Guess,' Art said.

'Well, if you ask me, they all look doolally.'

'Again with the fucking raised voice. Shout a bit louder, I don't think they heard you out on the fucking green.' He tutted and shook his head. 'The one with the flat cap on.'

'Figures,' Cameron said. 'He looks like he's not playing with a full deck.'

'Which would have been amusing if they were playing cards.'

'Help you, Art?' one of the old boys asked.

'Aye,' Art replied, walking towards the table. 'Any of you boys in here last night?'

They looked at each other and laughed. 'We're in here every night,' Doolally said. 'Saves on our electricity bill.'

They all laughed again.

'More money for booze, boys, am I right?' Art said.

'Damn right, son,' one of the others said.

'When Dick was on last night, did he happen to mention if he wasn't coming in today?' Cameron said, cutting to the chase. 'We saw him, but were wondering if he said anything later on.'

They looked at Art before looking at Cameron. 'No, son. But he must have had a busy night after he left here. He likes a wee swally when he's finished for the night.'

'He's getting peace with his missus being away, that's for sure,' Doolally said.

'Did anybody try calling him to see why he didn't turn up for work?' Cameron asked.

'We only drink here, son, we don't run the place. Why don't you ask nice-but-dim Kim behind the bar?'

'She told us to ask the old coffin dodgers.' Cameron said.

'Did she fucking now?' one of the old boys said. 'Cheeky cow.'

'Does anybody know where he lives?' Art said.

'You drink here too, son,' Doolally said. 'You've as much idea as any of us.'

Art was just spinning his wheels now. 'Thanks, lads.'

'How about getting us old boys a drink?' one of them asked.

'I'll ask Kim to put it on Dick's tab.'

They walked away to the bar, Doolally looking over hopefully.

'You're not seriously getting the old farts a drink, are you?' Cameron asked.

'This you doing your bit for Help the Aged? Calling them old farts?'

'They hardly give off a vibe that they're one piece of coal away from freezing to death.'

Art whipped his head round to see if any of them had heard, but Doolally and his pals saw this as a signal that Art was indeed going to splurge for a round and he gave the thumbs up to the detective.

'Keep it fucking down. It's like when people get pished and start talking at the top of their voice, only you're fucking sober. Christ, you'll be singing "My Way" on the way out to the car next.'

Kim came over, her face doing a fair impression of a walking UTI. 'What now?'

'Do you know where Dick lives?' Art asked.

'Who's asking?'

'Well, I am.'

'Nope.'

'Can you find out?' Cameron asked.

'Nope.'

'We're conducting an investigation here, Kim. We need to talk to Dick,' Art said.

'Talk to your own dick, then.'

Art shook his head. 'What if he's fallen and can't get to the phone?' Cameron said.

'Tough shit. I'm not his babysitter. If he's fallen, he should be more careful. Besides, I'm not his secretary. I'm only here to serve drinks and packets of crisps.'

'Well, thanks for your help.'

Kim walked away, and Art turned to Cameron for a second. 'We'll get his address from control. They can get it from DVLA. But watch this.' He walked back over to the table where Doolally and his pals were, and he leaned in close. 'Sorry, lads, she wouldn't let me buy a round. She said you were a bunch of drunken old scrounging bastards and she wasn't going to encourage you. I did try.'

'She fucking said that?' Doolally said. 'The committee will hear about this. My son-in-law sits on it, and he'll make sure her arse is out the door. Thanks, son.'

Art nodded and walked out the door, followed by Cameron. 'How fast can you run?' he asked.

'Why? What happened?'

'Let's just say that nice-but-dim Kim might be getting her jotters soon.'

'At the end of the day, as long as I can run faster than you, that's all that matters.'

28

EDINBURGH

Brodie had his feet up on the couch, reading a book, when Ruth entered the living room and sat in a chair. The TV was on but he wasn't paying much attention to the show. He always thought that 7 p.m. was a dead zone when it came to TV.

He and Ruth were quite happy being in the same room as each other, without having to have a conversation every five minutes. He was reading a Stephen King novel called *Holly*. He had found it in the book exchange at his mother's café. Swapping it for the Dean Koontz he had left there.

Brodie liked reading horror novels. Some guys he worked with liked reading crime, but he wanted to steer away from that. He got enough of it at the office.

'Good book?' Ruth asked.

'It is. In my experience, you can't go wrong with a good King novel.'

'I've read them all,' she said. 'I enjoy his short stories.'

'Me too. "Everything's Eventual" is my favourite.' He stuck the bookmark into the book and closed it.

'What are you reading just now?'

'*The Silent Patient* by Alex Michaelides. It's about a therapist who tries to help a woman who won't talk. It's one of the best books I've ever read.'

'It must be good. You said you don't read books about psychiatrists.'

'I'd heard good things about it from a woman at work,' Ruth said. 'Word of mouth works wonders.'

'I can see that.'

'I put the kettle on if you want a cuppa.'

'Great. I don't feel like a beer tonight. I'll make them.' He got up and went into the kitchen and poured two coffees after the kettle switched off. 'I have to go over to Fife tomorrow,' he said to her after he put the mugs down on the coffee table.

'To see Eric? Is he okay?'

'No, it's not that. It's with work,' he said.

'Oh really? Why are they having you do that?'

'Remember I told you I was seconded over to Fife about seven years ago? I was working a serial killer case.'

'Oh, yeah. You told me ages ago about that.'

'The papers nicknamed him The Embalmer. We didn't catch him. But this time, the MIT in Glenrothes is a man down. Their DCI has gone missing and they want me in as the senior officer in charge.'

'It must be a serious case.'

He nodded. 'They found a skeleton under some floorboards, apparently.'

'Oh no. Who would do that? Put a body under the floorboards?' she said.

'You would be surprised,' Brodie said.

29

EDINBURGH

Wednesday

The Reader was enjoying the warmth as he strolled along the Shore, down in Leith. It was early morning. Not too early but at a time when people who worked office hours started hopping on buses.

This part of Edinburgh was very cathartic for him, being Nancy's home town, as it were. She had been brought up here, and had shared her memories with him, but she had had ambitions to move up in the world and had worked hard to get where she was.

Sometimes, he could feel her spirit if he closed his eyes. He stopped opposite Isobel's. He laughed inside at the thought of the book Sylvia had taken from there.

He felt his mood darken as he replayed her words in his head, but then it was like the clouds had parted and the sun shone through when he replayed the gravestone falling on top of her.

It bothered him when he remembered that her arm was sticking out. If he had had a tool with him, he would have chopped it off, but it was a gamble; what were the chances of somebody going into that old part of the cemetery and discovering her anytime soon?

Quite high, he thought. He hadn't thought that way last night, but then he remembered the newspeople talking about Kane being in the cemetery and there were ghouls who might want to go and have a look to see where the body was. If they did that, then they would find Sylvia.

It would be coming to a close soon anyway. That was the whole point. He wasn't going to be like the American serial killer Zodiac, who had simply disappeared. No, he, The Reader, would just kill who needed to be killed.

It was something he had told himself over and over, but then again, there was something deep inside him that enjoyed watching them die. Would he be able to stop? He would have to.

After they found Sylvia and then Marianne Taylor, they would know. But he would be away by then.

He walked over to the café and stepped inside to the smell of rolls and coffee.

'Hello again,' Isobel said, smiling at him. The Reader had his hat and sunglasses on, and made no move to take them off.

'Hello,' he said, putting a slight English accent into his voice.

'What can I get you?' Isobel asked, but The Reader's attention was caught by a young woman coming out from the back of the café.

'A new member of staff?' he asked Isobel.

'This is my daughter, Moira.' She smiled and turned to look. Moira smiled at him.

'Pleased to meet you...?'

The question was there, hanging between them. He knew *her* name and, in return, she wanted to know *his*. 'Peter.'

'Pleased to meet you, Pete.'

'Peter. Never Pete,' he said.

His smile stayed in place. It was the name he had given Sylvia. Not his real name, of course. That would be suicide.

'Sorry. Peter,' Moira said.

'Coffee?' Isobel asked.

'Please. No sugar. And I may as well have a bacon roll,' he said with a smile.

Nancy had always said his smile was his best feature. That and the blue eyes, but of course, these two women couldn't see his eyes for his sunglasses.

'Why don't you have a seat, love, and I'll bring it over,' Isobel said.

The Reader sat down without glancing at the bookcase. That might bring back memories of yesterday when he had been in with Sylvia.

Instead, he sat back and took the newspaper out of his pocket and unfurled it, starting to read, but he kept his eyes on the young woman.

Liam Brodie's sister. It had taken a little while to track her down, but here she was. She was already dead.

She just didn't know it yet.

30

FIFE

Wednesday morning, Ruth thought. Halfway through the week. It was all downhill from today to Friday. The older she became, the more she appreciated the weekends. She loved being with Brodie, doing fun things with him. They would go over to Burntisland in July when the carnival was there, and take Eric and his girlfriend, Chrissie. Eric couldn't do any of the rides, but he would still enjoy himself.

She looked at her watch. Plenty of time. She stood looking out of the window, over to Fife, drinking her coffee.

Brodie came in, fresh out of the shower, playing with his tie as usual.

'We should get a dog, then you could put your tie on him then transfer it,' she said, putting her mug down. She walked over to him and adjusted it for him.

'Thanks, honey.'

'You having a coffee?' she asked.

'I'll take one in my Stanley.'

She made it for him, thinking about her first patient of the day. Normally, she didn't get emotional about them, but she couldn't help feeling sorry for this one.

'Right, I'm off. I'll speak to you later.' He gave her a kiss, and left her alone with her thoughts.

* * *

The drive to Glenrothes took over an hour, over the Queensferry Crossing and up the M80, connecting with the A92.

Brodie got there just after 10 a.m. He was shown into the incident room by a young female uniformed officer. There was a small group of people sitting in front of computers when he walked in.

The oldest-looking of the bunch, a man, stood up and walked over to him. 'DI Art McKenzie. I'm assuming you're DCI Brodie.'

'It's wrong to assume anything, DI McKenzie,' Brodie said. 'I might have been some nutcase walking in to murder you all.'

Art smiled but there was no humour in it. 'They called up. Told me you were coming. Gave me your description. Otherwise, we would have all been over you like a rash.'

'Good to know you're keeping on your toes.' He looked at the others. 'Introduce me to your team.'

Art turned round to see the others watching them, like they were in the front row of the big top.

'DS Freya Munro. DS Cameron Reid. DC Morven Fraser. This is our temporary DCI. From Edinburgh.'

He said the city's name like he was informing everybody that one of them had dog shite on their shoe.

'Det Supt Cross from my division filled me in on what's been going on. You can fill in any blanks on the way to the crime scene. I want to see that first before we go to the mortuary. Somebody call and give them a heads-up that we'll be coming later this morning.'

'I'll get on it,' Morven said.

'Thank you. DI McKenzie, you and Reid can drive me to the scene. No point in taking two cars.'

Art nodded sideways to Cameron and the younger man stood up, grabbing his jacket from the back of his seat.

'You drive, son. I'll sit in the back. That way, I'll not see it coming when you shove us in front of a bus.'

Cameron looked at Brodie. 'He's kidding, of course, sir. I'm a very proficient driver.'

'I'm about to find out, I suppose.' Brodie watched as Art tossed Cameron the car keys and they left the incident room. 'Fill me in,' Brodie said as Cameron roared out of the car park.

Art was thrown back in his seat. 'There's an old cottage about to be put up for sale, apparently. The owner wanted it fixed up before selling. Two contractors dropped a chimney through the roof, and it went right through the floorboards, revealing a mummified corpse of a child in the crawl space. The pathologist is calling it murder. The boy has a hole in his skull. Blunt force trauma, he reckons.'

'Near St Monans?' Brodie asked.

'Aye. Not that far as the crow flies. Or the way Cameron drives either.'

Cameron looked over to Brodie. 'DI McKenzie said you've worked here before, sir?'

'I have. Years ago. I was seconded over here after we became a unified force. I was a DI at the time.'

Art snapped his fingers. 'I thought I recognised the name! We worked on the case where a guy was killing women and draining their blood and replacing it with bleach. The Embalmer, the press called him.'

'Did you catch him?' Cameron asked.

'Did we fu... er, no, we didn't,' Art said. 'He stopped. He's maybe in prison, or died.'

'Or maybe he just decided to have a rest,' Brodie said. 'It's been seven years, I think. Something like that. I still have a photo of his last victim on my desk. I promised her mother I'd catch the bastard. I know I shouldn't have, but I couldn't look her in the face and tell her I couldn't. Her mother died last year. The girl's name is Emily Blair. Don't ever let that name leave your brain. Or the others.'

'He might have moved out of the area,' Art said.

'That too. We had thought about that; what job could he have taken that would have made him move? There are endless possibilities.'

'Maybe he joined the military,' Cameron said.

'No,' Brodie said. 'I mean, he's clever enough to have passed a psych evaluation, but he doesn't have the personality to fit into the military. From the profile we had made up.'

Brodie didn't tell them that Dr Gabriel Kane had talked to Brodie about The Embalmer. At Kane's request. One nutjob talking about another. The blind leading the blind.

Cameron drove through Windygates, casting a glance in the rear-view mirror at Art, as if silently asking, *Should we tell him about Pat?* He then looked out of the windscreen and spotted the A915 before driving north-east.

'What's happening in Edinburgh?' Art asked. 'Anything exciting?'

Brodie shook his head, not wanting to go into it. 'Nothing right now. Just looking into old cases. Like the Fife side, I imagine. When there's nothing new. Like the bones you just found.' Brodie looked out of the window for a moment before looking round at Art. 'What's the story with the missing DCI?'

Art was silent for a moment, staring at the back of Cameron's head, before making eye contact with the temporary boss. 'He went on holiday to Tenerife, then arrived back in Scotland, but didn't go home and didn't show up for work.'

'Is he ill? Or had some sort of a breakdown or something?'

'Not that we know of. He lives with his sister and hasn't returned there or come back to work, and nobody's heard from him. It's been over a week now.'

'You should have been acting DCI until he came back,' Brodie said.

'I'm not going to take Alan's place,' Art said, his tone sharp.

'You obviously need somebody at the helm. That's why they asked me to step in.'

'No disrespect, sir, but I'm sure Alan will be back before you know it.'

Brodie looked at him. 'You always call senior ranks by their first name?'

Art shook his head. 'No. We were friends out of work, too. I've known Alan for a long time. We moved up together. He's a few years older, but we were friends.'

Brodie sensed that he had rubbed the man the wrong way and didn't speak again. Cameron took some minor B-roads until they came to a T-junction that had two signs pointing right, one for a castle and gardens, the other for Arncrouch.

He turned right and slowed at the 20 mph sign.

The cottage was on the left as they entered the village. A quiet, unassuming place, but where a young boy's life had ended. Now it wasn't quite unassuming.

31

FIFE

Brodie stood outside the cottage, looking at the white walls and the roof. The chimney had obviously fallen through the other side, as this side looked intact. There was a garage door further along that had seen better days. He thought the place would look pretty good after being refurbished. And a new roof put on.

'You alright, sir?' Art asked. 'You look like you've seen a ghost.'

'I'm fine. Let's get inside.'

Cameron made a face and shrugged but followed their temporary boss up to the front door. A Uniform stood guard and Art was glad to see it wasn't McCoy, but somebody he didn't recognise.

Brodie showed his ID. 'We need to go inside and have a look.'

'No problem, sir,' he said, stepping to one side.

The hallway smelled like an old person had lived in here, which was indeed the case.

White-suited people were bustling about, taking photos and video. Brodie turned to Art. 'What room was it?'

'To the annexe along on the left,' Art said.

'How do you know it's an annexe?'

'Just a guess. From the way this place looks laid out. Back in the day, it would have been just a regular shape, I reckon.'

Brodie nodded, and made his way along the hallway to where the techs were working.

'Help you?' a man in a white suit said.

'DCI Brodie. I'm here to examine the crime scene.'

He held out a hand. 'I'm Kevin Carnie, head of forensics.'

Brodie shook the man's hand, and Carnie nodded to Art and Cameron.

'Come on in and have a look.' Carnie led the men into the room, where Brodie was seeing it for the first time with wrecked floorboards.

'I spoke to the pathologist, Sherlock,' Carnie said. 'Doctor Ronald Holmes. Everybody calls him Sherlock for the obvious reason.'

'We'll be going to speak with him after this,' Brodie said, 'but give me your opinion.'

'Looks like a small boy was killed with a blunt instrument, from what the doc says. Then wrapped up in plastic and hidden under the floorboards. Carpets were put in and probably changed. The contractors said the carpets were old but not ancient.'

'What about a smell? Surely somebody would have smelled a dead body in there?'

'There are ventilation bricks in the foundations. Helps keep the house breathing. I'm assuming that any smell would have ventilated to the outside. Otherwise, somebody would have reported the smell, surely?' Carnie said.

'You would think,' Brodie said. 'How long do you think that he was down there?'

'Not sure. Decades, I would say at a guess.'

'Maybe we could ask the owner,' Art said.

'We could. Do you have a name for me?'

Cameron took his notebook out and flipped through it, then looked at Brodie. 'A woman called Margaret Wallace.'

'Anybody know where she lives?' Brodie asked.

'In Dunfermline,' Art answered.

'That's handy. We can go and talk to her then we can go to the mortuary.'

'In a home,' Cameron added.

'You might have led with that,' Brodie said.

'Sorry. That part was on the next page. It's a nursing home. She's eighty-five.'

'We can still go and talk to her,' Brodie said. 'But let's get to the mortuary first.'

Brodie looked back at the cottage as they went back to the car. He pictured a little boy playing outside in the sunshine, waving to him as they left. Then the image faded and he felt a sudden feeling of sadness.

No matter how long he was in the job, he could never wrap his head around how some people could kill children.

He shivered as he got into the car and Cameron drove off.

32

FIFE

The nursing home was in Townhill, just outside of Dunfermline. It looked relatively new and well maintained. They made small talk on the way down, Brodie trying to keep the talk light.

'Tell me more about DCI McRae,' he said to Art as they walked across the car park to the main entrance.

'He's a good guy. Firm but fair. Everybody likes him.'

'Is this unusual for him to take off like this?'

'It is. I've worked with him for years and he's never done anything like this.'

'You checked out his family?'

'We did. He lives with his sister after his divorce. They were joined at the hip, but Alan was starting to get out a bit more. You know, singles nights at the bowling club we go to in Windygates.'

They went inside, where the temperature seemed just as high inside as it was outside.

'I'm fucking sweating,' Cameron complained to Art as Brodie walked forward to the reception desk.

'You shouldn't have put your woolly long johns on then,' Art said.

Cameron elbowed him. 'You going to tell his nibs about Pat dying in her car?'

'If the moment presents itself. One step at a time, Cam. We don't know this bloke. He hasn't earned our trust yet.'

Brodie turned back towards them. 'Room 302. Lifts are over here.'

They followed Brodie. Upstairs, there was the universal smell again. Brodie hated it with a passion. Life and death mixed into one.

A nurse stopped them. 'Can I help you?'

The three detectives had their warrant cards out and showed them to the woman who looked like she might be in her thirties but had enough miles under her belt to not take any guff.

'Mrs Margaret Wallace, room 302,' Brodie said.

'Down that hallway to the left, second room on the right.' She walked away, efficient and in control.

They stopped at the doorway to the old woman's room and looked in. The first person Brodie saw was a woman who looked to be in her fifties. Not Margaret Wallace then.

He knocked on the open door. The woman looked at them.

'Help you?' she said, her eyes bright and fierce. Her hair had blonde streaks, but was mostly mousey brown, turning grey. Although well kept, it wasn't stylish. She wore a dress that was fashionable last year.

'DCI Brodie. I was hoping to have a word with Margaret Wallace. You are?'

'Laura Forrest. I'm her daughter. She's unfortunately about to get down for a nap.'

'I'm old, Laura, but don't treat me like I'm demented,' a voice said from out of sight. 'Let him in.'

'There are three of them,' Laura said.

'The more the merrier.'

Brodie didn't hesitate and entered the room fully, followed by Art and Cameron.

'Mrs Wallace?' Brodie said. 'I'm DCI Brodie. These are my colleagues, DI McKenzie and DS Reid.'

'Three fine young men come to visit me. How exciting. And call me Margaret. You do have first names, I assume?'

Brodie smiled. 'Liam. Art and Cameron.'

'Well, there's only one seat but you're welcome to stand.' Margaret looked at Laura. 'Can you get us some coffee and tea?'

'You're not supposed to have tea in the afternoon, Mum. It makes you pee.'

'Language, Laura.'

'It's only pee.'

'There you go again. Perhaps young Cameron wouldn't mind going with you to the vending machine? Tea or coffee, gentlemen?' Margaret said, smiling at them. She was sitting up in her bed, pillows behind her back. She was a slight woman with grey hair and wrinkled skin, just like any other eighty-five-year-old might look. But there was still a spark in her eyes, and a smile played on her lips.

Brodie turned to look at Cameron.

'No problem, sir.'

'I'll have a coffee,' Brodie said.

'Tea for me, Cameron,' Art said. 'Milk.'

'I don't think it's actually milk that comes out of the machine,' Laura said, making a face.

'What is it, then?' Cameron asked.

'Your guess is as good as mine,' Laura said, leaving the room.

Brodie looked at Margaret, momentarily turned away from the other two men.

For fuck's sake, Cameron mouthed to Art, who gave a slight grin, before straightening his face and looking away, then Cameron left to catch up with the sour-faced daughter.

'Now that Laura is away, why don't you tell me why you're here?' Margaret said. 'I might be old, but I'm not ready to be put in a straitjacket just yet.'

Brodie smiled. He imagined the old woman would have been a formidable mental opponent, back in the day.

'It's about your house. In Arncrouch.'

'I only have one house.'

'Well, it's about that one.'

She locked eyes with him. 'What about it?'

'I believe you're going to put it up for sale and wanted it refurbished before that happened.'

'That's right. Is everything okay with it? There hasn't been a fire or anything?'

'No, no, nothing like that,' Brodie said. He looked at Art to jump in.

'The contractors knocked a chimney over,' Art said, looking at the old woman. 'It went right through your roof, through the floorboards and into your crawl space.'

Margaret put a hand on her chest, and Art wondered for a moment if her heart was going to give out.

'Is there a lot of damage?' she asked.

'Yes, there is, I'm sorry to say.'

She looked at each of them in turn. 'They wouldn't send three police officers to tell me a chimney fell. Was somebody killed?'

Brodie shook his head. 'No. It was rather something that was found.'

'Found in the crawl space?'

'Yes. We found a body,' Art said.

Margaret gasped, and Brodie stood silently for a moment, watching her, just in case he needed to shout for help, but then she stared at him.

'Do you know who it was?' she asked.

'We were hoping you could tell us,' Art said. 'It's the body of a young boy.'

Margaret screamed.

33

EDINBURGH

The Reader walked into the bookshop, careful not to look up at the camera. Karen Blair was behind the counter. A mousey woman who was always talking about how she needed to lose some weight, all the while snacking on a chocolate bar. He had listened to her rabbiting away while he waited for Sylvia.

He made sure he put his red-coloured eyeglasses on when he wasn't wearing sunglasses. He slipped them out and put them on after he closed the door behind him. *Retinal dysfunction* he had told Sylvia the first time she saw him with them on.

'Just like Bono,' Karen said, smiling and nodding at his glasses. 'You haven't always worn them, have you?'

'I have to when it gets sunny outside. My retinas can't take the brightness. It's a level of blindness.' He kept a straight face, wiping the smile off hers.

'I'm sorry, Peter. I didn't know it was so serious.'

He waved her apology away and then smiled. It was important to win her over now. 'No need for an apology. I have to wear a different tint in the winter. Maybe that's why you've never seen me with the red ones on.' It was all horseshit, but this woman looked like she couldn't tie her own shoelaces without the aid of a YouTube video.

'If you're looking for Sylvia, then she isn't going to be in today. She said she was going to have a few days off and asked me to step in. In fact... weren't you supposed to be with her?'

'That's why I'm here. Sylvia needs your help. She wants you to come round to her house tonight for dinner, but she's making some Italian dish, and she's not confident it will come out right. She knows you're a good cook. Would you mind coming round and helping her? You can close the shop early, she says.'

Karen smiled, both at the thought of getting wired into some Italian food and going somewhere else for dinner rather than back to her dull house.

'I'd love that.' She smiled at him, and he thought she was attracted to him. If he tried hard enough, he knew he could sleep with her, but that wasn't the job at hand. Besides, she wasn't his type.

Nancy was his type. His sweet, beautiful Nancy.

'We can close up now.'

'Oh, right.'

Karen busied about, doing whatever it was she had to do to prepare the shop for closing, then they were ready to go. The Reader made sure to keep his hat on.

'Oh, one thing I have to pick up for her,' he said.

'What's that?'

'A book.' He walked over to one of the shelves and plucked one from the shelf. 'One of her favourites,' he said, smiling.

Five minutes later, they were outside and in his car. 'Before we go to Sylvia's, I was wondering if you would mind coming with me?' He pointed to the clock on the dashboard. 'Sylvia called me before I came into the shop and said she had popped out for something for dessert, so she isn't home just now. We have time. If you wouldn't mind.'

He looked round at the bunch of flowers on the back seat. Karen followed his gaze and her eyes went wide. 'They're beautiful. Sylvia's going to be so pleased.'

'Oh, they're not for Sylvia.'

'Oh? Who are they for?' There were two bright spots on her cheeks.

The Reader forced himself to smile. The fat old bitch thought they were

for her. That he was going to cheat on his and Sylvia's fictitious relationship.

'I'd like to put them on my sister's grave. She died a year ago today.' The
lie came easily. He'd had ample practice now, and it was a line he'd
rehearsed so much, he could deliver it in his sleep. 'You don't mind coming
with me, do you?'

Ask it in a way that they find awkward to say no to.

'Oh. No, that's fine. Sorry to hear about your sister.'

'Thank you, Karen. This means a lot to me. I've been dreading this first
anniversary all week. I was hesitant to ask Sylvia.' He looked over at Karen.
'But I look on you as a friend. Somebody I can trust.'

'That's so sweet,' Karen said.

They chatted as he drove down to the cemetery. Inside, he
followed the track round to the entrance to the old part. The grass
and weeds were taking over, growing tall, which was good camouflage. This made him think of the song 'Camouflage' by Stan
Ridgway. Just another random thought that popped into The Reader's
head.

'Here we are,' he said, still singing the song in his head. An earworm, he
thought. Fucking things. He'd need to start singing the *Postman Pat* theme
to get rid of it.

They got out into the shade provided by the tall trees in the cemetery.
He reached in and grabbed the flowers from the back seat.

'What was her name?'

The question caught The Reader off guard for a moment. He should
have had one prepared, but didn't. Had Sylvia asked? No, he didn't think so.
She was too self-absorbed.

'Caroline.' He made it sound real, even though it had just come off the
top of his head.

'Was she young? Like you?' Karen asked as they walked under the
archway.

'Karen, that's very kind. I'm not young, and neither was Caroline. I
suppose she was what one might say, middle-aged. Just along here.'

They walked past the large gravestone that had hidden Ivy Jack all
these years, and the others that held some surprises of their own.

'It's a disgrace,' Karen said, and for a moment he thought she was talking about his little adventures in here.

'I'm sorry?' he said.

'This.' She swept an arm around. 'The council pushing all the gravestones over. It makes the place feel disrespected. Why not repair them?'

Why not indeed? At least it helped hide his crimes. For the most part. 'It's shocking,' he said.

'Here we are.'

'Who's this?' Karen said as The Reader gently placed the flowers onto the ground in front of the gravestone. She looked at him.

'I don't have a sister called Caroline,' he said. Then he turned to look at her. 'In fact, I don't even have a sister.'

There was no smile on her face now as she realised she had come into a cemetery with this man and nobody knew where she was. Her phone was in her bag, which she'd left in the car.

'What... what's going on?' she asked.

He smiled at her. 'Have a look. Nancy Simpson. You remember the name, don't you?'

'Nancy Simpson,' Karen said out loud, rolling her eyes up and to the side, as if the answer lay in the ivy bushes that had climbed the boundary wall. 'Nancy...'

'Oh, for fuck's sake. It's a name that should be etched into your mind like it was written with indelible ink. Nancy Simpson. The woman who I buried on the day we were to get married.'

Her eyes went wide. She fucking well knew. She was just stalling for time. The fat bitch knew as soon as she'd seen the name chipped into the granite. Then she turned and ran.

The Reader was expecting it and bolted after her. Karen made it ten feet before a strong hand grabbed her by the hair and pulled her back, half dragging her, literally kicking and screaming.

He bunched his fingers in her hair and made her look at the names. 'My Nancy,' he said, then let her hair go, then punched her hard in the face, breaking her nose, then punched her on the jaw, knocking her sideways.

Karen fell in a heap and it took him a few minutes to get her into exactly the correct position. He took the paperback from his pocket and laid it on her chest before going round to the back of the tall gravestone that was a few spaces along from Nancy's.

This one was bigger than the one Sylvia was under so it took extra work. But the adrenaline was coursing fast through his veins now, so pushing the heavy gravestone was easy.

It fell with a sickening thud onto Karen, and all moaning ended.

He was sweating now, his breath coming in rasps, and he knew he would start shaking when the adrenaline was gone. He hurried back to his car, sweating and out of breath.

He saw the handbag still sitting on the passenger seat. Then he looked in the back of the car and saw Nancy sitting there. He smiled. 'Hello, sweetheart.'

'Hello, my love.'

'I did it. I took care of the fat one.'

'Thank you.' She smiled at him.

'You know I love you, don't you?'

'Of course I do.'

He looked at her beautiful face, her shining eyes, the gorgeous lips. Then the blood started to seep out of her mouth and her eyes went wide. He closed his eyes for a second and when he opened them again, her face was pure once more.

'You'll be waiting for me, won't you, my love?' he asked her.

'Of course I will. I'm waiting now.' She smiled that smile of hers but as he stared at her, she started to fade again. 'We'll talk again soon, my darling...' she said, then she was gone.

He started the car and drove out of the cemetery. He still had a lot of work to do.

34

FIFE

'Mum! What's wrong?' Laura Forrest said, rushing into the room, trying not to burn herself with the cup of coffee.

Margaret couldn't get the words out but instead was flapping her hand in front of her.

As soon as the old woman let out the scream, Art bolted out of the room to get a nurse while Brodie tried to calm her. The nurse came rushing into the room, brushing past Laura and Cameron, the latter holding two cups of hot coffee, trying to envision how he would wipe his arse after he had skin grafts on his hands. He spotted the elevated wheeled bed tray that would be swung over the old woman's bed and put the cups down, going over to a small sink and running cold water over his hands. He stepped back with Art as the nurse attended to Margaret, with her daughter by her side.

They stepped out of the room. 'What was she screaming about?' Cameron whispered.

'Brodie told her that we found a body under her floorboards, then she went off her nut. Not unexpected, especially when he said it was a bairn.'

'Fuck me. That daughter shoved into me when she heard the scream and I nearly burnt my fucking hands off. I'm not going to that bastarding machine again. It probably tastes worse than that pishwater lager in the bowling club.'

'Just drink lemonade next time we go.'

'What makes you think I'll go there again?'

Art made a face and looked at him. 'You're living with your maw. Do you want to stay in and exchange patterns? Or do you want to have a few beers after work?'

'Knitting or crochet?'

'Fine, help her ball up her wool for all I care.'

Cameron laughed. 'Easy, pal. I get your point. Maybe we could grab a pint in some boozer one night.'

'That's all fine and dandy until they find out we're coppers. Then one of them leaves through a window.'

'Aye, good point,' Cameron said. 'Hopefully when we go back, that moaning old hag won't be serving.'

'Fingers crossed. I got Drever's address from the DVLA. We'll pay him a visit later.'

'We can check it out later after the high heid yin goes home,' Cameron said.

'What do you think of him?' Art asked.

'Efficient. Probably doesn't do stand-up at a comedy club.'

'Come back, Alan, all is forgiven.'

The nurse came back out. 'Is everything okay?' Art asked her.

'I gave her something to calm her down. Getting bad news will often shock them like that, but it's especially bad in her state.' The woman looked frazzled and walked away quickly.

'In her state?' Cameron asked. 'Old and infirm?'

Art shrugged and headed back into the room. 'Everything okay, boss?'

'It is now. Mrs Wallace is asleep.'

Laura was standing beside her mother, holding her hand. 'She's a remarkable woman, isn't she?'

'Aye, she is that.'

'Is your father still alive?' Cameron asked.

Laura looked at him and shook her head. 'He died a long time ago.'

'What was his name?'

'Toby Wallace.'

'What did he do for a living?'

'A miner, before he retired on ill health.'

'How old was he when he died?'

'Fifty,' Laura said.

Brodie nodded at her. 'We told your mother that we found the body of a young boy under the floorboards.'

Laura gasped and put a hand to her mouth. 'What boy?' Her eyes were wide now.

'We don't have an identification.'

'Marcus,' she whispered.

Laura took a few deep breaths before carrying on.

'He was my little brother. He disappeared. He was a runner, you see. I remember he had my mother worried sick. He ran away for some reason. Nowadays they would say he had ADHD or something. Maybe he was on the spectrum, but whatever it was, he just had these fantasies about running away to sea on a pirate ship, and one time he wanted to go in a rocket up to space. Then one time my mother was running about like a headless chicken when I got home from school. He had run away again, but the police caught him at the bus station.'

'How did he get there?' Art asked.

'At that time, there was a bus that went through the village. He would get on like any other kid. This particular bus went to the station. The control room at the bus company put out an alert for him after Mum discovered he was gone, and they got him at the station and brought him home. There was no malice or anything. He would tell the police that he wanted to go on adventures, just like my dad. But the thing is, my dad used to tell him stories, like he was an African explorer or an astronaut. He would spin these tall tales to us. Marcus wanted to be like him. My dad was told to stop, and he did. No more tales of climbing Mount Everest, but then one day, Marcus was gone again. And he didn't come home this time. We never heard from him again.'

'No sign of him was ever found?' Brodie said, matter-of-factly.

'Correct.' Her lips started to tremble. 'To be honest, my father was distraught. He would drink and take pills to sleep. He did this the night Marcus disappeared but he miscounted and died of an overdose.'

'Do you think your father had anything to do with Marcus's disappearance?' Art asked.

'No. He loved his son, and he was usually too drunk to lift a hand to wipe his nose, never mind lift a hand to us. He was never violent, and he was always worried sick when Marcus took off.'

'How old were you when he disappeared?' Art asked.

'Sixteen. It was in the summer of 1987'

'How did he get under the floorboards?' Brodie asked.

'I have no idea. That's something you'd have to ask my mum.' Tears rolled down her cheeks.

'We're going to have to get a statement from you, Laura,' Brodie said. 'Do you have a number I can reach you at?'

She gave him her mobile number and he put it into his phone.

'What about your address?'

She gave him her address in Leven.

'We'll be in touch, Laura.'

She nodded back at them, and then the three men left the room.

Downstairs in the car, Brodie looked at them. 'What do you think?'

'It's a strange one,' Art said. 'Obviously somebody killed him and wrapped him up and hid him under the floorboards. And there were technically three adults in the house, if you count Laura because she said she was sixteen at the time, but how would you kill somebody and then lift up the floorboards and put them back without anybody noticing?'

'Maybe they didn't have carpets?' Brodie said.

'We can find out. Meantime, I want to get some Uniforms going door to door, asking the neighbours about the family who lived there. Especially Margaret and her husband, Toby. Make a phone call to your team, Art.'

'Will do.' He sat in contemplation for a moment. 'You think one of them killed the boy?' Art said.

'Well, there's another explanation: somebody took him, killed him, brought him back and then put him under the floorboards. But that's an outside chance.'

They sat in silent contemplation as Cameron drove away.

35

EDINBURGH

Det Supt Rob Cross reclined the passenger seat a bit more, hiding his face behind the B-pillar as he rolled the window down. 'See? This is why smoking in the summer is okay. Nobody would look twice at a car with its windows rolled down.'

'Unless there was the barrel of a gun sticking out of it,' Lucy Warren said.

'What are the chances of that happening in Morningside?' Cross took a puff on his cigarette and blew the smoke out, nipping the ciggie as Lucy pulled into the car park of the psychiatric hospital. She parked the car and they got out after the windows were rolled up. 'I've been here that much recently, they'll think I'm a fucking patient,' Cross said, pulling his jacket on.

'It's the hairstyle, sir, if you don't mind me saying.'

'I do mind; what do you think the chances are of you getting a good annual report this year?'

'As I was saying, you're too smart, suave and sophisticated for anybody to think you're a nutjob.'

'Too much, Lucy. There's a fine line between impressing the boss and being an arse-licker.'

'Really? Arse-licker? And you don't want your wife to find out you've been smoking again?'

'That's blackmail.'

'I expect an A-Plus on my annual report.'

'You got it, sister.'

They made their way up to Gabriel Kane's level, Cross popping a couple of mints and offering one to Lucy, who informed him where he could shove his manky mints, despite his assurances that he had just bought them and hadn't fished them out of his office wastebasket.

'Some day you'll be gagging for a mint, and don't come running to me when you are,' Cross said.

'I wouldn't dream of it.'

They were shown into the conference room and didn't have to wait long before Kane was escorted in, the two orderlies waiting outside.

'Why do they need two to escort me along here?' Kane said, tutting and sitting down.

'Oh, I don't know,' Cross said. 'Maybe because you fucking kill people by pushing a huge gravestone on top of them?'

'There are no gravestones in here,' Kane said, sitting down. 'Miss Lucy. How are we today?'

'Peachy,' Lucy said.

'Good good.' He stretched his back. 'I must be getting old. The back isn't as supple as it used to be.'

'Just wait until we get you a lovely new bed, with hardly any springs in it,' Cross said.

'Robert, you really need to try anger management. You're driving yourself into an early grave. Maybe you and I could have a one on one sometime?'

'I don't think you would want to be in a room with me on your own, Kane.'

'That just proves my point about you needing therapy.'

'I get therapy every night when I go home and see my dog.'

'Really? What kind of dog do you have?' Kane asked.

'Never you fucking mind what kind of dog I have.' Cross locked eyes with Kane, thoughts of his dog jumping into his mind, and what he would do to Kane if the lunatic ever laid his hands on his boy.

'Just making conversation, Robert. I'm an animal lover, believe me. Save a dog or a busload of nuns about to drive over a cliff? No contest.'

'Not a religious man, then?'

'I love animals more than humans, more like. But let's get the party started. Did either of you bring any snacks? I'm feeling a bit peckish.'

'Ivy Jack and Marianne Taylor are guests of honour. Why don't you tell us a little bit more about them?' Cross said.

'I thought we had done this one to death, if you'll pardon the pun.'

'Now is not the time to get flippant, doctor,' Lucy said.

'What else do you want to know?' Kane said.

'You seemed to be at a loss when we spoke last,' Cross said. 'Then you told us what you knew about Ivy and Marianne. Which we now know was total pish. Why was that?'

Kane smiled. 'When you've killed as many women as I have, you sometimes get the little details mixed up, that's all.'

'Why did you choose them?' Lucy asked.

'Because of going into the bookshop. You know I was in there as you have that lovely portrait of me courtesy of the CCTV.'

'You went to a bookshop to buy a book to leave with your victims,' Cross said. 'You then murdered women associated with that same bookshop. You're a lot smarter than that. That was a huge risk you took. Why not kill somebody random?'

'I don't do random,' Kane said, and Cross could see the man's jaw tighten, like he had made a mistake and he knew it but it was too late to backtrack.

'You once told us you picked them at random. Now it's every one of your victims was planned out...' Cross said. 'Which is it?'

Kane smiled and shrugged. 'I didn't say every one was random, did I? I meant it's fifty-fifty.'

'Did you choose that bookshop in particular?' Lucy asked.

'I just happened to go in one day and saw Ivy and Marianne chatting and I thought, hmm, they would make nice victims.'

Cross gave a brief laugh. 'Belligerent as ever. However, my bosses upstairs want me to convey a message: if you think we're fucking about when we say you'll have privileges taken away, think again. Starting today, you'll have your books taken away and you'll have zero access to any more. We know you foam at the mouth when the volunteer comes round with your library books, but foam no more.' He looked at Lucy. 'What's his name again? This volunteer?'

'Dermot Hume.'

'Hume. Yes, we'll tell him to bypass your room, Dr Kane. No more books.'

'I'm telling you the truth, Mr Cross. They were picked at random, then I studied them, that's all.' He shrugged. 'I don't know what else to tell you.'

'What is Ivy's brother's name?' Cross asked.

'She doesn't have a brother. She has a sister called Alice. I remember now; they lived in Liberton.'

Cross stared at him, observing his eye movements, looking for any tics or shifts that might reveal his true feelings. There was nothing. He looked dead behind the eyes.

'Can I still have my books?' Kane asked, like a lost little schoolboy.

'It's your lucky day,' Cross said, standing up.

Outside in the corridor, the two attendants escorted Kane through to his wing. Cross watched through the wired glass door windows as the volunteer, Dermot Hume, approached Kane and gave him a paperback book.

'He almost pissed his pants when we said he couldn't have his books,' Cross said.

'Did you believe him when he said he picked women at random and then studied them?' Lucy asked.

'Did you?'

'He has that uncanny knack of being convincing.'

'Let's leave the sad bastard to his manky paperbacks. At least he doesn't get hardbacks. He'd have some bastard's eye out with one of those.'

36

FIFE

Dr Ronald 'Sherlock' Holmes was doing paperwork in his office when Brodie entered with Art and Cameron after three o'clock.

'DCI Brodie, this is Dr Holmes,' Art said. 'A legend in his own lunchtime.'

'Thanks for that, Art,' Sherlock said, standing up. Then to Brodie: 'Everybody calls me Sherlock. Whether you do or not, that's up to you.'

'Sherlock it is. Liam.' Brodie held out a hand for Sherlock to shake.

'You're new here,' Sherlock said.

'On secondment. I was here seven years ago too, but you weren't the pathologist here at the time.'

'I worked in Dundee seven years ago. I've only been here about six months.' He smiled. 'I hope I'm fitting in with the natives?' He looked at Art and Cameron.

'Absolutely, doc,' Cameron said. 'After old Angus, anybody is an improvement.'

'Angus Kennedy?' Brodie said. 'I remember him. He seemed alright.'

'He went off the rails a bit,' Art said. 'Started drinking a fair bit. The high heid yins were starting to get worried he'd make a mistake. So he told me. They retired him, and he started drinking in earnest. He liked to drink in the bath, apparently. He finished a bottle and slipped under the water and drowned.'

'Jesus. What a way to go,' Brodie said.

'You know what, though, sir?' Art said. 'I don't think he would have had it any other way. He loved the drink, and he always said he would rather die happy than live to a hundred and be ill.'

'How old was he?'

'Sixty. He used to drink at our bowling club, with me and DCI McRae. He was a great guy.'

'DCI McRae is still missing. I'm hoping it's nothing serious,' Sherlock said.

'We're still looking for him,' Art said.

'Maybe he went on some kind of bender,' Brodie said. 'It happens.'

'Alan was a civilised drinker,' Art said. 'He liked a good drink, but he wasn't an aggressive drunk. I don't think somebody would have skelped him.'

'It's true,' Sherlock said. 'He was a happy drunk.'

'He and his wife loved socialising,' Art said.

'And now his ex-wife was found dead of an apparent suicide,' Sherlock said.

'What's this?' Brodie asked.

Art shuffled his feet. 'We went round to have another word with Alan's ex and found her in her car in the garage with a hosepipe running from the exhaust into the car.'

'Is that information something you were going to share with me?' Brodie asked, his tone sharp.

'It's early days in the investigation. We were going to discuss it when we heard what Dr Holmes had to say about the post-mortem. Detective Super-intendent Breck knows. He was there at the scene with us. Maybe you could ask him.'

Brodie looked at Sherlock. 'Is the post-mortem done on this woman?'

'Is is. We finished it last night. The toxicology report came back earlier.'

The three of them stood around, waiting for the magician to pull the rabbit out of the hat.

'And?' Brodie said. 'Don't keep us in suspense, doc.'

'There was a high amount of sleeping pills in her system. Painkillers, too.'

'Enough to kill her?' Brodie asked.

Sherlock nodded his head. 'There was enough in her system to make her feel woozy, and clumsy at first, then they would shut her body down. Looks like she was dead before the exhaust could kill her.'

'Maybe she wanted to dull the pain before going out to the garage,' Cameron said.

Art stepped forward. 'Could somebody have forced her to take those drugs and then put her in the car?'

'I suppose. They would have to have put a fair bit in a drink, for example, then she could have been manipulated. As she was impaired, her thinking would have been affected, and difficult – but not impossible – for her to get the hosepipe on the exhaust and into the car. It might have been meant to look like a suicide, or even a mistake, but there was no sign of carbon monoxide poisoning. Meaning she was dead by the time the fumes were noxious enough to kill her. Cause of death: overdose. Manner of death: undetermined.'

'Fuck's sake,' Art said. 'I've known Pat for a very long time. First Alan goes missing, now Pat is dead under mysterious circumstances. And that fucking Dick Drever doesn't turn up for work.'

'Who's Drever?' Brodie asked.

'We went to talk to Pat, and she told us she was dating Drever, the bar manager at the bowling club that Alan and I are members of. We went to talk to him this morning but he hadn't turned up for work. We know where he lives now. We got his address.'

'You think he had anything to do with Mrs McRae's death?' Brodie said.

'We won't know until we can talk to him.'

'When we spoke to Mrs McRae,' Cameron said, then saw Art shake his head slightly, 'she didn't seem to have any concern with Drever.'

'Check him out anyway,' Brodie said. Then he spoke to Sherlock. 'What about the skeletal remains of the boy that were found in the cottage?'

'Let me show you.' Sherlock went over to the fridge drawers and slid one out. A white sheet covered the boy underneath. He gently lifted it and pulled it back. 'He was covered in clothes that had degraded but were most likely intact when he was wrapped in black plastic bags and taped. Any smell would have been minimal, but there are also air vent bricks in the foundation. When I first inspected him in situ, the chimney that had fallen through the roof was partially laying on him. I opened up the plastic and had a look and I could see a hole in his head.'

'Blunt force trauma?' Brodie asked.

'That's what I thought, but after a thorough exam on the table here, I could see old wounds that had healed. Fractured ribs, a broken collarbone and even a broken finger.' Sherlock looked at the big detective. 'It looks like the poor little boy was beaten regularly.'

'Jesus,' Brodie said. He thought about his own stepson Eric, and how he, Brodie, had brought him up with nothing but love and affection. 'We need to go back and talk to Margaret Wallace, maybe tomorrow, and I don't care how much she screams the place down.'

'Have you any idea who might have done this?' Sherlock asked Art.

'We're talking to the family just now.'

Brodie looked at Art as if waiting for something else to follow, but nothing did.

'Thanks, Sherlock. I think we've got some busy times ahead,' Brodie said.

37

EDINBURGH

The Reader looked at his watch as he parked the car in Burgess Street, just off Shore. Quick pint or a quick coffee? Although alcohol was very tempting – after all, he'd had a physically hard day and it was just gone 5 p.m. – he opted for a coffee. He turned left and headed for the café, knowing it closed in half an hour.

Inside, there was a young couple sitting drinking a coffee, and it was obvious that the place was winding down for the day.

'Hello again,' Isobel said from behind the counter. Despite the long hours, she was still smiling. A stray hair hung down the side of her head, as if she had attempted to sweep it back up with little success.

'Hello,' he said to her.

'What can I get you?'

'I'd like a coffee, please. Flat white.'

'Coming right up.'

Isobel busied herself with making the coffee when Moira came through from the back. 'Hi!' she said, genuinely pleased to see him. 'Busy day?'

'Always,' he said, smiling at her. He'd put his red sunglasses on again. 'What about you? Mum keeping you on your toes?'

'Absolutely, I'm finished for the day, though.'

'Join me for a coffee, if you like.'

She smiled. 'You're okay if I knock off now, Mum?'

Isobel smiled. 'Of course. Flat white?'

'Sounds great.'

'Go and sit down and I'll bring them over.'

They sat at a table looking out onto the Water of Leith.

'Isn't this the most beautiful place on earth?' he asked with a smile, looking into her eyes.

'It is. I'm a Leither through and through. My dad's grandparents were alive when Leith was separate from Edinburgh, and there was an outcry when it was absorbed by Edinburgh. They wanted to remain independent but that didn't happen.'

'I was brought up here too,' he lied. It was only a small lie; he was brought up along the road in Newhaven, in a large house with loving parents who had money. But he did like Leith. Nancy came from Leith.

They chatted for a little while, Moira telling him about her impending divorce.

He feigned interest until it was almost closing time for the café.

'Why don't you come and have a bite with me?'

'Oh, I don't know, Peter.'

'It can be in a little restaurant.' He smiled sheepishly at her. 'I'm sorry, I didn't mean to sound so forward. I just thought that if you wanted, I could cook us dinner, but I realise you don't even know me. Sorry. Forget I asked.'

She laughed. 'Your wife wouldn't mind you bringing a strange woman home?'

There was a slight tightening of the jaw as he maintained his smile. 'I'm not married. You're quite safe. In fact, you could invite your mum along if that eases your mind.'

The Reader smiled inwardly; telling her she could invite her mother along instilled a bit of trust in him. What man would be some kind of nut if he were actually inviting her mother along on a date? Or, if not quite a date, then certainly a cosy get-together?

'I'd like that. And let's not involve my mum. She and my dad will be sitting in front of the TV, snoring their heads off in a little while.'

'Fine then. It's the first block of flats, the new ones. Number twelve. I'll go and get things started. A pasta dish okay?'

'Sounds good.'

They talked books over coffee as The Reader mentioned the bookcase in the café and how it was a good idea.

'I love reading,' Moira said.

'What do you read?' he asked, expecting her to tell him it was romantic stuff.

'Crime books. I love them. I try and figure out who the killer is before the halfway point.'

'And are you successful?'

'Most of the time. You get to know how a writer thinks. What about you?'

'An eclectic mix. Everything from poetry to thrillers. There are not enough books in the world.'

'I agree.'

They chatted some more until their coffees were finished. Then they got up.

'See you in a little while. I'll just nip back home to get freshened up,' Moira said.

'That's fine. See you in an hour or so?'

Moira smiled. 'Absolutely.'

As The Reader got up and left he felt pleased with himself. He'd finally made a decision.

38

FIFE

It had gone five now, and Art was thinking about what he was going to have for dinner, but food would have to wait.

'Fuck me,' Art said as Cameron took a corner too fast. 'I saw my life flash before my eyes there.'

'That's 'cause you're getting older. Old fogies always shite themselves in a car when it's going more than ten miles an hour.'

'Cheeky bastard. Just keep your eyes on the fucking road.'

Cameron grinned. 'What do you think of this new boss of ours?'

'Well, he's no Alan, that's for sure, and he's not our new boss. He's our temporary boss. I'm not sure if I like him or not. He's just another suit. Whether he cuts the mustard or not remains to be seen.'

'He seems professional enough.'

'Aye, but Alan was more than just that. He was our team leader, some-body who would go the extra mile and put his neck on the line to back us all up.' Art shook his head and turned to look out the window.

Cameron drove the rest of the way in silence until they got to the modern detached house in a new development.

'There's a nice wee bowling club here,' Art said.

Cameron shook his head. 'Do they water the beer down there too?'

'Give it a rest.'

Cameron looked out the window at the red-brick house before turning the engine off. 'Nice wee house, right enough.' He looked at Art. 'And he can afford a house like this by working as a bar manager in a wee bowling club?'

'Unlike you, I'm not a nosy bastard. I don't go in and say, "Half of lager and a packet of crisps, Dick. Oh, and by the way, are you fucking the taxman or something?" I don't know how I can introduce that into the conversation.'

'I just envisioned him living in a two-up, two-down sort of affair, not something as nice as this.'

'Maybe he had an inheritance or something. Maybe I'll let you ask him if we get invited inside.'

They walked up to the front door, where a small driveway sat empty. A few steps led up to the door.

Cameron walked up to the door and hammered on it.

'Fuck me, how about trying the bell first?'

No matter how much ringing or banging they did, nobody answered the door.

'Have a wee look round the back,' Art said. 'We have reason to believe he may be in danger.'

'Aye, from us, the bastard.'

'Aww, Jesus, keep it down, for fuck's sake. There's always one old nosy bastard in this sort of development. Just hop over the fence at the side of the house and have a gander round the back.'

'What if I slip and rip my trousers?'

'Sake, Cameron, you're a young laddie. You should be able to hop that in your sleep.'

'If I rip my trousers, I'll be putting in a claim.'

'Aye, aye, just get your arse over there.'

Cameron tutted as he approached the wooden fence and managed to haul himself up and over without doing irreparable damage to his reproductive area.

'Right, Art, your turn,' he said, looking back over the fence, which was only about five feet high.

'Watch me. Just get round and check through the windows.'

Cameron stomped off, muttering to himself, and disappeared from view round the back of the house.

Then Art heard him come rushing back. 'There are sliding doors that are open, Art. It's stinking in there.'

'Define "stinking".'

'You know, the stink that after you've smelled it for the first time, you never forget it.'

'Oh, magic.' He looked at the gate. 'How the hell am I going to climb that? The front door is one of those plastic ones where there won't be a key hanging out of it—'

Cameron clicked the latch and the gate swung open.

'Pity you didn't check that before you climbed over it, son,' he said, following his younger colleague to the back.

The sliding doors weren't wide open; one was open just a couple of feet. Enough so that it wouldn't draw attention from the casual onlooker.

Art took his extendable baton out and flicked his wrist out until the weapon was fully extended. Cameron did the same.

'Watch your back in here, son. Anybody comes at you with a knife, let the bastard have it.'

'Too fucking right.'

Art swore he could see Cameron's eyes lighting up at the prospect, and decided he would let the younger man charge in since he was already revved up anyway.

Cameron slammed the sliding door open and stepped in past full-length net curtains, Art right behind him.

'Dick!' he shouted. 'Police!'

They were in the kitchen. Nothing seemed out of place and it was deadly silent.

'Dick! It's Art and Cameron. You alright in there, pal? We're coming in.'

They found Dick Drever in his bedroom, in what could be seen as auto-eroticism gone wrong. He was sitting with his back against the en-suite bathroom door with a tie round his neck, the other end round the door handle. His discoloured tongue was protruding out of his mouth. He was naked from the waist down, his right hand holding his flaccid penis.

'Jesus. I didn't take him for one of those people who whack one out with a necktie round their neck,' Art said.

'I did. I thought he was a wanker the first time I clapped eyes on him.'

'Here, now, a bit of respect for a dead man.'

'How do you know he's dead?' Cameron said. 'What if he has a pulse?'

'Pulse my arse. Look at the colour of his skin.'

'I've seen people come back from worse than that.'

Art shook his head. 'Where about? On *Night of the Living Dead*?'

'Seriously. There was this one guy who'd been run over by a tractor—'

'Right, zip it. I don't want to spoil my dinner. I'll call this in, and they can send in the doc to pronounce him.'

Art walked away to make the phone call. Two people connected to Alan McRae, both dead by suicide. He didn't believe it, not for one minute. Pat McRae, taking sleeping pills and hooking up a hosepipe to her exhaust; and Dick Drever, dying after playing with himself and putting a tie around his neck? No, something was way off here.

And if the bloke from Edinburgh was any good, he could pull his finger out of his arse and solve this. Whatever *this* was.

39

EDINBURGH

Brodie was sitting at the dining table with a folder open, the papers spread out in front of him. They had ordered takeaway for dinner, but it wouldn't be there for another half-hour. It was already gone six but he could wait a little while longer.

Ruth came up to him and put a hand on his shoulder.

'Busy day?' she asked.

'You wouldn't believe the half of it. A woman who might have been murdered, and the skeleton of a little boy found under the floorboards of a house. Poor little bastard had been tortured long before he was murdered.'

She sat down in the chair next to him, horror on her face. 'How do you know he was tortured?'

'He had broken bones that had healed. Ribs, clavicle and a finger. Somebody gave him the works before they killed him with a blunt instrument.'

'Poor thing. How long was he in there?'

'A very long time,' Brodie said. 'It was a nice little cottage in Arncrouch. The last place you would think a murder had taken place.'

'Arncrouch? Are you sure?' Ruth asked.

Brodie looked at her. 'Of course I'm sure.'

'Was it... was it on Castle Street?'

'Yes. How did you know?'

Ruth sat down heavily on the couch beside him. 'I used to live there. When I was fostered.'

'What? You lived in the white cottage?'

'Yes. There's only one in the village. My foster mother was Margaret Wallace.' She looked at him, her eyes bright with tears. 'Is it Marcus?'

Brodie nodded. 'We think so, but it has to be confirmed.'

'Oh God.' She covered her face with her hands and started crying. Brodie put his arm around her shoulders and pulled her in close until her sobbing subsided. She gently prised herself away from him.

'What do you remember of Marcus?' he asked her quietly.

Ruth composed herself. 'I was around seven when he disappeared. I had been there for two years or so. I don't have strong memories of him, but I remember him being there. Then one day he wasn't.'

'There must have been a lot going on at the time he went missing.'

She sniffed and nodded. 'I remember a lot of policemen in the house, coming and going. Margaret was a wreck, crying all the time. Then they explained that her husband had gone to heaven. Everything seemed to happen at once.'

'I'll have to call Rob Cross and see if he wants me off the case now there's a personal involvement.'

'I'm sorry, Liam.'

'Nothing to be sorry about. But let me ask you, did she ever raise a hand to you?'

Ruth looked away for a moment, and Brodie saw tears running down her face again. He reached over the table and put a hand on hers.

'I know this is tough,' he said, 'but we need to know what we're facing here.'

She sniffed and wiped away the tears. Her eyes were like those of a dragon, red and fiery. 'She wasn't physically violent to me. If she thought I was misbehaving or was late for lunch when I was out playing with my friends, she would get upset and shout at me. I remember being terrified of her. I was there for five years and was mostly miserable.'

'Do you think Margaret could have been capable of killing Marcus?'

Ruth looked into his eyes and her lip started trembling before she answered. 'Yes. If our life was anything to go by.'

'Our life?' Brodie asked.

'Laura and I. She's much older than I am, but I remember Margaret getting wired into her too. Laura was a teenager, and I didn't know it at the time, but she was just developing into a young woman, and maturing, but thinking about it now, Margaret didn't like that. She was very controlling. Laura stayed out late, past her curfew time. And they would argue. Laura was very aggressive, getting very angry all the time. To be honest, I was glad that I got adopted. My new parents were so much better to live with than Margaret Wallace.'

'Did Laura keep in touch after you were adopted?'

'No. I didn't see her again until I was about eighteen and I bumped into her one day.'

Brodie looked puzzled. 'She didn't reach out to you after you were adopted?'

'No. We never had any communication. I didn't see Margaret again. To be honest, I was glad. Don't get me wrong, I was grateful for Margaret taking me in, but it was nice to be with a family who didn't shout and argue all the time. Laura was a bloody nightmare, arguing with Margaret all the time, and it got worse the older she got.'

'Her last name is Forrest. I'm assuming she got married.' He looked at her. 'I wonder what her husband is like.'

'I have no idea, but I don't think it would be a healthy environment when he found out what she was really like.'

'She looks the bossy type,' Brodie said.

Ruth sighed. 'It isn't really her being bossy. It was only after being a psychiatrist that I learned what was really wrong with Laura.'

Brodie looked at her, waiting for her to go on.

'It's called Reactive Attachment Disorder. Where a child can't form a bond with his or her parents.'

'You think Laura has that?'

'I'm convinced of it. They can have mood swings, and be nice to their parents one minute, then go berserk the next.'

Brodie sat silent for a moment. 'If I'm still on the case, I'm going back in to the home to see Margaret tomorrow. Ask her some more questions.'

'Give her my best,' Ruth said sarcastically.

Brodie didn't think he would bother. He'd already heard the woman scream once and that was enough.

40

EDINBURGH

Moira looked at herself in the compact mirror as she took the lift up to the top floor of the apartment complex. Since when were flats in Edinburgh called apartments? Since the prices went way up, she thought.

She studied her face; a little bit of powder, a bit of lippie, a pluck of the eyebrows (and that had hurt like a bastard), and a few squirts of the perfume, just to give a hint of what might come later.

She looked at her watch; a few minutes until seven o'clock.

She liked Peter, and although he was a bit older, he seemed wise, funny and intelligent, on the exact opposite end of the scale from her husband, who couldn't crack an egg, never mind a joke.

She had stopped at an off-licence to buy a bottle of wine. White to go with the pasta. Nothing too expensive, nothing too cheap. Just the right one to wash the food down with.

The lift came to a halt, telling her she was indeed at the correct floor, so she snapped the compact closed, fired it into her bag where the paperback lay, and she ran her tongue over her teeth once more, just to be sure, but the view in the compact had told her she had nothing to worry about. No stray bits of food and no errant lipstick.

She stepped out and saw number twelve. She walked up and knocked on the door. She knew he was inside because he'd just buzzed her in, but now she thought he might be finishing off building the indestructible head-board, the one where she couldn't break it with the handcuffs, no matter how hard she tried. She laughed to herself; like he would be able to persuade her to do that.

She looked at her watch. Where the hell was he? Had he nipped to the lav on the way from the living room to the front door or something?

Then the sound of the door being unlocked and the door opened, and Peter was standing smiling at her.

'Sorry! I was about to come to the door when I heard the sauce bubbling away, then I checked the pasta and thought it wasn't cooking fast enough. Come in, come in.'

He stepped aside to let her in, and she could smell some sort of body spray. It wasn't repugnant, but she would have chastised Roger for putting it on. She thought she had smelled better air freshener.

He was wearing his red glasses again.

The hallway was light and small, veering to the left where the rooms were painted in a cream colour, the walls matching the carpet. Something similar to what Roger would say: do the curtains match the carpet? Dirty bastard. She didn't get that vibe from Peter, but the night was young.

She heard the door closing behind her and turned to hand over the wine.

'What's this?' he asked, his face lighting up.

'I like a little wine to go with dinner sometimes,' she said.

'Well, thank you so much. Please, go through to the living room.' He indicated with a hand where the room was, but she could see a couch and went through the door.

A TV was on but muted. In front of the window was a little table with two bistro chairs.

'Make yourself comfortable. The pasta should be ready.'

He scuttled away after putting the wine on the table. Moira noticed there were two glasses already there and she wondered if he had something chilling in the fridge, or whether he was just being fancy and was going to pour tap water.

'Here we are,' he said, coming through with two plates of spaghetti Bolognese and putting them down on the table.

He sat down opposite her. 'May I pour?' he said, smiling.

'Of course. This is a great view,' she said.

'Where does your brother live?' he asked casually.

'In the new apartments along at Newhaven.'

'Very nice. They have a better view than I do.'

'Different, Peter, different. This is beautiful. I can imagine what it's like at night, with the floating restaurant along the road lit up.' She turned to face him. 'I love being down here.'

'Where did you live with your husband?'

'Drylaw. Nice little house. I loved living there, but my heart was always in Leith, so I moved into a flat on Leith Walk.'

'Do you think you'll move back here permanently?'

'No doubt. My family's here, and some of my old friends. I would love to move back here.' She tasted the pasta dish, and it was terrific. 'This is so good. What's your secret?'

'A good chef never reveals his secret ingredient.' He smiled at her. If he told her what his secret ingredient was, she might run out of the flat screaming.

Then Moira's phone rang. She took it out of her pocket and looked at the screen. 'Oh, Jesus. It's him. My soon-to-be ex. I'm sorry, I have to take this. I'm going to tell him to stop calling me or the lawyer will ream him a new arsehole.' She pushed the chair back and looked at him. 'Can I use your bedroom?'

'Of course. The first door on your right.'

She left the living room and found the bedroom. The room was painted the same colour. It must be a bachelor thing, she thought. There was no sign of a woman's touch. No photos, no flowers, no nothing.

She shook her head and answered the phone. 'What?'

'I had a call with my lawyer today. He said your lawyer hasn't been in contact about dealing with the finer details.'

'So?'

'So, hurry up, for fuck's sake.'

'You know what, you brought this all on yourself.'

There was silence at the other end. 'Well, we need to talk, to sort out things. Like selling the house and stuff.'

'I can't come over right now. I'm having dinner.'

'I don't want to put this off,' Roger said, a note of resignation in his voice.

'Too bad. I'll call you tomorrow then we can discuss when we'll meet.'

He hung up on her.

'Wanker,' she said in a low voice, putting her phone away before walking back through to the living room. 'Sorry about that,' she said. 'I have to go and meet Roger so we can discuss our impending divorce.' She sat back down at the table. 'But not tonight.'

'Don't worry about it. Do what you have to do.' He smiled and they ate, chit-chatting with small talk.

The Reader was planning ahead, making split-second decisions.

'How about a little tour of the place where I work part-time?' he said. 'Somewhere that no member of the public ever gets to see?'

'Oh, I love the sound of that.'

The Reader smiled. 'Good.'

41

FIFE

Thursday

The morning was warm, despite it only being half past nine, with only a few clouds threatening to spoil it. Art McKenzie stood looking at the cottage in Arncrouch, the tranquillity spoiled by the presence of the patrol car and the forensics van.

'What a fucking place, eh?' PC Don McCoy said, striding over to their car as Cameron got out from behind the wheel. 'You couldn't pay me to live in a little fucking place like this. I mean, where's the local boozer?'

Art looked at Cameron to see if he had the answer, but the DS seemed to be just as flummoxed as he was.

'I'm not familiar with this place,' Cameron said.

'How about you, Arthur?' McCoy asked. 'You're a drunken old bastard. You should know all the watering holes around here.'

Art bit his tongue, metaphorically if not physically, and silently wondered if he could knock the big bastard out if he crept up on him and swung when he wasn't looking.

'I prefer to call myself "well travelled", Don.'

McCoy laughed. 'Is that what we're calling it these days? Not a fucking alkie or something?' He guffawed.

Art didn't have words for the big man, so got down to business. 'How is the door to door going?'

'Fucking hell. This is one of those creepy fucking places where every bastard knows everybody else's business. I couldn't live like that. Me? I prefer my business to stay my business, if you know what I mean.' He winked at Cameron, and neither detective knew what McCoy was on about, unless he was a secret drug dealer.

'Right, but how is it going?' Art said. 'Anybody know anything?'

'One baldy old cunt started getting a bit stroppy. Started giving me lip. Me. Fucking lip. I told him right off the bat to cool his fucking jets.'

'Did you tell him what might happen to his bollocks if he didn't calm down?' Art asked.

McCoy gave him a puzzled look. 'Aye. How did you know that? Got a fucking crystal ball or something?'

'I just had a feeling,' Art said. 'Where does this man without hair live?'

'That house just there.' McCoy pointed to the house directly across from the cottage. 'With his missus, loudmouth.'

Fucking hell. 'Leave it with us, Don. We'll have a word with him. Anything else come to light?' Art said.

'Nah. Fuck all so far. Although some of these twats look like they could do with being wired up to the mains.'

'Right. We'll bear that in mind.'

'Catch you later, Arthur.' McCoy saluted with two fingers and turned on his heel, shouting at one of the other Uniforms. 'Hey, fucking knob face! I've already spoken to them. Dozy cunt!' He went marching off, tutting and mumbling.

'How?' Art said. 'How in the name of God is he still wearing a uniform? He should have been booted out long ago.'

'Det Supt Breck is his uncle.'

'What?' Art shook his head in disbelief. 'Pair of twats, both of them.' He drew in a deep breath and let it out. 'Come on then, let's go and talk to baldy.'

They walked over to the other detached house and up the path to the front door. The front of the house faced a garden and was side-on to the main street. Art was about to knock when the door opened a couple of inches, and Art could see the chain across it.

'Is he gone?' an old man asked. Art couldn't help but look at the man's receding hairline.

'Is who gone, sir?'

'That police officer.'

They heard a shout from further up the street. 'The one next to it, ya dozy wank biscuit!'

'That one,' the old man said. 'He's not coming back here, is he?'

'No, sir. But my colleague and I were wondering if we could come in and have a chat? I'm DI McKenzie, and this is DS Reid. Can I ask your name?' They both held up their warrant cards.

'Ted Carr. Oh, right, I suppose so, but you'll have to hurry. That officer said some nasty things about my privates.' He closed the door, and they heard the chain sliding and then the door opened further. 'Come in quickly. My wife is terrified.'

Both detectives stepped into the hallway, which was dull and dingy and smelled musty with a hint of cat piss. The man slammed the door shut and put the chain on.

'Through here.' He scuttled along the hallway and turned into the living room. Two big, overstuffed leather sofas were on either side of a fireplace that lay dormant, while a leather chair that had seen better days sat over on the other side of the room. The carpet was dark, and the walls had wood panelling on them, but nothing in the room looked recent. Maybe they didn't want to buy new furniture in case they expired soon and didn't get enough use out of their purchase.

A cat walked into the room, its tail up, and went over to Art and rubbed itself on his trouser legs. He looked down as it walked over to Cameron and saw the animal had left some of its fur on his right leg. Fuck's sake, he thought. Swipe the fur off now or pretend he hadn't noticed?

There was a woman sitting in the chair, a cotton hanky in her hand.

'Police officers,' her husband said.

The wife gasped like they were really a couple of stripper grams, but not in a good way.

'They seem to be the good ones,' Ted said, not quite ready to believe it, but willing to give them the benefit of the doubt. 'This is Penny.'

The woman was of a bigger size, and he assumed this was the woman McCoy had called loudmouth. Which was a complete exaggeration.

'We're here to ask a few questions, Mrs Carr,' Cameron said, in his best placating voice, which was only really a watered-down version of, *Get your fucking hands where I can see them.*

'Do you know that other officer who was here before. The sweary one?'

'No,' Art said, maybe a little too quickly, while Cameron shook his head.

'He's an awful man. I thought at first that he had stolen a uniform and was pretending to be an officer.' Penny wiped at her nose again.

'I'll put in a full report,' Art said, noticing that the cat had also shed some fur against Cameron as well.

'Thank you. The man's a clot,' Ted said.

I'll tell him that, will I? Art thought, but then wondered which of them would be getting the full force of McCoy's wrath if he did so. 'He must be. Not from our division, but I'll get to the bottom of it.'

'Thank you,' Penny said.

'Sit down,' Ted said, sweeping an arm between the two sofas, giving them a choice.

They sat on one, Cameron in the middle. Art nudged him. 'Budge, ya fat bastard,' he said in a low voice.

Cameron tutted and scooted over to the opposite end, and Art saw Ted attending to his wife, and hoped he hadn't seen the younger detective having to move.

Then Ted turned round, his face slightly flushed, as if he'd just said to Penny, run like fuck, while he fought the two imposters. He didn't say anything but sat on the other sofa, the one that the cat had disappeared behind. Art heard it clawing at the leather, imagining what a state it was in. This, he assumed, was the reason for the lack of new furniture. The sofas were doubling as scratching posts.

'As you may know, we're investigating an occurrence in the cottage across the way,' Art said.

'Yes. We did notice the commotion,' Ted said. 'We moved here for peace and quiet many years ago, and there's been nothing but bloody trouble.'

'Language, Ted,' Penny said, fanning her face with the now-damp hanky, as if her husband had started in on the filth like the uniformed officer had.

'Sorry, but that man got my blood going. It was almost fisticuffs, policeman or no policeman.'

'Oh, Ted, don't talk like that. You're lowering yourself to their level.'

Art didn't know if she meant him and Cameron, or the force in general. 'We'd like to know more about your neighbours in the cottage,' he said.

'Dysfunctional lot,' Ted said.

'Can you elaborate?' Cameron said, suddenly looking down and noticing the cat hair on his trousers. He looked over at Art's trousers. 'Jesus,' he said in a similar low tone to the one Art had used.

'That old one, Margaret Wallace, she was a real hussy,' Penny said. 'And the voice on her. Goodness. She could have rented herself out to be a foghorn. Always shouting at the kids and her husband.'

'How old were the kids when she was doing this?' Art asked.

'Margaret fostered one. She must have been about five or six at the time. The other girl, the oldest one, was about sixteen. Marcus was six or seven at the time. He was eight when he ran off.'

'There I was,' Ted said, cutting in, eager to tell the story, 'trimming the bushes, when the man came walking over. He had a whisky bottle in his hand. And he offered me a swig from it. Can you imagine?' Ted made a face. 'I refused his kind offer,' Ted said, 'and the drunken galoot shrugged and drank some more. Then he started spouting off about his family life. How Margaret had ruined him. And how the daughter, Laura, was a little bast—' He looked at Penny. 'Not a nice girl.'

'Do you remember much about the son, Marcus?' Art asked.

Ted stared up at the ceiling and put a thumb and index finger on his chin, like one of the emojis on Art's phone. 'Yes. He was also a little... rumbunctious. Got into all sorts of mischief. I remember Toby telling me the boy had run away a couple of times, and it was hard looking after him. Then he ran away once more and nobody ever saw him again.'

'Then what happened?' Cameron asked.

'There was a huge search for him. Police everywhere. Fortunately, none like that madman out there, the one who was shouting. They searched everywhere, but they couldn't find him.'

'And he was never found?' Cameron asked.

'Not that I know of.'

'You said Margaret Wallace was loud,' Art said. 'In what way?'

Ted made a face like he was chewing a piece of pineapple with the skin on it. 'She had a temper. She would shout at all of her family. Her husband, her kids, everybody. Then, when she came out and met a neighbour, you would think butter wouldn't melt in her mouth. It was like she had some mental problems.'

'Did Mrs Wallace drink?' Cameron asked.

Penny shook her head. 'Not that we saw. If she did, it was behind closed doors. But she had another vice.'

Ted looked at his wife, giving her a look that suggested that maybe they shouldn't go down this road. But she wasn't about to give up on any juicy gossip.

'What was that?' Art asked, prompting her, and now she was like a snowball rolling downhill.

'Men. She liked men. And I don't just mean her husband. She had numerous affairs.'

'We don't know if it was numerous,' Ted said. 'We only knew of one.'

'That's not what was said at the knitting club. There was one in particular who was there for a long time.'

'Penny, don't. Things might come back to haunt us,' Ted said, but then Art and Cameron saw who wore the trousers in the house.

'Nonsense. The man's wicked.'

'He was very popular.'

'Who are we talking about?' Art said.

'MSP Rory Farmington. Nasty man. Thought he owned Fife.'

'And Mrs Wallace was having an affair with him?'

'Yes she was,' Penny said.

'We don't know that for a fact, Penny,' Ted said.

Penny tutted and gave him a side-eye look, and she pursed her lips, as if questioning her husband's intelligence. 'I told you years ago that I saw his car parked up the street, a little bit away from her front door. I saw him going in. With my own eyes. He stayed for an hour and then left.'

'You don't know what they were doing,' Ted said.

'He looked flushed and her hair was a mess. I don't think they were playing Scrabble, unless it was a very intense game.'

Art had heard of the MSP a long time ago. An old windbag, just like most politicians.

'How long was this going on?' Art asked.

'I'm not sure,' Ted answered.

'Years,' Penny said. 'I was a homemaker, bringing up our two children, and I managed not to have any men around when Ted was at work.'

Art didn't tell her that the old woman was in a nursing home. 'What happened to her husband?' he asked instead, knowing the answer but wanting to hear Penny's perspective on the matter.

'He committed suicide,' Ted said. 'Stupid man. I don't know if he found out about his wife's infidelities or not, but he took a bottle of sleeping pills washed down with a bottle of whisky, went to sleep and never woke up. His daughter found him. Serves her right if you ask me.'

'Ted, have some respect for the dead,' Penny said.

'As much as I'd like to, they were an awful family. That Laura one.' Ted shook his head. 'Awful, wretched girl.'

'Maybe she redeemed herself,' Cameron said. 'She got married after all.'

'Did she?' Penny said. 'That's news to me.'

'Her last name's Forrest, so I assumed she did.'

Penny gave a little chuckle. 'You've got that wrong, dear. The little besom didn't get married; she changed her name.'

'Do you know why she would do that?' Art asked.

'She was adopted. She told me she wanted to use her birth name. Her original name was Carol Forrest. She decided to keep the name Laura, as everybody knew her by that name, used Carol as her middle name and changed her name to Forrest.'

'Did she tell you all this?'

'No, Mrs Wallace did. She was upset with Laura, and of course, they had a huge fight about it, but what's new? They weren't having fun unless they were arguing. But Laura said she was proud to change her name.'

'Did she ever get married?' Cameron asked.

'Who would have *her*? Unless he was as daft as she was. But I think it was her temper that kept any men away from her. And now she must be in her fifties, and still sitting on the shelf.'

They chatted some more before leaving.

Outside, they could hear McCoy, shouting in the distance.

'Let's get out of here before that twat finds us again,' Art said. He took his phone out as Cameron drove away.

'Freya?' DS Freya Munro. 'I want you to do a little bit of research.' He told her what he wanted and they managed to escape the village before McCoy waved them down again.

42

EDINBURGH

Ruth was tired this morning. It was almost ten, her first patient was due and she couldn't stop yawning. She had gone to bed at a reasonable hour, but some primitive part of her brain kept her awake. She understood that there was a subconscious instinct in humans that made them desire to feel safe and secure in their environment at night, so when the house wasn't locked up tight, it made the brain more alert.

Brodie had had no problem getting to sleep, but no matter how hard she tried, it had eluded her. She had put her Kindle on again and eventually fell asleep with the device running. She knew she would have to reread the last couple of pages later that night.

It was the thoughts of when she was a little girl that had kept her awake last night. Things that she hadn't thought about in a very long time...

* * *

It was a hot summer's night when it first happened. Five-year-old Ruth Mason – she wouldn't become Ruth Campbell until after she was adopted – loved to read. All sorts of books. She couldn't get enough of them. She would go into the children's book department when they went over to John

Menzies on Princes Street in Edinburgh, and go through a load of books before Margaret bought her one to take home.

The series she was reading now was about a little boy who went on adventures with his dog.

Ruth devoured the first in the series, and Margaret bought them all for her. She knew she was being spoiled, but so was the older girl who lived here, Laura. Ruth couldn't bring herself to call Laura her sister, because the girl wasn't. She was sixteen and she had a boyfriend – yuck! – and she was noisy when she was in the room. And she argued with Margaret. A lot! The more Margaret argued, the more belligerent Laura became.

Ruth lost herself in her books. She let the fictitious characters take her into their world where she could roam as much as she wanted.

Her teacher said she was a dreamer and would get on better if she concentrated more. But it was hard to concentrate when you were being abused.

The first time it happened, the door had opened quietly and the hallway light was on, and all she could see was the silhouette of the man coming into the room.

Then he was on the bed, and a rough hand was put over her mouth, and he leaned down closer to her and the smell of the booze hit her.

'You'll be old enough one day, and when you are, Daddy will take care of you.'

She lay rigid in bed, fear gripping her like no other fear she had ever felt. Then he got up off the bed and gently left the room. But he hadn't closed the door all the way.

Then she heard a commotion coming from Laura's room. Almost like an argument, but not quite. It went on for a few minutes, then she saw Marcus sneaking past, then quickly running back.

Then the Dark Man went rushing past her doorway, and then she heard shouting. She pulled the covers over herself and then took her pillow and covered her head with it. The shouting continued until...

* * *

Ruth shook her head, realising that she was sweating. She had thought that the dark thoughts had gone for good, but what had happened in real life was now invading her dreams. It wasn't a good sign. She used to think that it was only a nightmare, but as she got older, she realised that it was something that had happened, and she kept having recurring dreams about it.

She was in her office at Astley Ainslie Hospital, waiting for her next patient. Right on time, there was a gentle knock at the door. Usually, she would open the door and announce the next patient, and there was generally only one waiting, with the next one overlapping by a couple of minutes. However, she had been making strides with this patient, building his confidence.

'Come!' she shouted.

The door opened, and his head poked round first. He was smiling as Ruth stood up with her notebook and moved over to the chair.

'Come in, Dermot,' Ruth said.

The man came in, nervously rubbing his hands together. He smiled a weak smile and kept himself slightly stooped. Ruth had told him before to walk with confidence, upright, chin up, chest out, but it was a work in progress.

'Good morning,' Dermot said.

Ruth smiled, but it was a smile on the outside only. Ever since Brodie had told her about the skeleton under the floorboards in her old house, she felt like she had been punched in the stomach.

Was it Marcus who had been murdered and hidden under the floorboards? It had to be. Unless... there was somebody else who had come into the house and didn't leave. But who?

'...distracted today.'

She snapped out of her reverie. 'I'm sorry, Dermot. What did you say?' she asked as he sat down on his usual spot on the couch.

He smiled wider and gave a small laugh. 'I said, you seem distracted today.'

'I'm so sorry. I had a rough night. One of those nights where sleep eludes you, no matter what you do. Counting sheep, walking along an endless corridor. Nothing worked.'

'I have nights like that,' he said, still smiling.

Ruth smiled back, admiring the man. He had come so far in the past few years, from standing on the ledge, waiting for the right moment to jump, to coming in here, smiling. He wasn't at the end of the road yet, but he was getting there. He'd got over the blind bump in the road and was making his way down the other side, where everything was open and clear before him.

'Not too many now, though?'

He shook his head. 'No, thanks to you, Ruth. Getting better every day. In fact, I haven't felt this good in a long time.'

'That's good to hear. Do you think volunteering at the hospital helps?'

'I do. Knowing that dishing out books to patients might help them get better makes me feel better inside. Except...'

'Except what?' Ruth asked.

'Except that doctor. Kane. He scares me.'

'Why is that?'

'I don't like getting close to him. He gives off a... vibe. Everybody knows who he is. We all know who he is and what he did. To those women.' He shuddered. 'Yet, to look at him, you wouldn't give him a second look if you passed him in the street.'

'That happens everywhere, Dermot. Those monsters that walk among us don't look like monsters. They look like you and me. And that's why Dr Kane was able to do what he did. But if you're unsure of him, I can request the hospital move you to another department.'

'No, no, it's fine. I mean, who would take my place? Benny from the kitchen? He can whizz that mop around like nobody's business, but if he was delivering books to patients? He'd need the mop to wipe up after himself. No, doctor, that's fine. I don't feel as nervous as I was when I started. I'm getting better at it, but it's just Kane.'

'He always has attendants with him, doesn't he?'

'Yes, he does,' Dermot said. 'But it's my imagination running away with me.'

'Is the volunteering helping you with your day-to-day life, Dermot?' she asked.

'It is indeed. Also, working part-time helps a lot. I get to meet people,

and although some of them aren't very nice, most of them are. It's a plea-
sure dealing with them.'

'That's good, Dermot. I'm so proud of you. You've come far.'

'I think the end is near, Ruth. I feel confident that I won't need to come
back any more.'

'I think so too. But we can still go to once every two weeks to help you
transition, and remember that my door is always open.'

'Thank you, Ruth. I couldn't have done this without your help.'

Ruth didn't have another patient after Dermot, so she sat at her desk
with a pad in front of her and doodled and jotted thoughts down. She tried
hard to remember more details about Marcus. Things that Margaret and
Laura might have talked about.

She would have to go and talk to Laura herself. Not something she
looked forward to. Not after getting away from them both many years
before.

43

FIFE

Brodie had called Det Supt Cross the night before. 'Sorry to call you at home, boss, but there's been a development in the Fife case.'

'Oh aye? What's that then?'

'I was talking to Ruth about the case and it turns out that's the house where she was fostered when she was a child.' He told him what age Ruth had been when she was at the house and how old she was when she left.

'What? Oh fuck.' There was silence for a few moments, Brodie hearing the TV on in the background wherever Cross was. 'Listen, I'll call Assistant Chief Annie Leslie and tell her. She'll make the decision and I'll call you tomorrow.'

'Okay, sir. Enjoy the rest of your night.'

'I'm watching TV, having a beer with my dog lying next to me. Life doesn't get any better, son.'

It turned out that the assistant chief had run things past the chief constable, and because Ruth was only a toddler when she lived there, it wouldn't affect the case, so Brodie was to stay on board. He was happy to.

Thursday morning, he got up early and drove over to Glenrothes. He was pulling out the desk drawers when Art walked in. The incident room was full and there was a buzz of activity.

'I don't think Alan keeps his Hobnobs in there,' Art said. Cameron was standing behind him.

Brodie turned to look at him. 'Just making myself at home,' he said. 'Not that it's any of your business, mind.' He looked at him. 'And it should be DCI McRae, surely?'

'I told you Alan and I go way back.' Art stepped into the room like he wanted a fight. 'And I give him his rank when we're on duty.' *Not that it's any of your fucking business*, he thought, but kept that part to himself.

'Glad to hear it.' He picked up a mug and drank from it. 'Morven made it for me. She said this was your spare mug. I hope you don't mind?'

Art stepped closer. 'Let's just clear the air a wee bit here; you're a DCI, higher rank than me, but you're also an outsider.'

'Nobody's a fucking outsider in Police Scotland, pal. That's why they had me come over from Edinburgh. Years ago, they would have found somebody from within, but they want me in here.'

'In case there's any shenanigans, I get it. But we're a tight-knit team in here. There's no shenanigans.'

'I hope not.' Brodie sipped his coffee. 'I'm glad you got that off your chest.'

'Talking of DCI McRae, the bar manager at the bowling club, the one his ex-wife was seeing, was found dead in his house.'

'Who found him?'

'We did. Me and Cameron. He was hanging from a door handle with his willy in his hand.'

'Auto-eroticism gone wrong?'

'It might be. Sherlock will tell us what he thinks.'

'Don't you think that's what it was?' Brodie said.

'Both of them commit suicide after Alan, I mean, DCI McRae, disappears? I'm sceptical.'

'If it was foul play, do you have any idea what the motive would be?'

Art hesitated. 'Alan's ex, Pat, said when she met him at the trail car park, he was scared about something. He didn't tell her what he was scared of. Maybe he got himself into trouble or something.'

Brodie shook his head. 'I'm not here to help you look for your missing

DCI, I'm here because of the bones found. But you could keep me in the loop.'

'Sorry, sir. We're a tight-knit team, and we're all worried about the boss. I didn't mean to give you a hard time. Feel free to write me up.'

'Shut up. Listen, I understand, Art. But don't keep anything else from me. You too, Cameron.'

'Yes, sir,' Cameron said.

Art nodded.

Just then, DS Freya Munro knocked on the open door. 'Sorry to disturb, sir, but you told me to tell you right away if I found anything,' she said, handing over some papers to Art.

'What's this?'

'The house report about the cottage. Everything to know about it, including its owner's details.'

'Margaret Wallace?' Brodie asked.

'No, sir. Rory Farmington. Ex-MSP.'

Art looked puzzled. 'That's the second time I've heard his name mentioned.'

'What was the first time?' Brodie asked.

Art turned to look at him. 'Mrs Wallace's neighbours gave us a rundown on the Wallace family, including the fact that the lady of the house used to... entertain some men. Rory Farmington being the main protagonist.'

'Is he still alive?'

'I think so,' Art said. 'He's ancient though.'

'I'll find an address for him.'

'Thanks, Freya,' Art said. Then to Brodie: 'You don't mind if I call my DS by her first name, do you, sir?'

'Don't be a smart-arse, inspector.'

'Sir.'

Art left the office without saying another word. Freya was at her keyboard.

'He's a charmer, if you don't mind me saying so, sir,' she said to Art.

'Let's just hope that Alan walks in through that door sometime soon and tells us he's back for good.'

'Here it is now, sir. An article from the *Fife Independent*. Former MSP

Rory Farmington's son to enter politics.' She scanned the article. 'It says Farmington senior is living in a nursing home in Townhill, just outside of Dunfermline.'

'What?' Art looked closer at the screen. 'Jesus. That's the same one Margaret Wallace is in.' He turned round and walked back to Brodie's temporary office. Knocked.

'Art. What's happening?' Brodie said.

'You said we were going along to the nursing home in Dunfermline.'

'I did.'

'Former MSP Rory Farmington is in there, too.'

'Interesting. Let's go down there now and maybe we could have a talk with him too. But first, I want to declare something.' He told Art about Ruth living at the cottage when she was a girl. 'The chief constable herself has given me the green light to stay on the case, so everything is above board.'

'That's fine, sir.'

Art filled him in on the conversation with the couple across from the cottage, then left the office and shouted at Cameron. 'With me. And DCI Brodie.'

'Yes, sir,' Cameron said, giving thought to finishing the sausage roll that was half eaten, but deciding it would still be there when he came back.

'I'll catch up in a minute,' Brodie said. 'Don't fuck off without me.'

'Wouldn't dream of it,' Art said. 'How can you eat that for breakfast?' he asked Cameron on the way out.

'It's Greggs.'

'It's fucking carbs.'

'When I get to your age, I'll start worrying about my health.'

'If you don't start worrying about your health now, you might not get to my age. Besides, we're not that far apart in years, cheeky bastard.'

'Fourteen years. A lot can happen in fourteen years.'

Art thought back fourteen years, and saw his wife there. He was happily married to her back then, and they had a few years left together. They just didn't know it at the time.

'Aye, go ahead, son. Eat as many sausage rolls as you like. You never know what's round the corner.'

Cameron started the car up and they waited for Brodie.

'Here he is, now. Fuck's sake,' Art said, looking at their temporary boss in his side-view mirror.

'Ease up on him, boss. I don't suppose he asked to come through here,' Cameron said.

Art looked at him. 'If we piss him off enough, maybe he'll go running back through to poshland.'

'I'm not going to piss him off. I don't know if you've noticed, but he's a big bastard,' Cameron said.

'The harder they fall, eh?'

The back door opened and Brodie got in. 'You pair of bastards talking about me again?' he said.

'Sausage rolls, sir,' Cameron said. 'We were discussing the merits of having one for breakfast.'

'And why you'll be a fat bastard when you get to my age,' Art added.

44

FIFE

They were almost at the nursing home when Brodie's phone rang. He took it out and looked at the number, before deciding to answer it or not. His mother. What if something had happened to his dad?

'Hello?'

'Liam, it's Mum. I was just wondering if you've heard from Moira this morning?'

'No. Why would I? She's supposed to be working with you, isn't she?'

'She didn't turn up for work. I can't get a hold of her. Your dad went round to her flat but there was no answer.'

'Was she sick yesterday?' Brodie asked.

'Not that she said. She got talking to one of our customers, a regular, and he left and then she said she was going home for a quiet night. There was nothing unusual. The only thing different was talking to the man.'

'Do you know his name?'

Silence on the other end for a moment. 'He said his name was Peter, a little while back. He's not been coming here for very long though, so I don't know anything about him.'

'Maybe she went out with some friends. You know how she used to be, going out in that group of friends of hers. Getting drunk, partying.'

'That was a while ago,' Isobel said.

'Not that long ago. She would go out and Roger would go out with his pals. Moira liked a good drink, Mum.'

'Don't say that. She wasn't an alkie or anything.'

'My point is, she likes going out with her friends. You shouldn't worry about her. She's forty-two, well able to look after herself.'

'You know, all this working for us is all good and well, but if she's not going to be punctual for anything, then perhaps she should return to working in an office.'

Brodie's mind was on other things, and he tried to think of a way to cut the call without offending her. 'I really have to go.'

'Can't you pop back home and check on her?'

'I'm in Fife right now. I won't be home for a while yet.'

'Okay. Your father is worried sick. You know how he gets.'

'I know.'

'I shouldn't worry like this, but you know how it is, having Eric.'

'I know. I'm sure she'll turn up soon.'

'I hope so. Let me know if you hear from her.'

Brodie hung up, wishing his mother wouldn't worry so much. Moira had had a small group of friends that she would go drinking with a few years earlier. She had been carefree, even though she was married. Five or six of them would go out on the town on a Friday and get hammered, falling about drunk. He wasn't sure if she had seen them recently but, Roger, her husband, had called him one night a few years back, saying she was out and hadn't come home until late. It was daylight when she got in and he had been worried that she had been fooling around on him, but she had assured him that she wasn't. The thing was, she had a cut above her eye, almost like she'd been mugged, but she said she had fallen. And she flat-out refused to get it looked at.

Moira had changed after that, and when he had spoken to her, she told him she decided to cut back on going out after the fall. The thing was, Brodie hadn't believed she had fallen, not back then and not now.

If she hadn't been out drinking, then where had she been? And where was she now?

Cameron pulled the car into the car park and slipped in between a cheap hatchback and a Range Rover.

Upstairs, they made their way to Margaret Wallace's room. The bed was made, but there was nobody in it.

'Maybe she went for a walk,' Cameron said.

'She's dying of cancer, son. It saps your energy. I'll go and find a nurse.' Brodie walked back to a nurse's station and saw a young woman sitting behind the counter.

'DCI Brodie. I was here speaking with Margaret Wallace yesterday. I don't see her in her room. Is she still...'

'Alive? Yes. She asked one of the nurses to take her to see her friend, Mr Farmington.' She looked at her watch. 'It's just after eleven, so they'll be having their morning cup of tea.'

Brodie nodded. 'Where is his room? Would he be up for getting a visit?'

She smiled. 'I think he would. His room is at the end of the corridor. That way.' She pointed in the opposite direction from Margaret's room. Brodie waved to the two others to follow him, and they all trooped along to Farmington's room.

Margaret was sitting in a wheelchair, having a laugh with the old man when they appeared in the doorway.

'Mrs Wallace,' Brodie said, and the smiles dropped off both of their faces.

'Who are you?' Farmington asked.

'DCI Brodie.' He introduced the other two. 'We'd like to ask some follow-up questions about the boy found under the floorboards.'

'Floorboards?' Farmington said. 'What are you talking about, man?'

'Under the floorboards in Mrs Wallace's house.'

'How dare you,' Farmington said, his face growing red. 'Coming in here accusing her of stuff. I personally know the chief constable of Fife Constabulary. I'll make a call.'

Brodie thought the man must have dementia. Fife Constabulary hadn't existed for twelve years, since Police Scotland had been formed and all police forces had been amalgamated.

Brodie could tell this man was used to getting his own way. 'It's not a crime, no, but it's a crime to kill a child, wrap him up and hide him under floorboards.'

There was a voice behind them, and they turned to look. 'It's you lot again. What do you want now?' Laura said.

'We're just having a chat,' Art said. 'Come in and join the fun.'

'Don't be facetious, inspector. I'll be reporting the lot of you for bothering a couple of elderly patients who are in a nursing home.'

To Fife Constabulary, just like Farmington? Brodie wanted to say but kept his mouth shut.

'We're conducting a murder inquiry here, Ms Forrest,' Art said.

Laura gave him a look that might have killed lesser mortals, as she realised he knew her marital status and the name change when he called her Ms.

'You want to question them, but it needs three of you?' She was holding a Tim Hortons disposable cup in her hand, and Brodie thought for a second that she was going to throw it.

'It's operational procedure,' Brodie said, staring her down.

'What is it you want now?' she said, drinking from the cup.

Brodie saw the hardness around her eyes, the crow's feet that he was willing to bet had been there for a long time. 'Just follow-up questions.'

'You don't mind if I stay and listen?' Laura said with a tone in her voice.

'Actually, we were hoping you would be here so we could talk to you as well, Ms Forrest,' Art said. 'If you wouldn't mind stepping out of the room where my colleague and I could have a little chat?'

'Sake,' she said, turning on her heel. Art indicated for Cameron to come out with him, and Brodie nodded his appreciation.

Brodie then turned to Farmington. 'Sir, I'd like to ask you what you remember about young Marcus disappearing.'

'What makes you think I would know anything about what went on in Margaret's house?'

Brodie walked over and sat in the one chair in the room: a large, high-backed affair. 'Do you really want to do this dance?' he asked Farmington.

The old man chuckled. 'I really don't have any—'

'Rory, he knows,' Margaret said quietly, and Farmington dropped the façade.

'Yes, I suppose he does,' he said.

'Right, let's reset this conversation; what do you know about Marcus?' Brodie said.

Farmington looked at Margaret, who nodded, and then he began to speak. 'Margaret worked for me at one time. We started dating, but my work took me all over the place, and we drifted apart. She could have been a rising political star, but she met a fine young man and fell in love with him. However, after they got married, the veneer began to crack, revealing his true character. He was a drunk and couldn't keep a job.'

Brodie looked at Margaret, who nodded slowly.

'Then one day, I bumped into her at a function,' Farmington said, carrying on, 'and we hit it off, like we had never stopped seeing each other and, to be honest, I fell in love with her at that moment.'

'Let me guess; you were married?' Brodie said.

Farmington nodded. 'Yes. I was married to Cecilia, and we had one child, a boy. I wanted to be with Margaret, and to hell with my career, but she wouldn't hear of it. She said we could still see each other. It was something she was happy with. Just being with each other was magical. Then Margaret started working in my office again, and there would be trips. If anybody suspected anything, they damn well didn't say anything. Margaret and I kept on seeing each other for years. I even went to her house a few times, and if Toby should come home early, then I would have a stack of papers that we would be reading through. Unless we were in bed, then we'd be royally screwed. But that never happened.'

Margaret smiled. 'And then it happened; I fell pregnant. Laura was about eight at the time, but I had told Toby a long time before that I couldn't produce children.'

'Walk me through the pregnancy, which I'm assuming was Marcus,' Brodie said.

Margaret nodded. 'I told Toby that stranger things have happened. He believed it. I really believed I couldn't conceive, but there it was. I was pregnant by another man.'

'Then Marcus was born,' Brodie said. 'How did Toby take that?'

'We had a plan to have Margaret leave Toby, and we would take the kids,' Farmington said.

'Then you would get divorced, is that it?' Brodie said.

'I wanted that, but Margaret was so selfless, weren't you, my dear?' Farmington said to Margaret.

She smiled at him. 'You had your political career to think of.' She looked at Brodie. 'I made sure that Rory saw Marcus as often as he wanted. Toby was drunk most of the time, so he didn't care if I took Marcus and Laura out.'

'Very clever,' Brodie said. 'Except things didn't work out that way.'

Margaret took a deep breath and made a grunt as she exhaled, as if fighting back a sob. 'No, it didn't. He was about five or six when he changed. He became withdrawn and then one day, he ran away. He had never run away before. He began acting out at school and getting into fights. Then one day, I returned after a trip to London with Rory. I had been away for a few days. When I got back, I was told by the police that Toby was dead. They were sure it was suicide. They also told me Marcus had run off again. On the same day that Toby had died. He left the house, and we never saw him again.'

'What year was this?'

'Nineteen eighty-seven.'

'Where were Laura and Ruth at this time?'

'Next door. They have a couple of spare bedrooms, so they kindly took them in until I got home.'

'There was a manhunt for him, wasn't there?' Brodie asked.

'Oh, yes, I was on the bloody phone making sure every resource was at their disposal,' Farmington said.

'And still nothing,' Margaret said. 'They asked Laura about the last time she saw him, and she said the day before. She was in her room, watching videos with Ruth, and they saw Marcus, who said he was going to play in his room. That's the last they saw of him.'

Brodie tapped his foot for a second. 'Your husband liked a drink, we know that now, but do you think he could have come home and done something to Marcus?' Brodie asked.

'Kill him, you mean?' Farmington said.

'Yes. Somebody killed him with a blunt force object. Could it have been Toby?'

'I mean, it's possible. Maybe he committed suicide because he couldn't live with the guilt. But Toby shouted at everybody.'

'How was Laura with Toby after you told her she was adopted?' Brodie asked. 'Did she still look on him as her dad?'

'Laura was Laura, always very strong-willed. She would do whatever she wanted to do. But it didn't seem to faze her, being adopted. She just shrugged and went on with life. She didn't know anything different. We adopted her when she was a year old, so we were really all she knew.'

'When she was older,' Brodie said, 'how was she with Marcus?'

'She was fine.'

'How about the arguments?'

Margaret looked at Farmington, then back to Brodie. 'Toby and I would have the odd argument, but nothing outrageous.'

'You and Laura would have arguments, we heard.'

'I tried to make her see sense, but as she slipped into her teenage years, she got worse. She was very, how shall I put it, independent when she got to about fifteen, sixteen. Started going out with boys – older boys, mind – ones who had cars who would pick her up. She would come in at all hours. She would drink, especially on a Friday night. She had left school by then and was waiting to go to college. She didn't even attempt to look for temporary work. That's when the arguments started. And poor Marcus, he had to witness that. He was scared at times, but I reassured him that everything was fine.'

'How did your husband react at that time?' Brodie asked.

'He was supportive. He would back me up when I told Laura about her behaviour. She would tell him to get lost. Then he grounded her and things got worse between them.'

'Can I ask you, what do you know about Laura's birth mother and father?'

'Not much. I think Laura was an unwanted pregnancy.'

'Do you know their names?'

'Steven and Ashley.'

'Where was Laura born?' Brodie asked.

'In Dunfermline. May 2, 1971. She just turned fifty-four.'

'How did Laura and Ruth cope with Toby dying the way he did?' Brodie asked.

Margaret looked at Farmington before looking back at Brodie. 'Laura was almost inconsolable. She cried for weeks afterwards. Ruth was too young to understand.'

Brodie looked at them both for a second. 'It must have been hard for Laura, her brother disappearing and then her father dying.'

'It was.'

Brodie looked at the old woman and thought about the stories Ruth had told him about how horrible her foster mother had been. Obviously, Margaret had selective memory.

He stood up and looked at Farmington. 'Where would I be able to find your son?'

'Why?' the old man asked.

'Covering all of our bases. I want to talk to him.'

'I don't have to tell you where he is.'

Brodie nodded. 'That's right, you don't, but it would make life easier for me. Since he's running for a seat in the Scottish Parliament, he won't be hard to find, but if I have to go the extra mile to find him, I'll make sure it gets leaked to the press that a potential candidate is being investigated in a decades-old murder. See what his chances are after that.'

'That's fucking blackmail,' Farmington said, his voice barely a whisper.

Brodie smiled. 'Yes, it is.' He turned and walked towards the room door.

'Wait.'

Brodie turned. Farmington gave him the address.

'You certainly are a bastard, chief inspector.'

Brodie smiled again. 'And proud of it.'

45

FIFE

Brodie took his coffee over to a desk and sat on the edge. The others looked at him. It was lunchtime, and they generally ate at their desks if they were in the office at that time. Art McKenzie, Cameron Reid, DS Freya Munro and DC Morven Fraser.

Morven was eating pizza and it smelled wonderful, making his stomach growl. 'From what we can gather,' Brodie said, 'Margaret Wallace had a temper on her. At eighty-five now, she doesn't show signs of it, but from what some of the neighbours tell us, she used to go at it with Laura. DI McKenzie spoke to the neighbours across the road, and they said arguments would happen all the time. This was also confirmed by other neighbours. According to them, they all thought that Mrs Wallace had mental health issues.'

'What was your impression of her, sir?' Morven asked.

'I could see it. Even though she's elderly, there was an underlying tone there.'

Freya was sitting at another computer off to one side, typing and drinking her coffee.

'What we didn't tell her was we knew about the little boy having broken bones from previous injuries, breaks that had healed. Somebody used to batter the wee guy, and God knows how they got away with it for so long.' He looked at Freya. 'How did the social work search go?'

She looked at him. 'There's nothing in the system, but since he went missing in 1987, and the injuries would have been before that, it doesn't surprise me. Not every record would have been digitised. They would be on paper, and if they were kept, they would be in a central storage place somewhere. But we're talking forty years ago, so the chances of finding anything like that are slim.'

'How about Laura's biological parents?' Art asked.

'This is interesting,' Freya said. 'I couldn't find any information on Laura's parents regarding the adoption, but I did find a newspaper story about a Steven and Ashley Forrest who were killed in a car crash.'

'When did this happen?'

'Nineteen eighty-six.'

'A year before Margaret's husband died in 1987, which we now know to be a murder,' Art said.

'Is there any way we can find out if she had treatment for mental health issues?' Morven said.

'Probably not,' Brodie answered. 'It's all privacy laws nowadays.'

Just then, the incident door opened and Det Supt Chris Breck walked in. 'Brodie. I need a word,' he said, holding the door open.

Brodie stood up and walked towards the man. Breck was as tall as Brodie, but not as well built. 'Sir?'

'Outside,' he said, as if he meant to take the DCI out to the car park for a fist fight. Brodie stepped into the corridor.

Breck let the incident room door close before speaking to him.

'I've had a phone call,' Beck said.

'Let me guess; from Rory Farmington.'

'Give that man a cigar. He might be a pain in the arse, but he's still a powerful pain in the arse. He told me you are going to interrogate his son about the murder of Marcus Wallace.'

'Interrogate is taking it a bit too far. I was going to talk to him about that time.'

'Leave it alone. He too has powerful friends. Besides, what can he tell us after forty years?'

'You'd be surprised. Margaret Wallace remembers quite a lot. So does old Farmington.'

'Just leave it, Liam. This is an old case. It might never get solved.' Breck patted him on the shoulder and walked away.

Brodie fought to contain his anger. If there was one thing he hated, it was politicians who thought they could walk on water.

'Problem, sir?' Art asked.

'Cancel talking with Farmington's son, Keith. The old boy made a phone call. It was a long shot anyway, seeing what he could remember from those times.'

'Unless there is something that we can get DNA from, this is a case that might never get solved,' Morven said.

'That's what worries me,' Brodie said. Then he looked at Art. 'How did it go when you were talking with Laura when I was talking to her mother?'

'There's an air about her. She's tough, as you saw for yourself, and when I asked her about that day, she told us she was busy doing homework and didn't really take notice of Marcus.'

'Unless there's a smoking gun, this case might stay unsolved,' Brodie said. 'But we have to keep on trying.'

A phone rang and Cameron picked it up. He listened and held out the receiver.

'It's for you, sir.'

'Hello?'

'This is Sergeant Foster at the front desk, sir. Somebody here asking for you. A Mr Keith Farmington.'

46

FIFE

Brodie was outside in the station car park. Next to him was Keith Farmington.

'Sorry about all the fuss, DCI Brodie,' the older man said. 'I'm running for the Scottish Parliament, not to be the first man on Mars, as my father might think.'

'I apologise for the way I spoke to your father. I was just keen to get your viewpoint from back then.'

Keith laughed. 'Don't apologise. I just wanted to walk out here because I don't want to be seen talking to you on camera. Things that get recorded have a habit of getting out, even in dear old Fife.'

'Understandable.'

'When my father called, he once again spoke to me like I was fucking five. He forgets I turned sixty last year.' He held up a hand. 'I know, I know, it's a bit old to be running for MSP, but I feel that I have a lot to offer. I'm a lawyer and I've decided to retire. And when I see how this country is going sometimes, I want to do something to shape its future for the better. Does that make sense?'

'Perfectly.'

'Now, you wanted to ask me about 1987. Ask away. Anything you like.'

Brodie stopped for a moment. 'Did you know your father was having a long-term affair with Margaret Wallace?'

Keith smiled. 'Yes. My sister didn't know, or at least, if she did, she never said anything. I heard him and Margaret talking about the boy one time. I was surprised, but my father was a bit of a lad, and he seemed to care for Margaret more than he cared for my mother. There was no love lost between my parents.'

They started walking again. 'Margaret said she couldn't get pregnant, but she did with your father,' Brodie said.

'I know. He told me when I was an adult. He and Margaret had talked about whether she should keep him or terminate the pregnancy. But Margaret was delighted she was going to have her own baby, even if it wasn't her husband's. She told my father that she loved him and to have his child made their love complete. It's a cliché of course, but she loved their son.'

'I heard that when he got a bit older, he would run away,' Brodie said.

'Which would be a good cover story for whoever murdered him. Make it look like he had just taken off, never to return,' Keith said.

'Toby Wallace committed suicide, I believe,' Brodie said.

'He did. Bottle of pills and a bottle of whisky. Classic move when you want to go out quietly.'

'It's the old adage, but a policeman doesn't believe in coincidences. There we have Marcus, missing, later to be found to have been murdered, then Toby Wallace is found after committing suicide on the same day that Marcus was last seen. I'm paid to be suspicious of things, and that makes me question things.'

'You mean, did somebody help Wallace on his way?'

'Exactly.'

'Are you suggesting my father might have wanted Wallace out of the picture?' Keith smiled. 'That's what I would think if I was you. But you would be wrong. At the time Wallace died, my father was visiting America. He wasn't even in the country. Besides, Wallace didn't know about his wife and my father. And let's face it, even if he found out, my father could have bought him off. The man would have been glad of the money. There would have been no need to kill him.'

'Margaret Wallace might have seen things differently.'

'No. She and my father talked. She didn't want to break up his marriage. I know that for a fact because my father told me this. After we had argued one night, I mentioned that I knew. He assured me that his marriage was safe. It wouldn't benefit his political career to be seen having an affair, and Margaret was simply happy to have him in her life. Neither of them would have anything to gain from killing Toby Wallace.'

'Did your father ever stop seeing Margaret?' Brodie asked.

'Never. Even after my mother died, he still saw her. They've been friends ever since. More than friends, but as they got older, I imagine just friends.'

They walked back to Keith's car.

'Thank you for talking with me,' Brodie said.

'Just don't tell the old man, eh? He's a moaning bastard as it is. But he still has influence, so I don't want to rock the boat.'

'You got it.'

47

EDINBURGH

Det Supt Rob Cross sat with his elbow out of the passenger window and flicked a cigarette out into the street.

'What happened to the mints?' DI Lucy Warren said as she floored the car down the long street to the entrance to the cemetery.

'I thought I'd have one last one before you take us into the stone pillars and kill us both.'

'I have the siren on,' she said.

'Oh good, we can go out in style.'

Lucy slowed down as she approached. There was a patrol car not quite blocking the entrance. Cross held out his warrant card.

'Thank you, sir. It's down—'

'We know. We've been here before,' he said as Lucy drove in at a more sedate pace. 'This is fucking unbelievable,' Cross said as Lucy navigated her way down to the archway where other emergency vehicles were parked. 'I mean, we're sure Kane is still locked up, right?'

'He is,' Lucy said, slowing down. 'I checked.'

'Wonderful. Now we have a copycat. I told those upstairs we should have had a news blackout, but what do I know?'

They got out and were recognised by the Uniform standing guard at the archway.

'My wife wonders why I go home and scran all the teacakes. I stress-eat,' Cross said. He looked at Lucy. 'You don't think I'm a fat bastard now, do you?'

'What do you mean, "now"?'

'I feel that you and I were married in a former life.'

They walked towards a group of police officers and the pathologist from Cowgate, a young woman named Dr Crystal Main.

'Dr Main,' he said.

'Rob. Lucy.' She was dressed head to foot in a white suit with the hood pulled up.

'Hi, Crys,' Lucy said.

'What have we got here?' He looked down at the piece of material sticking out from underneath the gravestone.

'It looks like somebody's under there. The weight of the stone would have impacted them into the ground, but the edge caught a piece of this material. On further inspection, there's a fraction of an arm caught in the material.'

'Jesus,' Cross said.

'We have the Bobcat operator on his way again,' Lucy said.

'Wracking up bloody good money on the taxpayer, so he is,' Cross said. 'He probably gets paid more for driving that machine than I do.'

'You could always try lifting the gravestone by hand,' Crystal said.

'And do that laddie out of some overtime?'

Crystal smiled at him. 'That's what I thought.'

'Who found it?' Cross said to a Uniform standing close by.

'A man and woman walking their dog, sir. They're outside.' He led them back through the archway to where an elderly couple were standing with a little brown dog that wasn't interested in standing still.

'Thanks, we'll take it from here,' Cross said. Then he looked at the man as Lucy stood by his side, and introduced them.

'I'm Mark Bishop and this is my friend, Trudi Brough. We already spoke to one of the officers and gave our details.'

'I'm his girlfriend, actually,' Trudi said.

'Trudi with an "i",' Bishop said, just a hint of sarcasm in his voice. 'And this little fella is Percy.'

Cross nodded as the dog gave him the once-over and then stood back and barked at him.

'Can you tell me how you found that item under the gravestone?' Cross asked Bishop.

'We were here walking the dog and he sort of pulled us through the archway. He sniffed at that gravestone, and we noticed the material. I knew a body had been found under another grave from watching the news, mind, not because I was responsible. I wanted to do my civic duty and call you lot.'

Trudi snorted a laugh, like this was some sort of game show. 'That's not quite true, is it, Mark?' Trudi said.

Bishop looked like he could quite happily strangle her, even in front of two police officers.

'Well, it really is,' Bishop said, gritting his teeth, wondering what prison food tasted like. Maybe if she rattled on, there would be a chance for him to turn the tables on her and put the blame on her, taking the copper aside and telling him that he really didn't know this woman, that he had met her online.

'Silly billy. We wanted to come down here and look at the crime scene,' she said, the smile still playing on her lips. Bishop wondered if she went home at night and put lipstick around the edge of her mouth as well as on her lips. Just before she sacrificed an animal.

'Is that true?' Lucy asked. 'You wanted to come down here and get a close-up of where a body was lifted from?'

Bishop knew he never wanted to see this mad fanny ever again. Or maybe that choice would be made for him when they carted him away to give him a lobotomy.

'I'm a true-crime addict,' he said in his own defence. 'This was right on my own doorstep. I was just interested, that's all. I never thought in a million years that we would find another one.'

Cross looked at him. 'You see, the problem we have now is that you started off with a lie. That throws everything else you say into question. We're going to have to crawl through your life with a fine-toothed comb now, just in case you *are* the man we've been looking for.'

Bishop's mouth fell open. 'I didn't fucking kill anybody. And you, we're fucking done,' he said to Trudi with an 'i'. Then he looked at Lucy. 'If you want any more answers, you can talk to me in front of my lawyer. Come on, Percy.'

He started walking away when Trudi called after him. 'Wait, Mark.'

'Don't call me ever again,' he said and started walking faster.

'Do you think he's the one, sir?' Lucy asked as the couple were out of earshot.

Cross shook his head. 'Any man who calls his dog Percy isn't capable of doing something like that. Also, did you see his body language when she called him out? He nearly shat himself. No, he wouldn't have brought her here if he had shoved a gravestone down on top of somebody.'

'Unless he planned to do it to her too,' Lucy said.

Cross gave an amused chuckle. 'Who would have held his dog? He doesn't look like he could fight his way through wet tissue paper.'

They heard the truck coming, pulling the Bobcat behind it.

'Here we go again,' Cross said.

Fifteen minutes later, the gravestone was moved and the body of Sylvia Green was revealed, in a horrendous state.

'Just like Kane's victim, with a book on top of her,' he said to Lucy. 'That's all we need.'

'I'll call DCI Brodie and give him a heads-up,' she said.

Cross looked at the gravestone with the material sticking out of it and then a thought hit him like a freight train.

'Jesus, Lucy.'

'What?'

'Take a look,' he said. 'Notice anything different from when we took the first body out?'

Lucy looked at the stones. 'Fucking hell.'

'Exactly. There's not just one more gravestone been knocked over, but two.' He looked at her. 'Make that laddie with the Bobcat earn his overtime. Get all those other stones next to the first one moved. I want to see what's under the others.'

48

FIFE

Brodie was in DCI Alan McRae's office with Art and Cameron sitting in chairs opposite him.

'Give me the full rundown on the DCI McRae investigation,' he said. He drank more coffee, feeling the tiredness creep into him.

'Maurice Duvall, a property solicitor, reported seeing Alan just before Alan went on holiday. Technically, he wasn't missing at that point. He was seen getting into a small blue Volvo. I asked his sister if she knew anybody who owned one. She did. Alan's ex-wife.'

Brodie put his mug down as Art looked at Cameron for a moment.

'As I already told you, sir, she told us he had met her at the trail car park outside Cupar. He was scared of something. I wish I knew what of. She told us that she was seeing Dick Drever, the bar manager at Windygates bowling club. When we returned to speak to her the following day, we found her dead in her car, as you know. Then we discovered Drever dead in his house. And that's you up to speed, sir.'

Brodie kept quiet for a moment. 'The way you tell it, you're either the unluckiest pair of bastards I know, or you're a fucking jinx,' he said.

'I think we're getting closer to something, sir,' Cameron said.

'You think something happened to McRae, and that what happened to his ex and this Drever character is also connected?' Brodie asked.

'It's highly possible,' Art answered, 'but we don't know what he was scared of.'

'How straight of an arrow was McRae?'

Art hesitated for a moment. Alan was a friend of his as well as his boss, but he had started thinking just how little he might have known about him.

'I would have trusted him with my life,' Art said. 'I've known him for a long time. I can't see him getting into anything dodgy, but you never truly know somebody, do you?'

'What's the next step in the inquiry?' Brodie asked.

'I was going to say, I'd like to go and talk to Alan's sister, Daisy, again, but as you say, somebody could be watching us. What if we put her in danger?'

'I think it's important to talk to her again. Call her and set up a meet in a public place, make sure you don't get followed.'

'What if somebody follows her?' Cameron asked.

'I doubt that will happen,' Brodie answered. 'If they wanted to harm her just like they did McRae's ex and Drever, then they would have already done it.'

'You've got a good point,' Art said.

'Tell her who I am and I'll meet her.' Brodie's phone rang, and he nodded for the other two detectives to leave. He answered it when his door was shut. 'Lucy. What's happening?'

'You're never going to believe this, sir; we found two more in the cemetery. Right next to where Ivy Jack was found.'

'Jesus. Do you think it's a copycat?'

'It must be, sir. There was a book left on top of her. We haven't identified her yet.'

'Was it a Bible?' Brodie asked.

'No, it was a John Sandford book.'

Brodie was sweating in this office, and he reminded himself to bring in a fan if he was going to be working here much longer. 'That is completely different from the other one.'

'It's strange.'

'Listen, I have another call coming in. I'll meet up with you tomorrow morning before I come across here.'

'Okay, sir. See you at the station.'

Brodie hung up and pressed the button for the other call.

'Liam, it's Ruth.'

'Hey, honey, how are you doing?' He listened for a second as she didn't answer right away. It sounded like she had been crying.

'I'd like to go and see the cottage. Can you take me there?'

'Of course. Are you on your way up there now?'

'I am. I'll meet you there. Wait for me, will you?'

'I will.'

'My satnav says I should be there in about fifteen minutes.'

'I'll leave now, Ruth.'

He hung up and stood up from behind his desk. He called Art over and told him he had to run an errand.

'Hold the fort while I'm away. If Breck is looking for me, tell him I won't be long.'

'No problem.'

Brodie took off from the car park.

49

FIFE

Ruth was standing outside the cottage when Brodie pulled up. And still he hadn't eaten. He got out and walked over to her and saw the tears streaming down her face. She barely noticed as he stopped and put an arm around her shoulders. She leaned into him and started sobbing.

After a few moments, she sniffed and stopped, gently pulling away from him.

'Bittersweet,' she said.

'Good memories and bad?' he said, as she took a paper hanky out of her pocket and wiped her eyes with it.

'Yes. I was five when I arrived forty years ago, and I can still remember some of the details. Mr Wallace was tall and skinny, and he looked like a giant. Laura was fourteen at the time. Big and mean-looking. I remember how she couldn't care less that I was there. I hated being here.'

They walked towards the door where a patrol car sat. The forensics van was there. A Uniform stepped out of the car as they approached, and Brodie took his warrant card out.

'We need to see the crime scene,' he said.

'No problem, sir. Let me know if you need anything.'

'Will do.'

Brodie stayed behind Ruth as she stepped through the open doorway.

'Nothing much has changed,' she said, looking around. She stopped and turned to look at him. 'You know when you go into a house, and it has a unique smell? My adoptive grandmother's house was like that. Not smelly, but like somebody wearing cologne. You just associate it with that person.'

'I know what you mean. My grandmother's house smelled exactly like that. Most of the time, there was also the aroma of her baking biscuits or rolls. My grandfather was a baker, so it was great.'

Ruth ventured further in, and a pair of figures in white suits came into view before disappearing again.

'What are they doing?' Ruth asked.

'Looking for other evidence. They'll pull up other floorboards too.'

'Which room was Marcus in?' Ruth said, her voice slightly hoarse from the crying.

'It's along to the left,' Brodie said.

Ruth knew where she was going and walked slowly along the hallway and saw where the men and women were concentrating their efforts on.

'Laura's room,' she said simply.

'I spoke to Margaret and Rory Farmington.'

Ruth turned to look at him. 'How did that go?'

'She seems like a tough old bird.'

Ruth shook her head. 'That's her alright. She is one scary lady. I haven't seen her since I left when I was ten. I did not like her at all. One minute she was happy, the next, going off her head at something. Always lashing out at her husband. No wonder he was a drunk.'

'I wonder why he didn't just leave instead of taking his own life.'

'I hate to say this, but some people see committing suicide as a permanent way out. They won't ever have to see their aggressor again. If they just left, they would always wonder if that person was going to show up in their life again. It was a classic move by Mr Wallace.' She locked eyes with him. 'Unless somebody helped him along.'

'The post-mortem showed pills and alcohol in his system,' Brodie said.

'You're a detective. You know, some killers can make a death appear as a suicide. I'm not suggesting that occurred in this instance, but considering someone murdered Marcus and concealed it, then it would have been quite easy for Mr Wallace's death to seem like suicide. Just saying.'

Brodie knew she had a good point.

'Do you feel better coming to see where Marcus was buried?' he asked her. She poked her head into the room and saw the lifted floorboards and bricks scattered, broken off from the big lump that was the chimney.

'I wouldn't say better. I can't even say I've found closure, as the Americans would say. But to think I lived here for five years and didn't know Marcus was buried under there. I can't get my head around it.'

'You were five when you got here, and Marcus was six. Laura was fourteen, is that right? In 1985.'

'Yes,' Ruth said.

'He went missing in 1987, so you would be seven, Marcus eight and Laura sixteen at the time,' Brodie said.

Ruth simply nodded.

They turned and walked back out into the sunshine to find the next-door neighbour standing with his hands on his hips. Ted Carr. With his wife Penny behind him.

'When is this going to be finished?' he demanded.

'When is what going to be finished?' Brodie said.

'This... mess!' Ted said.

'Yes, this mess,' Penny said, poking her head round her husband then withdrawing it back.

'This sort of thing takes time, Mr Carr,' Ruth said. 'Do you remember me?'

Ted looked Puzzled. 'No. Should I?'

'I lived here forty years ago. I'm Ruth.' She smiled at him.

'Yes, of course! Young Ruth. Look, Penny, it's little Ruth.'

Penny shuffled sideways. 'Hello, Ruth. Look at you, all grown up.'

'How are you both doing?' she asked, holding her hand out for Ted to shake.

'We're doing fine, Ruth.' He let her hand go, and stood looking at her. 'We heard on the news that a skeleton was found under the floorboards,' he said. Penny looked down at the ground.

Ruth nodded but Brodie cut in. 'We can't speculate any further on that matter,' he said.

'And who are you?' Ted asked.

'DCI Brodie. I'm Ruth's partner.'

'You're a police officer?' Ted asked Ruth.

'No, he meant partner, as in boyfriend.'

'Oh, you're not married.'

'I was, but I got divorced years ago.'

'Ah, I see. What is it you do nowadays?'

'I'm a psychiatrist.'

'She's Dr Ruth Campbell,' Brodie said.

'Well, that's wonderful, Ruth. I'm proud of you,' Ted said.

'Thank you. What do you do yourself these days?'

'I'm retired. I was an accountant.'

'Terrific. Peace and quiet now,' Ruth said. 'It's a beautiful place to live.'

Ted drew in a breath and let it out slowly. 'That's what we thought. Until your foster mother moved in with her husband. I told the other two detectives who were here that the peace was shattered when they moved in. Her husband was a drunk. I didn't like him at all. And their daughter. Good Lord, they couldn't keep her under control at all.'

'I remember Laura. I haven't seen her in a very long time.'

'She still lived there,' Ted said, nodding at the cottage.

'Where did she move to when the chimney fell?' Brodie asked.

'I have no idea. Margaret was already in the nursing home, and Laura stayed near it, I think. Don't quote me on that, but the best thing that's ever happened is that place is about to be put on the market. I might buy it myself, just to control who lives there.'

'It might be worth the investment, right enough,' Ruth said.

'Would you both like to come in for a cup of tea?' Penny asked.

'Thank you, no,' Ruth said. 'I have to get back to work.'

'Me too,' Brodie said, 'but thanks anyway.'

'Okay. Take care, Ruth. Good seeing you again,' Ted said. Penny waved as she followed her husband back into the house.

'They seem nice,' Brodie said.

'I have memories of them but a bit vague now. I remember him having a missing finger on his left hand. It used to creep me out.'

They walked back to her car.

'Have you heard from Moira by any chance?' he asked her.

Ruth shook her head. 'No.'

'She's having some holiday time to sort out her marriage, so maybe she was just having a lie-in. But mum can't get a hold of her, and you know what she's like when she can't get a hold of her bairns.' He smiled.

'Mother hen. I would be the same.' She unlocked the car and opened the driver's door. 'Are you going to see Eric later?'

'I'll call him.' He held the door for her as she climbed into the driver's seat. 'Are you really going back to work?' he asked.

She shook her head as she started the car. 'I was just being polite.'

'Lucky you. I had a call from Lucy earlier; they found more bodies under gravestones, right next to the other one in the cemetery.'

'Oh, no.'

'We think it's a copycat. I'm going to Edinburgh now too. See you at home?' Brodie said.

'Yes.' Ruth shivered, even though it was warm outside. She wished that seeing the place would bring back memories of that time, but they were vague. A young boy, older than her, was laughing. An older girl who was mean to her. Those were the memories she had, like seeing somebody through an opaque window. She felt empty inside to think that somebody had killed Marcus and buried him under the floorboards like a piece of rubbish.

Her heart felt heavy at the thought. She still couldn't believe that she had lived in that house for another three years before being adopted, with a dead body there.

50

EDINBURGH

The Reader unlocked the padlock on the door and slid it open. He had chosen this room since it had this door. One that opened outwards would give her a chance to rush at him, and inwards, she could be hiding behind it, waiting to pounce. That's if she had managed to get herself free from the chain, which was long enough to let her use the chemical toilet and drink, but not long enough to reach the doorway. There was also a bed for sleeping on and she would be comfortable on it. Mostly.

It was cool down here, away from the madness of the midday rush hour, people leaving their offices to go and get lunch.

He held a carrier bag in one hand with food in it.

The room was long and filled with shelving, but the nook at the back once had a table, though not any more. Only a couple of the light bulbs worked, which made the room appear danker and mouldier than it truly was. The walls were painted a light cream colour, but his red glasses gave them a reddish-pink hue.

He slid the door closed behind him and his footsteps echoed on the stone floor.

'Help!' he heard her shout.

He walked closer and stopped when he saw she was standing up, the chain still wrapped around the iron pipe that came in through the ceiling and went down through the floor. Which had to be the sewage pipes, they were so low down.

'I told you before, you can scream all you like. Nobody will hear you. The walls are two feet thick, and your voice won't carry all the way up the stairwell. And as you can see, there are no windows. You should just rest your voice and have a drink of water. I promise you there's nothing in it and the seal hasn't been broken. Here, let me show you.'

He put the carrier bag on the floor and lifted the water bottle. After breaking the seal, he took a sip and smacked his lips.

'It's up to you, of course. I mean, you can take a horse to water, and all that. I also brought you some food from Greggs, and sandwiches from Morrisons. They do a good deal, you know. My favourites are the tuna mayo, so I added some in. Are you hungry?'

'Fuck off. Shove your sandwiches up your arse,' Moira said. She spat at him and missed.

'Dear oh dear, Moira, love. That's very antisocial.'

'And what do you think this is? Keeping me chained up in here?'

'It won't be for long. This is going to come to an end soon.' He walked along and nipped behind a shelf where he had placed a folding chair. He made sure it was out of Moira's reach, and he sat down and picked up the carrier bag and started rifling through it. 'You want an egg sandwich or a tuna one? I got both in case you don't eat seafood. I have Scotch eggs and little Melton Mowbray pies too. I even bought you a bottle of Diet Coke. Less sugar. That's bad for you.'

Moira sat on the floor. 'Egg, please. Scotch egg. And the Coke.' Her anger had subsided.

He passed them over, and he watched as she tore open the packet. He opened a tuna sandwich and wolfed down the two sandwiches.

'Aren't you going to ask me why I'm doing this?' he asked after he washed down his own sandwich with a Coke Zero.

She ate a sandwich and had a drink. 'Don't you find it annoying that in the UK, the cap is stuck onto the bottle so you have to recycle it, but in the States, they do it the old-fashioned way and just let you take the cap off?' She let out a belch. 'Pardon me.'

'You didn't answer my question.' He nibbled on one of the little pies.

'I don't want to know. But if I were to hazard a guess, I'd say my ex-husband put you up to this.'

'Interesting theory, but you'd be wrong. I've never met him and have no intention of ever meeting him. No, this is all me, Moira.'

'Why do you wear red glasses?' she asked. 'I was starting to think it was a disguise, but if it is, it's not a very good one.'

He looked at her while he shoved the rest of the pie in his mouth and chewed. Then he washed it down. 'These are real. I have a slight brain injury. It affected my vision, so I need the red colour to stop my brain from frying itself through my eyes. Something like that. Red for inside, black in the summer sun, then back to red at all times when it's not sunny. Here, do you want to try them?' He put a hand up to the left arm as if he was about to take them off, and she nodded and held out a hand.

He handed them over and she immediately broke them, bending and twisting the frame.

'There. How do you like that?' she said to him and threw the glasses away as far as she could.

He laughed and reached into an inside pocket of his jacket, brought out another pair and slipped them on. 'They were old ones. My prescription changed slightly.' He looked around, left, right, up and down. 'That's better.'

'Okay, I give in; what am I doing here, Peter?' Moira asked.

'My name's not really Peter. My real name is not important. The name you should be thinking about is Nancy. That was her name.'

Moira's eyes grew wide, and her shoulders slumped.

'And now you know,' he said to her.

51

FIFE

Ruth was already halfway down the A982 when she decided to go to Townhill. She saw the signs for Dunfermline, and she just asked her satnav to take her to the nursing home.

She sat in her car in the car park, now unsure if she wanted to do this. But if not now, then when? It was already early afternoon and time was skipping along.

She got out of her car and walked into reception. 'I'd like to see my mum, please.'

The nurse at reception looked confused for a moment. 'Who's your mum?'

'Margaret Wallace.'

'Margaret? I didn't know she has two daughters.'

'Well, she does, and I'm one of them. Go and ask her if you don't believe me. I'm Ruth. The young one.'

Then recognition crossed her face. 'She talks about you, Ruth. Go upstairs. She should be in her room.' She told her the number and Ruth walked up the stairs instead of taking the lift. It gave her more time to think.

Ruth stepped into the corridor and started heading towards the room when she suddenly stopped. Coming out of Margaret's room was Laura.

She recognised the features even though they had aged a lot. Laura stopped and looked at Ruth.

Ruth anticipated a confrontation, but Laura merely walked towards her, started crying, and then threw her arms around her.

'Oh, Ruthie.' She pushed herself away for a moment, then hugged Ruth tighter. Ruth hesitated before wrapping her arms around her foster sister and holding her closely.

They both cried and then separated. Ruth pulled out a small packet of tissues and took two out, handing one to Laura.

'You know about Marcus, I assume?' Laura said.

Ruth nodded.

'When the police told us about there being a skeleton under the floorboards, I just had a feeling it was Marcus,' Laura said.

'I thought so too. My boyfriend is the one who told you about the skeleton. He's the detective in charge.'

'Really? Small world. Oh, Ruth, it's so good to see you. I didn't think I'd ever see you again,' Laura said.

'It's been a long time, I admit.' She felt her cheeks going red. 'How's Mum?'

Laura put out a hand and wiggled it back and forth. 'Sometimes she seems like she's thirty years younger, and there are days when she gets confused a bit. But generally, she's fine. I take it you're here to see her?'

'That was the idea, but now I'm not so sure.'

'Oh, why? She would love to see you.'

'I don't think she will like what I have to say, Laura.'

'What is it?'

Ruth looked at her. 'I know who killed Marcus.'

52

EDINBURGH

Brodie parked his car around the back of his mother's café and walked round to the front. The lunchtime rush was over and the mid-afternoon lull had kicked in, before later on when more people would come in.

'There he is,' his father, Dougal, said. 'The man who keeps us safe in our beds at night. And whatever it is they're paying you, it isn't enough.'

'Amen to that,' Brodie said.

'Have you heard from Moira?' his mother asked as she came in from the back, wiping her hands on an apron.

'Let the boy get a coffee, Isobel, for goodness' sake.' His father took a mug and poured from the urn.

'I haven't heard from her. This isn't like her. She always calls you for a chat.'

Isobel let her apron fall down. 'I'm really worried, Liam. Even when she's at the hospital, she calls. She's taking a week off from being a nurse and helping out here and that was her idea, so it's not like she doesn't want to come in. It's not like her.'

'There you go, son,' Dougal said, handing over the mug.

'Thanks, Dad.' He sipped at the coffee, enjoying the taste. 'I'll give her a call and see where she is.' He took out his phone and dialled her number but it went straight to voicemail. 'No answer.'

'See? I told you,' Isobel said.

'Maybe she's finally having some fun after being married to Roger for all this time,' Dougal said.

'Oh, for goodness' sake. She's not like that. This is unusual, even for her.'

Brodie nodded. 'I'll have a patrol go round to her flat on Leith Walk and see if they can get an answer.'

'She wanted a change of pace. She works hard in the Western, so coming in here and chatting with customers who don't want to throw up all over her makes a wee change. And to be honest, it's been great having her here. I'm worried sick,' Isobel said.

'I'll try and get a hold of her, don't worry.'

'Why would she switch her phone off?' Dougal said.

'Maybe her inbox is full, or something,' Brodie said.

Then his phone rang. He thought it might be his sister, but it was Lucy.

'DI Warren. How can I help you?'

'We're still at the cemetery. They haven't moved the bodies yet. Forensics are crawling all over it. Are you still in Fife?'

'No, I'm at my mum's café.'

'You need to come down here, sir. This is big.'

'I'll be there shortly.' He disconnected the call and drank some more coffee before setting the mug on the counter. 'Got to go, Dad, thanks for that.'

'If you get a hold of Moira, get her to call your mother, for God's sake. Let us know if the Uniforms get a hold of her.'

'Trust me, I will.'

'She was chatting with that nice man, Peter, who comes in here regularly. Perhaps she's away spending some time with him. She deserves a bit of fun in her life after being married to that dull sod.'

'Who is this Peter?' Brodie asked.

'Just a customer who's been coming in here. They were just talking, having a cuppa. He left on his own and she didn't say she was meeting him. She needs some male company, so maybe chatting with this bloke made her happy. I wouldn't read anything into it.'

'You don't think anything's happened to her, do you?'

'Let's just stay positive.'

He left the café and headed back up Ferry Road and to the main entrance to the cemetery, then down to the archway.

Rob Cross was pacing back and forward with his phone to his ear when Brodie parked his car. He got out into the sun and wished he had bought a cold drink before he left the café.

'That bad?' Brodie asked.

'Bad? This is as bad as it fucking gets. There are another three in there.'

'Christ. How did you find them?' Brodie asked as they started walking through to the smaller part of the cemetery.

'We were here with Kane the other day, and today I noticed there were more gravestones down. Somebody had reported they saw material sticking out from under a gravestone, so when we checked it out, I called in the guy with the Bobcat, and that's when it hit me, that there was more than just another one stone down. The guy lifted the stones and we discovered three bodies.'

He walked over to the row of graves and Brodie saw right away that more had been knocked over.

Cross stopped in front of a black granite stone. 'This one is well attended to,' he said, pointing out the cut grass around it and some flowers lying in front of it.

'Nancy Simpson,' Brodie said.

'She died five years ago today,' Cross said.

'Christ,' Brodie said. 'When I was talking to somebody about the case, she told us that she had killed a cyclist, five years ago today. This is too much of a coincidence.'

'You think this woman was the victim?' Cross said.

'It has to be. Any ID on the women you found today?'

'A driving licence in the back pocket of one has the name Sylvia Green. A bank card in the pocket of another says Karen Blair.' He nodded to another one, in a much worse state than the others. 'There's Marianne Taylor. Not confirmed but she has a necklace on. It has the name Marianne on it. Of course, we're not taking it at face value, and we'll need ID confirmed, but it's a start.'

'This is starting to make sense. The woman who killed Nancy Simpson,

Alice Jack, was Ivy Jack's sister. Karen Blair also worked in the shop that Sylvia Green owned. Marianne Taylor was a customer. They all knew each other. That's why they're all here. Buried beside Nancy.' He looked at Cross. 'But Alice Jack said she hit two cyclists. One of them survived.'

'Sylvia and Karen have only been there for a few days at most. Those stones were standing when we were here before. Which fits n with the copycat theory.'

Brodie shook his head. 'No. I don't think we have a copycat. I think Gabriel Kane had a partner.'

53

FIFE

Ruth's phone rang, and she was tempted to ignore it, but she knew she couldn't. She had many patients who relied on her to be at the other end of the line if they needed someone to talk them down off the ledge.

She looked at the caller ID. 'Laura, I need to take this. We'll talk later.'

'Are you going to come back?' Laura asked as Ruth walked away.

'Soon. I promise.' Ruth walked over to the stairs and answered the phone. 'Hello?'

The caller on the other end was crying, attempting to speak while stifling sobs.

'Take your time, Dermot. It's going to be okay.'

She heard him sniffing back the tears so he could talk to her. 'I'm sorry, doctor. I was doing well, I really was. Now I feel like jumping off a bridge.'

'Oh, don't do that. Please. Let me find you and we can talk.'

'Do you think you can help me?'

'Of course I can,' Ruth said. 'We can sit and talk as long as you like. I'm not in Edinburgh just now, but can you meet me at my office in an hour?'

'Yes, I can wait for you. I'm so sorry to bother you.'

'It's no bother. Just wait for me.'

'I will. Thank you for being here for me, doc.'

'It's honestly no problem. If you feel like you have to stay on the phone while I'm driving, then that's fine too.'

'No, no. I'll have to get the bus, and I don't want people to be listening in. I'll be waiting at your office. And thank you again.'

The call was disconnected, and Ruth put her phone away until she reached her car. The timing of the phone call was dreadful, but it couldn't be helped. When she started her car, she plugged a cable into her phone to connect it to the vehicle.

Then she made another phone call.

The drive took less than an hour. She would tell Brodie that she went one or two miles per hour over the 70-speed limit, and while the road was busy, it wasn't heaving, so she made good time. Then along the Edinburgh bypass and down through Comiston to the Astley Ainslie.

She pulled into the staff car park and sat back for a moment. Now she knew what race-car drivers must experience, albeit on a much lesser scale. She put the car into park and the doors unlocked.

That was when the back passenger door opened behind her and someone jumped in. She yelled and then felt her hair being pulled back, the cold steel coming round from her right side and touching her neck.

'Make a move, and I'll slit your carotid. You'll be dead before I even leave this car park. Do you understand?'

'Uh huh.' She didn't move her head.

'Drive. I'm going to take the knife away, and if you do something stupid, I'll ram it into your ear while you're driving.'

'Why are you doing this?'

'No questions. Just do as I say. Now move.'

54

EDINBURGH

'What do you mean, he had a fucking partner?' Cross said. The afternoon sun was high in the sky but they were in the shade from some trees.

'I've had this feeling, if you will, ever since I got stabbed by Kane. You see, that night, I was walking through the depository, and I saw him at the far end. Then he ran around the shelving, and I lost sight of him. But I've lived that moment repeatedly, because something wasn't right. I thought I was just delirious, but now I know what it was.' He looked at him.

'Don't keep us in suspense, son,' Cross said.

'His height. I see him running around the end of the shelving, and before he turned, his head was level with a shelf with a big red book on it. Fourth shelf up. But when I was stabbed and turned to see Kane, the red book was at shoulder level. When the first guy was running, he wasn't ducking. He was shorter than Kane. There were two of them there that night. And the first one got away. He could have been hiding somewhere in there and waited until we left before leaving. There were two of the fuckers that night.'

'Who would the other man be?'

* * *

Lucy walked across to them and looked at Brodie. 'Forensics had bagged the book that was lying on Sylvia,' she said, holding up the clear evidence bag. 'I flipped through it. It's a John Sandford. Latest paperback. But that's not the interesting point. I took a photo.'

Brodie pulled on a pair of nitrile gloves and reached into the bag, taking the book out. Inside the front page of the book, with a sticker from his mother's café. The name, phone number, address, and the fact they had a book exchange.

'You seen those stickers before?' Cross asked.

Brodie nodded. 'My dad puts them in the books. He reckons people will come to the café if they like books.'

'Considering this is a new book, it's safe to say it was in the café recently.'

'It would appear so.' He thought about his mother telling him Moira was talking with a customer. Somebody called Peter.

'Could be that this killer was in your mother's café,' Cross said.

'Let me call her.' Brodie walked away and called his father instead. 'Dad, it's Liam.'

'Have you heard about Moira yet? Did those Uniforms go to her flat?'

'Not yet. I'll chase them up. But I have to ask you about one of the books you had in your book exchange. You wouldn't happen to remember if you had the latest John Sandford, would you?'

'Of course. It was mine. I bought it and put it on the shelf when I was finished.'

'And you put a sticker inside, with the name of the café on it?'

'Always.'

'I don't suppose you know who took it?' Brodie asked.

'I do actually. A very nice woman.' He heard his father click his fingers. 'Now I remember, she was with the customer who was chatting with Moira. Peter.'

'Did they leave together?'

'They did, actually. Why? What's happened?'

'Nothing. It doesn't matter. Just don't tell Mum I asked, okay?'

'Sure, if that's what you want.'

Brodie disconnected then walked back over to Cross and Lucy. 'My dad remembers who took the book. A woman. She was with a man called Peter. The same customer who my sister was chatting to. Now nobody can get a hold of my sister.'

'There were other books on the women. One of them, the one on Marianne, had words in the book highlighted in yellow.'

'Highlighted?' Brodie said.

Brodie's phone rang again. It was control informing him that a patrol had attempted contact with his sister and got a negative response.

'Did you get a hold of her?' Cross asked.

Brodie shook his head. 'She's not at home. Or answering her phone. But my dad remembers this guy Peter was with the woman who took the book, more than likely it was Sylvia.'

'Right, again, who could his partner be, if we're working on your theory? This Peter. How would he know Kane?'

'It obviously has to be somebody he knows, but Kane doesn't have any friends. Who else would he be able to coerce into murdering?' Brodie said.

Cross glanced up at the sky for a moment, as if a plane were flying by with a banner trailing behind it bearing the answer.

'One of his patients,' Lucy said.

'Exactly. It has to be. We need to get a list of his patients that he worked with just before his arrest.'

'That could be a lot,' Cross said.

'I know. But I need to go and talk to somebody. Lucy, let's go.'

55

EDINBURGH

'Moira isn't at home, not answering her phone and she was seen talking to this Peter in the café, and now we find out Sylvia Green was with him,' Brodie said, driving over the speed limit.

'You don't know for a fact she met him after that,' Lucy said.

'We don't know that she *didn't*,' Brodie said. 'I have a bad feeling about this.'

'Could it be her husband is messing her about?' Lucy asked.

'Roger He's a windbag. Moira would knock the stuffing out of him. No, he wouldn't have touched her. It has to be this Peter guy, but who the hell is he? And if he took her, where would he have taken her?'

'Let's not assume the worst, sir.'

They drove the rest of the way in silence up to Liberton, Brodie not being able to get his sister out of his mind. The traffic was starting to pick up in the late afternoon, the prelude to rush hour.

Alice Jack was simply sitting back with a lovely cup of tea when the doorbell rang. She had added a splash of whisky to her drink, just to soften the memories a little. The memories of five years ago.

'Ms Jack,' Brodie said, standing large in her doorway. Beside him was the female detective who had been with him the last time.

'DCI Brodie. I thought you might come today,' she said, ushering them in.

'Why is that?' he said as she closed the door. It was cool in here, the late afternoon sun neither hitting the front nor the back of the house.

'Because of the anniversary. Five years ago today, I killed somebody.'

Brodie looked at Lucy as they walked into the living room. 'I know, you told me all about it the last time we spoke. You said it was almost five years to the day. And you're right, that is why we're here, but not because of the anniversary.'

'Today *is* the day.' They sat down on the couch, with Alice taking a chair. 'Why are you here? Is it because you know now?'

'We do know,' Lucy said. 'We need you to elaborate.'

Alice looked at her tea and wanted to down it in one go, but resisted the urge. 'I was sure she was going to tell you eventually, DCI Brodie. It wasn't my idea, it was all hers. She wanted to protect you.'

'Go on,' he said, not wanting to stop her talking now.

'She left the scene before the police got there. Nobody knew she was in the car when I hit the cyclists.'

'Who left the scene, Alice?' Brodie said.

'I thought you said you knew?'

'I think we've got our wires crossed here,' Brodie said. 'Who are you talking about that left the scene?'

Alice paused for a moment before answering. 'Your sister. Moira. She didn't want to cause any bother for you. She thought it might reflect badly on you, so she left before the police got there.'

'Moira was there?' Lucy said, unable to keep the shock out of her voice.

'Yes. She's one of our friends. We were all drinking, but I was the one driving. I wish we had taken a taxi that night, but we thought we could make it back here if we were careful. However, I was too far over the limit to drive safely. And then the accident happened.'

'Where did this happen?'

'On Liberton Brae. Not far from here. We were almost home...'

56

EDINBURGH

Five years ago

'What do you think now?' Alice asked, grinning.

Moira smiled. 'Not too shabby, m'dear. In fact, there's a bloke over there who's been giving me the eye all night.'

'You're a married woman,' Marianne Taylor said to Moira. 'I'm not, so he's fair game.'

'I'm the only one who's married, but I'm only after a little fun, not find somebody to run away with.'

Ivy Jack was sitting at a table, her back to the wall, if not quite unconscious, then well on her way.

'Look at her,' Moira said. 'Nobody can say she isn't having a good time.'

'Especially when she won't remember most of it tomorrow,' Alice Jack said. She looked around. 'Where's Karen?'

'On the dance floor,' Marianne said. 'Although you can hardly call it dancing. She's got her arms draped around that guy's neck. Another one who won't remember what went on tonight.'

Which wasn't true. The clock was ticking down to disaster, and each of them would have this day etched in their minds forever.

They were at the Royal British Legion in Penicuik, a place that was usually filled with ex-military men and women of an older generation, but this Friday night, the hall had been booked for a birthday party. The women had accepted the invitation and were ready to bale if the music was gash; they were surprised at what a good night it was. Especially since the drink was cheap.

At the end of the night, they were all the worse for wear, even Alice, who had been their designated driver. 'I'll only drink Coke,' she said, but then a man had asked her to dance, and had bought her a drink, and one turned into two, then a few more. She wasn't as drunk as the others, and they really should have got two taxis to take them home, but the last bus was gone, and Alice did have a car that seated seven, even though the last row was meant for kids. Marianne was thin and managed to squeeze into the back, sitting sideways.

Alice promised them she felt fine to drive, but she was anything but fine. Her head swam a little bit and she concentrated extra hard as they drove at the speed limit.

They were literally two minutes away from the house at Kirk Brae, where the party was going to continue, when the accident happened...

57

EDINBURGH

'I thought I was fine,' Alice told Brodie. 'But I think I dozed off. Ivy kept playing with the bloody heater, telling me she was cold, even though it was summer. The heat made me doze off more than once, and we started arguing about it. Ivy took a tantrum and turned the heat right up. I dozed off at the traffic light. Didn't even see the red light. Or the cyclists going through.'

'It was pretty late at night for cyclists to be out, wasn't it?' Lucy said.

'Later on, my lawyer told me the couple were out late because it was supposedly safer. They were doing a bit of training before going on a touring holiday. The woman was in front, and the man behind, but they were close together and I hit them square on. The car stopped and Moira jumped out. She said she couldn't be there when the police showed up, because you were a detective and it would look bad for you. She took off. The woman died, but the man survived, although he was badly injured. He had a brain injury. Last year, Moira went to Spain with some of her pals. She didn't want to be in Edinburgh on the anniversary.'

'I remember her going on that holiday a year ago,' Brodie said. 'I thought she just wanted a break.'

'What do you know about the man who was knocked down?' Lucy asked. 'And the woman?'

Alice sniffed, like she was either going to cry or her nose needed blowing. 'They were engaged. They were both wearing helmets but his flew off just before his head hit a stone wall. He had a concussion, a broken hip, and a shattered pelvis, so my lawyer told me. The woman died on impact. I'm so ashamed.'

'Was this man called Peter?' Brodie asked.

'No. He was a surgeon and he lost his job afterwards. It affected his eyes and he had to wear red glasses afterwards. I'll never forget that day as long as I live. But his name wasn't Peter.'

58

EDINBURGH

Brodie entered Alice's kitchen and dialled Moira's number, trying to get a hold of her again. When the call was answered, it wasn't Moira's voice.

'You do surprise me, Liam. I didn't think you would call on the day of the anniversary,' the man said.

'We found your latest victim. Karen. By chance, of course, but we did find her. There was a little piece of material sticking out from under a gravestone.'

'Ah. I was careless. It's always the little details that make you slip up. But it doesn't matter now. I presume you understand why this was done?'

'I do,' Brodie answered.

'Did you speak with Alice? She's the one who caused it all. I left her alive so she could tell you about things. Not so with Moira. However, I'll let her go if you come and meet me. Alone.'

'I can do that.'

The man laughed. 'That's what they all say. Then the reinforcements are in the background. I don't want that happening here, Liam, so I have a little incentive for you.'

Brodie listened to the sound of a struggle in the background, followed by a yell. He expected to hear his sister's voice, but he was shocked to hear another one instead.

'Liam. Don't come here. Fuck him,' Ruth shouted, then Brodie heard a slap and Ruth was quiet.

'Quite a fighter is our Ruthie, but there won't be any fight left in her if I see you with any other detective. I'll kill her and Moira both and I have a way out of here that not even the council knows about.'

'Where's here?'

'Where it all ended for Gabriel Kane, Liam. Where you first met me. And where it's going to finish. Come when it's dark outside. And remember, come alone.'

He hung up and Brodie stood looking at his phone for a minute.

Lucy approached him, the two of them alone in the quiet kitchen. 'You okay, boss?'

He looked at her, trying to get his breathing under control. 'He has Moira, but he also has Ruth. My incentive to go alone.'

'Where are they?'

'Where we caught Kane, he says.'

'I'm coming with you.'

'No, Lucy. I'm going alone. He wants me there after dark. That's because the traffic will be lighter then and easier for him to get away.'

'You're not going alone. He'll kill you if you do.'

'He'll kill Moira and Ruth if I don't.'

'Not going to happen.' She placed a hand on his arm. 'I have an idea, but if it's going to work, we need to move now. We have three hours. It's a very long shot, and it's going to require a lot of people to co-operate, but if we start now, it might just work. And if it doesn't, I'm still going with you. I'm not letting you go in there alone.'

She told him what she was thinking.

'If it all works out, then I won't be going in alone, will I?' he said.

'I'm still going to be there. There's nothing you can say or do that will stop me.'

He nodded. 'Okay. Let's get going.'

59

EDINBURGH

The sun had gone down now, which in Edinburgh was close to 11 p.m. Brodie felt exhausted, but the night was far from over. He'd been in a meeting with Cross and Lucy and the man who had agreed to this plan, albeit grudgingly.

Now he sat alone in the dark room. The door opened slowly and he looked at the figure standing silhouetted by the light from the hallway behind him.

The figure stepped forward and the door closed behind him.

'This is very cosy,' Gabriel Kane said. 'Except at my age, it's not a good idea to trip and break a hip. What about some lights, Liam?'

Brodie had his phone out and turned the flashlight on, setting the phone at the edge of a side table where the light shone down towards the carpet, illuminating Kane's feet. The Crocs that he had to wear in here. What all the patients wore. It wasn't easy to run in them, apparently.

'Why all the mystery, Liam?' Kane asked.

'We know all about him now, Gabriel. I just wanted your perspective.'

'You know about who?' Kane said.

'We don't have to play these games any more. We know you didn't kill those women. It was Dermot Hume. The volunteer who brings you the books.'

'Dermot. Dermot.' Kane pretended to think about the name. Brodie could see the man's face, bathed in shadow.

'We know how he was communicating with you. The book that was found on Marianne had words highlighted in yellow. When put together, it revealed a message. About killing.'

'Marianne?'

'Yes. You mistook what gravestone she was under. Dermot had put her under one closest to his fiancée's grave. Now we've got all his victims, because he was sloppy with one, and a dog walker saw part of her arm sticking out from under the stone. Now can we stop pretending you don't know Dermot?'

Kane gave a little chuckle. 'He's actually a very intelligent man. He was a surgeon before he got hit by the car.'

'I know all about him,' Brodie said.

'The head injury affected him. I don't think he would have made a mistake otherwise.'

'He wouldn't have been a patient of yours if he hadn't been injured.'

'You figured that out, too,' Kane said, again with a chuckle. 'I have to say, I underestimated you, Liam. I've known you for years, yet here I am, in awe of you.'

'You don't need to feel in awe of me. Anybody could have figured this out.'

'But not everybody did. *You* did, Liam. Your superior officers are going to be impressed.'

Brodie looked at the doctor. He knew what the psychiatrist was doing: stalling for time, trying to get the story worked out in his head.

'The thing is, Gabriel, I can't understand why Hume went from being a patient of yours to becoming a killer. And yet you knew about him.'

Kane smiled. 'Dermot had extreme rage issues. I was worried he would go out and do something stupid.'

'He did do something stupid.'

'Not quite. He channelled his rage. Under my guidance. I taught him how to focus. How to kill like I killed.'

'Makes sense. And please feel free to jump in and correct me if I'm wrong, but it looks like you helped him kill the women who were there the night his fiancée got killed. And to help him get away with it, you took the blame. Taking us to the cemetery to reveal one of your victims. Except you got it wrong. Somehow there was a mistake in translation, as it were. When Hume told you where he had put the women he murdered.'

'Seems like you've got this all sewn up, Liam. You don't need me any more.'

'The thing is, we could charge you with accessory to murder, but what good would that do us? You're already serving life in a psychiatric unit.'

Kane smiled and spread his hands. 'There we have it, then.'

'Not quite.' Brodie reached into his jacket and brought out a sheet of paper, handing it over to the doctor.

'What's this, Liam?'

'It's from the Crown Office, authorising your move to Carstairs State Hospital, where you will be put in a wing with extremely dangerous prisoners. You will be in a room with zero amenities. No books, no TV, nothing.'

'You've threatened me with this before. The no amenities bit.'

'I have. But as you can see, the move has already been approved. On my say-so. You have it in black and white.'

'Now my fate is in your hands, is that what you're saying?'

'That's exactly what I'm saying. Nine o'clock tomorrow, on the dot, I'm going to make a phone call. Whether you're transferred to Carstairs or not, is up to you.'

Kane was no longer smiling. 'What is it exactly you want, Liam? You obviously need something from me to prevent you deciding to ship me down south.'

Brodie leaned forward. 'I'm going to tell you. Then you have ten seconds to decide, then I'm out of here.'

Kane opened the letter and Brodie stayed silent while he read it. Then he locked eyes with the detective.

'Go ahead. I'm listening.'

60

EDINBURGH

Brodie hadn't been back to the depository since the night he had been stabbed, three years earlier. Memories of lying in the Royal Infirmary, his family and colleagues thinking he was going to die, ran back through his mind now.

Brodie could fight and had been in many fights, but a sneak attack from someone with a knife could kill anyone. Lucy Warren had saved his life that night, without a doubt. Yes, he had moved slightly, and the blade had not struck its intended target on his body, but she had jumped right in and taken down Gabriel Kane.

Brodie reached the spot in the depository where he had previously been attacked, and held on to the extendable baton, his senses heightened. It was always dark down here underground, and nobody could tell if it was night or day. No windows to illuminate anything, just a few bare bulbs behind cages, as if they were in a prison.

He saw the lamp on the small desk lit, as if it hadn't been extinguished in three years. He noticed the large red book still on the shelf. He idly wondered what its title was, but he couldn't allow his concentration to waver for a second.

He rounded the corner and walked on, preparing for the man to jump out, but he didn't. Then he saw the door leading into a stairwell, which he opened cautiously. Nobody was there. The dim light from this vast room partly illuminated the stairs on one side, but otherwise, it was pitch-dark.

He entered the stairwell, which descended only.

The stone steps were worn in the centre after many years of people treading up and down them. Brodie took each step gently until he reached the next level.

He reached a door with reinforced glass. A faint light illuminated this level, while darkness enveloped the passage to the lower floors. He pulled the door open and stepped inside. More racks of books filled the space, and it smelled even more musty. It was the place where books went to die.

He rounded a shelving unit, ceiling-high, which was about ten feet, and saw another doorway. He held the baton tight up to his shoulder, ready to bring it down fast.

It was a room with several doors. Sliding doors, one of which was open, revealed another dim light inside. At the far end stood a freight lift, featuring old-fashioned concertina gates. There was nothing beyond the gates.

Brodie stepped forward and peered inside. There was a bed and a portable chemical toilet, but nothing else.

He then heard movement behind him and spun round.

Dermot Hume stood facing the freight shaft, holding two women whom he had chained together. Their backs were turned to the shaft. He turned to look at Brodie.

'Glad you could make it.' Hume had his red glasses on and he was holding a large butcher's knife.

'I'm sorry about your fiancée, Dermot,' Brodie said.

'The only woman I ever loved. And Moira and her pals ruined our future that night. I wish I had died along with Nancy.'

Brodie could see that the man was now revved up, spittle flying from his lips. A walking stick lay close by, used by Hume after the surgeries to repair his hip and pelvis.

'Fucking brain trauma. Me! A surgeon. I couldn't walk properly afterwards, and I couldn't see clearly. There went my job. Thankfully, I sued and received some money, which I invested to make a living. No thanks to your fucking sister.'

'This isn't helping, Dermot. It isn't going to bring Nancy back. And she wouldn't want this, surely?'

'How the fuck do you know what she would have wanted? Besides, it's my decision. I'm the one who wanted revenge.' He laughed. 'Now you have a choice to make: Ruth or Moira. Who lives and who dies. Choose, Brodie. Which one is going down the lift shaft?'

Brodie had studied the engineering schematics before he came in and knew the lift used to carry books back in the old days, and that there was old heating machinery down there. All of it was redundant now.

'You don't want to do that, Dermot,' another voice said from outside the room.

'I told you not to bring any other copper here!' Hume shouted, waving the knife about.

'I'm not with the police, Dermot,' Gabriel Kane said, stepping into view.

Brodie looked at Hume, his face a mask of pure rage. 'You were the one I was chasing that night three years ago, weren't you, Dermot?'

Hume laughed. 'Yes, I was. It was brilliant. The idea was to kill you and escape down here, but things went sideways. You captured Dr Kane, yet I managed to slip away into the alleyway beneath the South Bridge. Dr Kane could have given the game away, but he didn't. Kudos to you, doctor.'

'I aim to please.'

'You were the one on the camera footage we captured from the bookshop,' Brodie said. 'The man who was there with Kane and Marianne Taylor.'

'Correct again. I was taught my skills by Dr Kane.'

'He was my patient,' Kane said. 'Then, when I was incarcerated, Ruth suggested to Dermot that he undertake volunteer work. And lo and behold, the position of patient librarian became available, and Ruth pulled some strings to help Dermot secure the job. We communicated by highlighting words in books to create sentences. He was my patient, and I taught him how to focus his anger.'

'By killing people,' Brodie said. 'That's why you forgot who was under the gravestone.'

Kane chuckled. 'Exactly.'

Brodie didn't want Hume to know they had already discussed this back in the hospital.

'Why there?' Brodie asked Hume.

'Those gravestones are next to my Nancy. It's almost as if she could see them being punished.'

Kane walked forward, and Brodie could see Hume visibly relaxing.

'You asked me to come along to talk to Hume tonight. Talk him off the ledge,' Kane said. 'But just like three years ago, you made a terrible mistake. There's two of us now, versus you.' He turned to look at Hume just a foot away now. 'Dermot, I think we should kill both women, don't you?'

Hume smiled. 'I do.'

'No, please,' Moira said.

Brodie took a step towards them.

'Uh uh, Brodie,' Hume said. 'One more step and I'll kill Ruth first.'

Brodie halted, feeling the sweat trickle down his back, even though it was cool in here. He realised he wouldn't reach Ruth in time if he lunged, yet he was determined to try anyway. Both women were gazing at him, their backs to Hume, awaiting the grab that would lead them to their deaths.

'Is there room for both of them down that lift shaft if we throw them down together?' Kane asked.

Hume turned to look, laughing. 'Yes, there—'

Kane stepped forward, reached out and touched Hume on the back. Hume fell down the shaft, which was three storeys high, screaming as he went, and they all heard the thump as he died when he landed on the roof of the parked lift.

'Come away from the edge, ladies,' Kane said, ushering them away from danger, just as Lucy ran in.

'What's going on?' she asked, running up to Brodie.

Kane looked at her. 'Hume looked into the shaft and fell to his death.' He looked at Brodie. 'I tried to grab him but missed.'

Brodie nodded. 'He fell.'

Kane smiled. 'Now I get a full Sky package as well, DCI Brodie.'

Brodie had no answer.

61

FIFE

'I wish I'd gone for a pee before we came here,' Cameron complained.

'I'm glad I did. And my bladder is a lot older than yours,' Art said.

They were sitting in a pool car in Arncrouch, a little bit down the road from the cottage.

'How long did Brodie say we had to sit here?' Cameron was hungry too. His mother had made fish and chips but now he felt like a teacake. 'You hungry?'

'No, I'm not hungry. What are you like? A fucking bairn would be sitting quieter than you. "I need a pish." "I'm hungry." What next? You going to start running up the main street naked?'

'You got any mints?'

'For God's sake. Get a fucking grip.'

'My arse is numb. I need to get out and stretch my legs.'

'Duck down. There's some bastard now.'

'Where's Brodie?' Cameron asked, slinking down further into the seat.

'He's five minutes out. He sent me a text.'

'When?'

Art looked at him. 'Five minutes ago.'

'Oh, right.'

Art kept his gaze just above the windscreen as he observed the figure, clad in black and moving quickly. He turned right into the quiet street where the entrance to the cottage lay and approached the front door. Tape had been affixed across the entrance: *Police – do not cross.*

The figure pulled the tape off, took a key out of his pocket and unlocked the front door.

Then he was inside.

Art sat back up, as did Cameron, and he got on his radio just as a set of headlights approached from behind and stopped right behind their car. Art's phone rang.

'Sir.'

'What's the latest, Arthur?' Brodie asked.

Fuck's sake. 'Somebody is now in Mrs Wallace's house.'

'Right. Warn the others and let's go.'

Cameron didn't need to be told twice and was out of the car. 'I think I can hear my bladder sloshing,' he said.

'Well, if we see any forest fires, I'll point you in the right direction.'

Brodie walked up and Art looked at the DCI. 'If you don't mind me saying, sir, you look like shite.'

'Let's just say, I've had a busy evening. But so do you. What's your excuse?'

'I look like this just to blend in.'

Brodie patted him on the upper arm. 'Let's get in there, Arthur.'

'Do me a favour, sir,' he asked.

'What's that?'

'Call me Art.'

'Okay, Art, but let's move before he comes back out.'

They crossed the road and walked over to the entrance where the figure had gone in, and entered the house, just as the headlights from a patrol car came round the corner.

Inside, they were as quiet as they could be in a cottage that was probably hundreds of years old and had all the stability of a house of cards.

Tarps had been fastened to the roof, making the house waterproof but not silent. This didn't really matter, as there was the sound of banging emanating from within the house.

Brodie followed the noise, turning down the hallway where the damaged bedroom was. The banging was coming from the room opposite.

Brodie gently pushed the door open and flicked the light switch.

Ted Carr was standing holding a hammer. An old, dusty one, not the one he had used to prise up some floorboards.

'Put it down, Mr Carr,' Art said.

'It's over now,' Brodie said, just as the two uniforms strolled along behind them. For once, PC Don McCoy wasn't shouting at the top of his lungs. He simply nodded to Cameron, poised to start kicking and swinging.

Carr sighed and put the hammer down.

'Is that the one Toby Wallace used to kill Marcus?'

'It is,' Carr said. He locked eyes with Brodie. 'The bastard deserved it. He battered that little boy and abused Laura. He would have abused Ruth too if I hadn't interfered. Laura told me what he had been doing, and Marcus came in when Toby was sexually assaulting her and he ran off shouting, but Toby was quick. He picked up a hammer and hit Marcus with it, killing him. Toby then slumped down and started crying. Laura came running over to my house and told me what had happened. I went back over with her.'

'Where was Margaret at the time?'

'Away on a trip or something. That's why Toby had no problem going into Laura's room.'

'Why didn't you call the police?' Art asked.

'And have him walking the streets again years later? No, you didn't see those girls' faces. They were terrified, especially Ruth. But we made sure she didn't see Marcus lying dead. I was incensed. I asked Laura if there were sleeping pills in the house. She said her mother had plenty. She had them prescribed but didn't take them all the time. So we crushed a lot of them and mixed the powder into a bottle of whisky. Then I told Toby it was going to be alright. We would help. He took the offered whisky and kept on drinking. We got him on his feet and into the living room. We put him in his armchair, wiped the bottle clean, and then placed his hand on it so only his prints would be on it, just in case. Then we left him. Laura begged me not to. It would mean the world would know her foster father had raped her, and then it would be her word against his. Except he would be dead. I agreed, and we wrapped the poor little fella up in plastic bin bags and taped it, then I lifted the floorboards and we put him inside. Then when they were nailed down, we cleaned up.'

'How long did it take Toby to die?' Art asked.

'I'm not sure. Laura went to bed. The next morning, she called for an ambulance, saying she couldn't wake Toby up. His death was ruled a suicide, and then Marcus was reported missing and soon Toby's death was forgotten about. I hid this hammer under the floorboards.'

'And now you're taking it out in case the forensics team find it,' Brodie said.

'Yes.'

Brodie turned round to the Uniforms. 'Arrest him. I'm going to talk to the procurator fiscal in the morning.'

McCoy stepped forward. 'Right, ya fuckin' baw bag. Get your fucking hands out in front of you.'

Brodie looked at Art, who just raised his eyebrows and shrugged. When Carr was taken out, he looked at the DCI. 'Det Supt Breck's nephew,' was all he said.

62

FIFE

A week later

'It's been a long time since I was in Anstruther,' Ruth said.

'It's beautiful here,' Laura said. Ruth held on to her arm as they walked along past the harbour, eating their ice cream cones from a shop called Scoop.

'Let's have a seat.'

They sat down, Brodie joining them.

'What's going to happen to Ted Carr?' Laura asked.

'He'll be charged with murder,' Brodie answered, 'but his lawyer will talk with the procurator fiscal and see what he can do. Mitigating circumstances, the amount of time that has passed, will all be taken into consideration. He might end up getting probation.'

Laura nodded. 'He saved me and Ruth both. Ruth was too young for Toby, but when she was older, she would have got the same treatment. I should have stabbed him.'

'Don't say that,' Ruth said, putting a hand on hers.

'When Ted talked about killing Toby, I didn't feel shock, just a sense of relief. If that makes sense?'

'As a psychiatrist, yes, it makes perfect sense. It's not like you're a mass murderer.'

'I know I acted up a lot when I was growing up, but my anger was directed at Margaret's lack of action when it came to her husband. But she was sleeping with Rory Farmington, so she didn't care.'

'It's over now, Laura. We can only learn from our mistakes.'

Laura nodded and licked more of her ice cream. 'I've decided I'm going to move away from Fife,' she said at last.

'Really? Where are you going to move to?' Brodie said.

'London, I think. It's far away from here, but I can hop on a shuttle when I want to visit.'

'What will you do for work?' Ruth asked.

'I've got a job lined up in a hospital as an administrator. Nothing exciting, but it will pay the bills. I've rented a room until I get on my feet.'

'Keep in touch,' Ruth said.

'I will.'

They finished their ice cream and stood up.

'I'm parked along that way,' she said.

'We're at the far end,' Brodie said.

Laura hugged them and walked away, Brodie and Ruth walking in the opposite direction.

It was a beautiful day, the sea calm and the view across to East Lothian unhindered. Brodie loved the smell of the salt air and stood for a few moments, inhaling it. Ruth held on to his arm before they turned and got into the car.

'Do you think you'll ever see her again?' Brodie asked, starting up the engine.

'No.'

They drove back to Edinburgh, connecting with the A982. 'What's happening with Alan McRae?' Ruth asked. 'Any sign of him?'

Brodie shook his head. 'Art McKenzie will keep on looking. That's a good team in Glenrothes.'

'If they have another major case, you know they'll put you back here.'

'I know,' Brodie answered. He could think of worse things that could happen.

* * *

MORE FROM JOHN CARSON

False Witness, the next instalment in the utterly gripping DCI Liam Brodie series, is available to buy now here:
https://mybook.to/FalseWitnessBackAd

ACKNOWLEDGEMENTS

It's the old cliché, but it really does take a team to get a book out, and I'm lucky to have been supported by a fantastic team at Boldwood Books.

First of all, I would like to thank: Amanda Ridout, CEO and founder, and Caroline Ridding, Publisher; Victoria Britton, Editorial Director who is a Godsend; Claire Fenby, Head of Marketing, and Ben Wilson; last, but not least, Ross Dickinson and Jacqueline Beard MBE; and everybody else who is involved in producing this book. I am glad to be part of the Boldwood team!

ABOUT THE AUTHOR

John Carson is the number one bestselling Scottish author of the DCI Liam Brodie detective series. Originally from Edinburgh, he now lives in New York State with his wife, family, two dogs and four cats.

Download your exclusive bonus content from John Carson here:

Visit John's website: www.johncarsonauthor.com

Follow John on social media here:

 x.com/JCarsonAuthor
 facebook.com/john.carsonauthor
 instagram.com/JohnCarsonAuthor

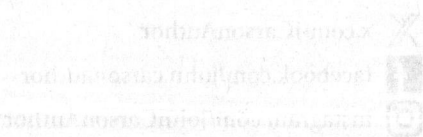

ALSO BY JOHN CARSON

DCI Liam Brodie

Broken Bones

False Witness

THE *Murder* LIST

**THE MURDER LIST IS A NEWSLETTER
DEDICATED TO SPINE-CHILLING
FICTION AND GRIPPING
PAGE-TURNERS!**

**SIGN UP TO MAKE SURE YOU'RE ON
OUR HIT LIST FOR EXCLUSIVE DEALS,
AUTHOR CONTENT, AND
COMPETITIONS.**

**SIGN UP TO OUR
NEWSLETTER**

BIT.LY/THEMURDERLISTNEWS

Boldwood

Boldwood Books is an award-winning fiction publishing company seeking out the best stories from around the world.

Find out more at www.boldwoodbooks.com

Join our reader community for brilliant books, competitions and offers!

Follow us
@BoldwoodBooks
@TheBoldBookClub

Sign up to our weekly deals newsletter

https://bit.ly/BoldwoodBNewsletter

www.ingramcontent.com/pod-product-compliance
Ingram Content Group UK Ltd.
Pitfield, Milton Keynes, MK11 3LW, UK
UKHW041551251125
9121UKWH00002B/8